TIPPING POINT

TIPPING POINT

BILL NOEL

Cover photo and design by Bill Noel

Author photo by Susan Noel

ISBN: 978-1-948374-41-5

Enigma House Press

Goshen, Kentucky

www.enigmahousepress.com

Also by Bill Noel

Folly

The Pier

Washout

The Edge

The Marsh

Ghosts

Missing

Final Cut

First Light

Boneyard Beach

Silent Night

Dead Center

Discord

The Folly Beach Mystery Collection

Dark Horse

Joy

The Folly Beach Mystery Collection II

No Joke

Relic

The Folly Beach Christmas Mystery Collection

Faith

Chapter One

Two extraordinary events occurred this morning. First, Charles Fowler convinced me to accompany him on a kayak adventure through the waterway as it weaves through the salt marsh separating Folly Island from the rest of South Carolina. The trip was extraordinary because of my fear of water, something there's no shortage of on a kayak ride. By fear of water, I'm not talking about panicking over taking a shower or getting caught in an occasional rainstorm. My fear, or as I refer to it in less-dysfunctional terms, extreme caution, involves water containing three-and-a-half-percent salt and in my mind roughly twenty percent sharks gathering to savor me for lunch.

I agreed to go because my friend said we'd rent a double kayak, plus he'd been kayaking many times on the same body of water. Nothing could possibly go wrong, or so he said. We'd paddled a couple hundred yards before he revised his kayaking experience saying this was the third time he'd been in one, but he'd thought many times about renting a kayak. I considered smacking him with my paddle or using my novice skills to turn the kayak around then head to shore. Either option would've capsized the vessel depositing me where the sharks were drooling over my meaty body. Falling for his story was on me since in the decade I'd known Charles, I couldn't recall him mentioning kayaking. He was also a master embellisher.

A few hundred yards later, I was feeling more comfortable using the fiberglass paddle, even started enjoying the scenery. It was early March, so the marsh grasses were beginning to change from winter brown to spring green. A handful of puffy cirrus clouds dotted the sky, the temperature a perfect seventy-two degrees. Large homes with walking piers ending at the river were to our right, where I recognized the residences of a couple of my friends. Even if I hadn't, Charles shared the name of the home's owner, who else lived in the house, including their pets. I became less comfortable when he insisted we take one of the tributaries branching to the left where the waterway narrowed. No manmade objects were in sight. The oyster-lined, eight-foot-wide passage appeared to become narrower with each paddle stroke. We came close to capsizing when a dolphin playfully arched out of the water close enough to splash me as it reentered the shark habitat. Charles thought it was way funnier than I had.

The only sounds I heard for the next fifteen minutes were a couple of terns laughing at me for believing Charles's story about how many times he'd been kayaking. I was beginning to relax, enjoy the marsh grasses, birds, and especially the dolphin gliding beside us.

Then the second extraordinary event occurred. My enjoyment of nature abruptly ended when the pleasant sound of the birds was drowned out by the roar of an airplane engine. It didn't take an aeronautical engineer to know the small, single-engine plane was in trouble. Its left wing dipped toward the water. It couldn't have been more than a hundred feet off the ground, or more accurately, the water. The plane was losing altitude and heading directly at us.

I didn't know if the pilot would or could gain altitude. It wasn't more than fifty feet from the marsh grasses when its nose pulled up. It still looked like it was going to crash. The deadly projectile was heading toward us when its front wheel caught in the thick marsh grasses, bounced once, then skipped across the narrow waterway. The aircraft continued in our direction. My fear of sharks was replaced by terror. I was about to be decapitated by the propeller with no time to paddle out of its way.

I screamed for Charles to bail out of the kayak. I did the same. We hit the water at the same time the plane's twisted landing gear filled the space our heads occupied seconds earlier. We were out of the overturned kayak in time to see the prop slam into the dense marsh three feet above the water. The nose of the aircraft burrowed in the pluff mud. The plane flipped and skidded, ripping a path through the grasses, before coming to a stop upside down and fewer than a hundred yards from where we were standing in waist-deep water.

The near silence that followed was eerie and consisted of a flock of birds squawking and Charles splashing around trying to find his paddle and Tilley hat. I managed to hold on to my paddle, but my hat was floating behind me. I grabbed it and my next thought was how we would get to the plane. It was high tide, the marsh grasses along with the island of mud was a few feet higher than the water, so I could only see the upside-down landing gear. It would've been impossible to walk through the mud without slicing our legs open on razor-sharp oysters along the bank before we'd sink knee-deep in the mushy surface. The waterway we'd been navigating meandered close to the plane.

Charles found his paddle and after what seemed like forever, we managed to climb back in the kayak, turned it around, then paddled to within six feet of the wreck. The right wing was above water and wedged into the side of the mud wall. That was all that prevented the cabin from being under water. Smoke was coming from the cowling, but there were no flames. That's when I heard banging sounds from inside the partially submerged fuselage.

Charles climbed out of the kayak to hold it stable while I gracelessly exited the vessel. I slogged through water and mud before grabbing a wing strut where I pulled myself up enough to see in the side window. Four men were in the cockpit, three upside down, held in place by seatbelts and shoulder harnesses. One was struggling with his harness; the other two, the pilot and the front seat passenger, were unmoving. Blood dripped from their heads. The cowling was mangled, the windshield shattered. Their heads had slammed into the upper section of the instrument panel. The fourth passenger had managed to get his restraints unhooked and knelt on the roof. He began shoving the unconscious man out of the way while ramming his shoulder into the door. It didn't budge.

Movement inside the cabin combined with my weight on the inverted wing dislodged part of the plane from the mud. It started tilting toward the water. If it slid much more, the cabin would be submerged.

We had to get the passengers out, and fast.

Chapter Two

The top of the door was wedged in the mud with the weight of the plane pressed on it making it impossible to open. I yelled for Charles to go to the other door to see if the situation was better. The backseat passenger who'd struggled with his harness got it unhitched before Charles waded around the plane. The passenger fell, landed hard. His impact rocked the plane enough that it slid closer to the tipping point which would drown anyone who'd survived the crash. The man pushing the door turned to help his friend. Charles yelled the pilot's door may open but he'd need help.

The tail was sinking, the rest of the deathtrap not far behind. The men inside the aircraft were attempting to unbuckle the unmoving front seat passenger.

"Stop moving!" I yelled, hoping to keep them from rocking the plane.

I grabbed the strut then slid off the wing and splashed to Charles who fought to open the stubborn door. My thigh scraped the side of the pluff-mud island as I moved beside him and wrapped my hands around the edge of the door. Charles managed to force it open a few inches. Both of us pulled. Nothing. One more yank and it swung open a couple of feet. The plane groaned then slid six inches toward deeper water.

The pilot, still strapped in his seat, blocked the escape route for the others. If we tried to free him, the movement could hasten the plane's slide. If we left him suspended, there was no way the others could get out. The choices were bad and worse. I opted for bad.

"Charles, can you hold the pilot in place while I unbuckle his shoulder harness?"

"I'll try."

Neither the pilot nor the front seat passenger had shown signs of life. From the unnatural way their heads were twisted, I didn't hold out hope.

"The plane's not going to stay where it is if there's much movement or weight shift."

"What are we waiting for?" Charles said, as he knelt under the pilot and pushed up.

It took three tries before I unhooked the restraints. The pilot's dead weight fell on Charles. He stumbled yet managed to lower the pilot. With help from the rear seat passenger, Charles and I dragged the pilot out of the aircraft and carried him through the water to where we could lay him on the mud. The other rear seat passenger scampered out behind his friend. He grabbed his shoulder cursing it was broken. It may be, but he was alive, climbing out under his own power. One unconscious passenger was still strapped upside down in a plane which was slipping with each passing second. The water was rising in the cabin and inches from covering his head.

There wasn't time to worry about him getting hurt if we unhooked his harness. Charles slid underwater then surfaced on the other side of the man. He pushed him up while I unhooked the harness. The man flopped down in the water filling the cockpit. I dragged him out of the wreck.

The plane creaked then slid the rest of the way into the murky saltwater before we reached the muddy, cordgrass covered plot of land.

We'd maneuvered the last man out toward a safe resting place when I heard the thump-thump sound of props. I looked up and saw a distinct orange and white Coast Guard helicopter swooping toward us. Someone must've seen the plane go down and called for help.

The man who'd helped his fellow passengers out of the plane collapsed beside the pilot. The one with the injured arm sat in the mud staring at the mostly submerged aircraft. Both appeared in shock.

I gasped to catch my breath as a Coast Guard crew member was lowered from the air-sea rescue chopper hovering directly over us. The rotor's turbulence had the marsh grasses swaying like they were in a hurricane. Seconds later, I heard another engine and saw a black jet ski moving around the mostly sunken plane. The wave runner had OCEAN RESCUE in yellow on the front and was manned by a member of the Folly Beach Department of Public Safety. We weren't in the ocean, but I wasn't about to complain.

I met the officer on the wave runner who asked if everyone was out of the plane. I told him yes then pointed to the two unmoving passengers. Folly Beach police officers doubled as firefighters; most were trained EMTs. He rushed to the closest passenger while the crew member from the helicopter was bent over the pilot. Charles was with the police officer and the unmoving passenger.

I walked to the other two passengers who'd scooted close to each other. Both were dressed in bright-colored polo shirts, one in Kelly green slacks, the other in bright-red shorts.

I knelt between them and asked what happened.

The man in shorts shook his head, the other said, "No idea. We were headed to Myrtle for a golfing weekend. Took off from Charleston Executive Airport." He pointed at the man being attended to by the Coast Guard member. "Gary, the pilot over there, was in the plane when we arrived. We were running late. We threw our clubs in and took off. Oh, I'm Tom, by the way. Thanks for saving us."

"I'm Chris Landrum," I said before pointing at Charles. "It's fortunate my friend, Charles Fowler, and I were nearby."

"Sure was," said the man in the Kelly-green slacks, grimacing while holding his shoulder. "I'm Richard."

"You took off, then what?"

Richard said, "Gary didn't say much. He had a cold, all stopped up, cranky. He was also mad because we were late. He's anal like that. It was my fault, so I apologized. It didn't help." He shook his head. "We take these golf outings three times a year. Gary, Tom, and I live on Folly, so each time we head out, Gary goes out of the way to fly over our houses. It's neat seeing Folly from the air. We took off then turned this direction. It's a beautiful day. Gary said it should be a smooth flight." He looked at the still-unmoving pilot. "Suddenly he turns chalk white. The plane starts down. He didn't say another word. None of the rest of us knew anything about flying." He slowly shook his head. "A couple of us screamed, not sure who. Umm, that's all I remember until you helped us out of the plane. We didn't ..." He stopped, grabbed his shoulder and winced.

Tom said, "You okay, Richard?"

Richard was in pain. He continued holding his shoulder. "I will be."

Tom said, "Good. Back to your question, I couldn't see Gary well, but he glanced back once. From where I was in the back seat it looked like his eyes glazed over. Then he turned, stared straight ahead. I could be mistaken, but it seems his head flopped forward seconds before we hit. Mark pulled up on the yolk, the steering-wheel looking thing in front of each front seat. It must've brought the nose up. That kept us from nosediving into the marsh. It saved our lives." He glanced at Charles and the police officer bending over the lifeless passenger. "Some of our lives." He lowered his head then whispered, "Mark's a hero."

Their stories were interrupted when Charles waved me over.

He removed his soaked hat and held it over the Naval Academy blue logo on his long-sleeve T-shirt. "He's gone."

The Coast Guardsman went over to the police officer and the deceased passenger. The two conferred as Charles and I slowly walked to the group. The Coast Guardsman then radioed the chopper, said there was nothing they could do, to send the harness down for him.

The police officer watched the Coast Guard copter retrieve its crew member and moved close to Charles and me, so we could hear over the sound of the rotor. I'd seen him around town but didn't know his name.

Charles said, "Chris, you know Officer Lane, don't you?"

Charles had lived on Folly thirty-five years and knew many of its residents. I had been there a decade and knew several people, but nowhere near as many as my friend.

"Don't believe I do."

We shook hands, he pointed to the pilot, then sighed.

The sound of an outboard motor got our attention as a white boat with Charleston County Rescue Squad on its side approached. It eased against the side of the elevated marsh mud. Two members of the volunteer rescue squad exited as the air filled with the thumping sounds of two approaching helicopters. They were marked with the logos of Charleston television stations and began circling the downed aircraft like buzzards preparing to descent on an animal's carcass.

Charles and I greeted the members of the rescue squad. The taller of the two asked if we needed medical assistance. I told him no, although I was feeling a sharp pain from a foot-long scratch on my thigh from when I scraped it on an oyster shell as I was helping Charles open the door. I pointed to the plane's surviving passengers and the paramedics headed their way to see if they could help.

The television choppers continued circling. They were so loud I didn't hear two more boats approach until the familiar voice of Cindy LaMond yelled my name. Cindy, Folly Beach's Director of Public Safety, was in the smaller of the two boats. The other watercraft held two more members of the rescue squad. Charles went to meet their boat while I helped Cindy out of hers.

I'd known Cindy since she moved to Folly several years ago to join the police department. She was in her early fifties, a five-foot-three bundle of energy, with a quick smile, and an irreverent sense of humor. She became Director of Public Safety, commonly called police chief, three years ago after her predecessor ascended to the position of mayor. Cindy is also married to Larry LaMond, another friend who owns Folly's tiny hardware store.

She glanced at the downed aircraft, then toward the others gathered near the scene, before saying, "Chris, what are the odds on you going anywhere without attracting a disaster?"

Cindy had exaggerated, although some would call it slight, at best. Since I moved from Kentucky, I'd stumbled across a few horrific situations. As unlikely as it had been, with the help of some friends I'd been involved in solving murders. What made it unusual was neither I nor any of my friends had worked in law enforcement, quite the opposite. Before retiring, I'd been employed in the human resource department of a large healthcare company. Most of my friends had equally unexciting careers.

"Cindy, Charles and I were—"

She waved her palm in my face. "Don't try to explain. Tell me what in the hell happened."

I described the crash and what the survivors had shared about the pilot losing consciousness. She told me not to leave, as if there was a chance of that happening, before she walked over to the rescue squad staff, talked briefly before stepping away from the group, then calling dispatch. I wasn't close enough to catch all her conversation but heard her mention the National Transportation Safety Board and the Federal Aviation Administration. Officer Lane stood a respectful distance from his boss until she finished her call, then cornered her as she approached the airplane.

Charles moved to my side and said, "What now?"

"Good question. Let's ask Cindy if there's anything we can do to help."

Cindy finished the conversation with her officer, shook her head, and said, "You two look like you've been mud wrestling."

Charles glanced at my soaked, mud-caked cut-off jeans and brown T-shirt, smiled at the chief, and said, "I won."

I ignored him. "Cindy, anything we can do to help?"

She looked at the plane then to the group of rescue workers huddled with the two survivors. "One of the rescue squad boats is going to take those two to an ambulance waiting at the dock. I suspect the one holding his shoulder and moaning will need more attention than the other guy. But, hey, I could be wrong. I dropped out of medical school. Wait, I never went to medical school. Anyway, I'll need to stay until the coroner arrives. I'm also waiting for a call back from the FAA and the NTSB. Somebody from the FAA will probably get here later today. The NTSB guy has to come from their field office in Atlanta. It'll be tomorrow at the earliest."

Charles said, "So, there's nothing we can do?"

Cindy glared at him. "Did I say that?"

"Umm, no."

"You two disaster magnets are going to hop in your cute little kayak and paddle back to wherever you got it. If you don't stumble across another plane crash or a hostile submarine peeking its periscope out of the marsh, you're going to go to a quiet place to write down what you saw, everything from when the plane headed your way until the cavalry arrived. When you're done, drop it at my office."

Charles let out a loud sigh before saying, "I hate homework."

Cindy wisely skipped over his comment. "Do either of you know the three guys who live on Folly?"

"I don't," I said and turned to Charles.

"I've seen Tom Kale around town. He's got a white poodle. Cute little thing, name's Casper. I introduced myself to him once, the guy, not the poodle, although it did lick my face when I knelt to pet it."

That didn't surprise me. I've suspected Charles thought more of dogs than he did of people. That was saying something since he's the best I've ever seen in getting along with almost everyone.

Cindy shook her head. "Other than having a dog named after a damned ghost, do you know anything else about him?"

"Not really. We didn't say much. He seems like a quiet guy."

"Neither of you know the other two who live here?"

We shook our heads.

"Hmm, that's unusual. Charles, I thought you knew everybody."

He sighed. "They must not have dogs."

Cindy rolled her eyes.

I was tired, sore, traumatized, and had heard enough canine talk. "Charles, ready to go?"

"Almost. Got another question for Cindy."

She rubbed her temples. "What?"

He pointed to the plane. "How're you going to get that out of here?"

"I'm not. It ain't flying out. I'm no expert since it's not a regular occurrence having an upside-down airplane in the marsh. I imagine someone'll have to get an aerial crane helicopter to haul it out. Nothing will happen until the NTSB and FAA clear the scene. Now get out of here. Let me start taking photos for the feds. The tide's starting to go out. I don't know what the plane will do when we reach low tide."

Charles looked down at his mud splattered red swim trunks, and said, "Cindy, one more—"

She pointed to the kayak. "Scat!"

Chapter Three

I was knocking on the door to my seventieth birthday, Charles a couple of years younger, so by the time we returned the kayak, a nap sounded more appealing than as Charles put it *doing homework*. I also knew our memories about what happened would never be better than now, so I told him we should go to my house to write our recollections. He mumbled something about he'd rather stick chopsticks up his nose and didn't think he would be at his homework best if he looked like he'd spent the afternoon in a pigpen. He was right about the second part of his gripe. I agreed to drop him at his apartment so he could shower. I'd pick him up in a half-hour to complete our assignment. I could've told him to come to my cottage, but that would've given him a reason not to show.

Thirty minutes later, I'd gone home, taken a quick shower, dumped my mud-covered clothes in the hamper, spread an antiseptic cream on my scratched thigh, and drove back to Charles's apartment in an ancient building on

Sandbar Lane. In true Charles style, he was outside leaning against the building as I pulled in the gravel lot. He looked at his wrist where most folks wore a watch. He didn't wear one, which didn't stop him from glaring at me as he walked to the car.

He pointed a gray, legal pad at me. "You're late."

When I'd dropped him off, I said I'd get back as quickly as I could. In his mind. I'd taken longer than *as quickly as I could.* "You're late," was one of his often-used phrases. Over the years I'd learned to ignore it. I again took that tactic.

Charles leaned his head back and closed his eyes during the short drive from his apartment to my cottage next door to Bert's Market on East Ashley Avenue. I would've done the same if I wasn't driving. We were too old for the day we were having.

We decided to write our recollections separately, then compare once we finished to iron out discrepancies. Over the years, Chief LaMond had beaten into my head how witness descriptions were suspect under the best circumstances. It wasn't unusual for three people to see a robbery then give the police three drastically different descriptions of the robber.

I asked Charles if he wanted something to drink before we began. He said water, so I grabbed two bottles from the refrigerator as he went to the spare bedroom I used as an office. He plopped down in a secondhand chair in front of a table to start writing. He looked like a student preparing to answer an essay question on a test, a very old student. I settled in front of my computer. My handwriting was so poor that not only was it illegible for anyone else to read, I couldn't decipher it. Keyboarding was my lone readable option.

"What kind of plane was it?" Charles asked before I started.

"It said Cessna on the side."

"What model Cessna?"

"Charles, I don't have a clue. I was sort of busy. Why?"

"Want to make sure I'm accurate."

"Did you see any other upside-down Cessnas out there? I think the NTSB will know the one you're talking about."

"No need to be touchy."

I sighed.

Ten minutes later, Charles said, "Would you call Richard's slacks Kelly or Crayola Green?"

I lifted my hands off the keyboard and rubbed my eyes. "Charles!"

"Just asking. I'll go with Kelly."

"Excellent choice," I said, not attempting to mask sarcasm.

Miraculously, the next thirty minutes passed without more questions. The streak was broken when he said, "What do you think happened to the pilot?"

"Don't know. I suppose they'll have to wait for the coroner's report. From what Tom said, it sounds like he had a heart attack or a stroke."

"He was in his forties. It seems strange."

I shrugged. "All I know is it's fortunate two of them are alive."

"Fortunate we are, too."

He was right. I started to agree when the phone rang.

"Is this Chris Landrum?" asked an unfamiliar female voice.

"Yes."

"Good. I'm Kylee Loftus with the *Post and* Courier. I'm following up on the fatal plane crash near Folly Beach."

It'd been fewer than five hours since I witnessed the crash, so I wondered how Charleston's daily newspaper learned my identity.

"How'd you get my name?"

The reporter hesitated before saying, "I was talking to one of the men from the Rescue Squad. He gave me your name, number, and that of a Charles Flowers who was with you."

"It's Fowler, not Flowers."

"Oh, thanks for the clarification, Mr. Landrum. Could I ask a few questions?"

My preference would have been to hang up, instead I said, "Not many. This has been an exhausting day."

"I can appreciate that, sir. I won't take much time."

"Go ahead."

"I was told you saved two of the passengers from drowning. Tell me about it."

"Charles and I did what anyone would've done under similar circumstances. We were nearby and helped them out of the plane. I'm only sorry we couldn't have done anything for the other two."

Ms. Loftus said, "That's not what, umm," I heard her shuffling papers. "Mr. Haymaker, one of the survivors, said. He told me if you hadn't helped at significant risk to your safety, he wouldn't be alive."

I repeated what I'd said about doing what anyone would've done, so she changed the subject. "Prior to the crash, did you know any of the men in the aircraft? My understanding is three lived on the island where you reside."

Charles had scooted closer as he motioned for me to put it on speaker. I did, and he leaned closer to the phone.

"No, Ms. Loftus, I didn't know the men."

"So, you and your friend risked your lives for strangers."

"You think if we didn't know anyone in the plane we wouldn't have helped?"

"No, no, sorry, Mr. Landrum. That's not what I meant. I was trying to put a lead on the story. Two men heroically risking their lives to help strangers has a positive ring to it."

I was tempted to hang up, but instead repeated what I'd said twice about doing what anyone would do. She must've figured she wasn't getting anywhere trying to put hero in front of our names. She thanked me for talking to her. She started to hang up. I stopped her figuring since she'd already managed to find me, she might have information about what caused the crash. I said, "Let me ask you a question. Do you know what caused the pilot to collapse?"

"Nothing official. The first responder with the Rescue Squad said it looked like a heart attack. Understand though, he was guessing."

She thanked me for talking with her and asked if she could send a photographer to the house to get my photo for the paper.

"No."

"But—"

I cut her off with another, "No."

She took my less-than-subtle hint, again thanked me for talking with her, and ended the call.

Charles took the pen that he'd been writing his description of the event with and pointed it at the phone. "At least you got my name corrected."

Chapter Four

Minor discrepancies existed between the narratives. The variations were where we were on opposite sides of the plane, and when he took credit for having us bail out of the kayak to prevent multiple decapitations. It wasn't worth debating, so I let him keep his memories. I dropped him at his apartment, illegally parked in a yellow zone in front of the police department, and scampered, okay, walked to the reception area. I was told Chief LaMond was still at the crash site, then handed our reports to one of the officers who said he'd give them to her when she returned.

My energy tank was running shy of empty by the time I got home. There was little food in the house, a common occurrence, yet I managed to scrounge up two slices of stale bread and a jar of peanut butter then using all my culinary skills, slathered peanut butter on the bread. I ate most of the sandwich before falling asleep in the recliner in the living room. I'd turned the television on to watch stories of the crash on the two stations that had aerial coverage. I slept through whatever was reported.

The phone jolted me awake. I couldn't imagine having slept too long until I realized the morning sun was filtering through the slats in my window shade.

"Chris, this is William. I know you're an early riser, so I trust I didn't awaken you."

William Hansel had been a friend since my first week on Folly. We'd also been next-door neighbors the first few weeks until an arsonist torched my rental house. Torched with me in it.

"Good morning, William."

I didn't tell him I'd been asleep and didn't dare ask what time it was.

"I saw on the morning news about an aircraft incident which occurred yesterday taking the lives of two gentlemen."

William, unlike most of my friends, spoke with the demeanor of a college professor lecturing his class. That was understandable since he was a professor at the College of Charleston and had been for many years.

"It was terrible."

"Correct me if I'm mistaken. From the angle shown by the camera on the news helicopter, it appeared you and your colleague Charles Fowler were near the inverted aircraft, the first responders tending to the injured, and to the unfortunate gentlemen whose lives were lost in the tragic occurrence."

I warned you he spoke like that.

I gave him an abbreviated description of what'd happened.

"As I suspected. The reporter gave the names of the

deceased victims yet didn't divulge the monikers of those who were at the scene of the misfortune."

"William, I appreciate your concern."

"Yes, of course, Chris. The news story not only showed two of my friends at the scene. But, how best should I say it, I am also acquainted with Mr. Tom Kale, one of the survivors."

"Oh. He said he lived over here. Is that how you know him?"

"To a degree. As you and I have lightly touched on over the years, there are a minuscule number of African Americans residing on Folly."

"Yes," I said, wondering where he was going with the story.

"And, I am certain you noticed Mr. Kale shares my racial human categorization."

"You're both black?"

William chuckled. "Yes. Additionally, you may or may not know Mr. Kale is a stockbroker by trade."

"All I knew about him was he survived the crash, and thanks to Charles, knew he has a poodle named Casper."

"I didn't know he possessed a canine."

"I can understand that."

"Chris, as you are aware, I'm not a wealthy man. I live by modest means thus keeping my expenses to a minimum. With that said, I have been able to accumulate a tidy sum of money to tide me over in retirement."

William had turned sixty-six a few months ago and shared plans to retire in the next two years.

Not knowing what to say, I gave a benign, "Yes."

"For the last five years, I have been investing utilizing the services of the brokerage firm in which Mr. Kale is a partner. I began working with his wife, Alyssa, then the Kales divorced a year ago, highly contested, I regret to say. Tom took over my account after Alyssa left the firm."

"Do you know him well?"

"Not much beyond his professional talents. He lives in a large house past the Washout. I seldom saw him in town. Most of my contacts took place in his office in Charleston. Truth be told, I knew Alyssa better. She seemed to always be concerned about my portfolio. She would contact me whenever adjustments were needed."

"Why didn't she take your portfolio with her?"

"I wish she could have, being as easy as she was to work with. It was prohibited by her contract, thus I remained with the firm. Mr. Kale, Tom, was always nice and appeared interested, but didn't have the personalized touch his wife exhibited. All, neither here nor there. I simply wanted to make sure you were okay and to share I knew one of the survivors. I'm certain you're busy, so I'll let you go."

William was overly generous saying I was busy. I wouldn't put retirement among the high-stress, demanding professions. I thanked him for calling and suggested we should have lunch soon. He said he would like that. Of course, he used multisyllabic words to express it.

I pushed out of the recliner, realized my neck was sore from sleeping in the chair, my back ached from yesterday's rescue, and my thigh stung from the encounter with the oyster shells. I was also starved. Unless I wanted another peanut butter sandwich, I'd have to leave the house to eat. I wasn't ready to encounter a restaurant full of people, so I headed next door. Bert's Market was a Folly icon, sold everything from beer to banjo strings, and prided itself on never closing.

Mary Ewing, a mid-twenties, single mother, greeted me. I'd met her a couple of years earlier when she was homeless and raising two young children while squatting in vacant rental houses. I introduced her to Preacher Burl Costello, minister of First Light Church, who helped her find more appropriate housing and the job at Bert's.

"Chris," Mary said, "I saw your name in today's newspaper. Did you and Charles really see that plane crash then save two men?"

I nodded.

"Wow, you're heroes. To think, I know both of you."

I repeated my story that we were in the right place at the right time doing what anyone would do under similar circumstances.

"You're still a hero. You know something else? I knew the pilot, well, I didn't really know him. He came in a few times."

"Know anything about him?"

She lowered her head. "I hate to talk bad about the dead. He, umm, he wasn't a nice person, not nice to me anyway."

"What do you mean?"

"He's a lawyer. Nearly every time he came in, he bragged about living in a big house on the beach. I think it was past the Washout. It seemed strange. Most folks treat all of us working here like we're friends. He was, how shall I say it, standoffish, snooty. Who talks about how big their house is or that it's oceanfront when all they're doing is buying a six-pack of beer?"

"That's strange."

"Not only that, I didn't like how he treated his wife. It was sort of like she was, umm, what's the word? Got it, she was subservient to him. She walked behind him like she was property. Sorry to ramble. He struck me as not being nice."

I'm glad Mary didn't like speaking poorly about the dead. No telling what she would've said.

"Thanks for sharing."

"I'm sorry he's dead, sorry for that other man who was killed. Enough about that, what can we get you?"

I thanked her again, said I knew where I could get what I needed, and headed for the cabinet holding pastries. I grabbed a cinnamon Danish and a newspaper from a nearby shelf. It would've been hard for Mary to have missed the story about the crash since there was a photo of the upturned airplane taking up most of the space above the fold. I drew a cup of complimentary coffee from the large urn then took my purchases to Mary who'd moved behind the counter. She took my money, grinned, and repeated, "My hero."

I tapped her on the arm, returned her smile, then headed home.

Chapter Five

The newspaper article filled several blanks about who was on the plane and their background. The deceased pilot, Gary Isles, a married, forty-three years old, was partner in Chapel Smyth & Isles, a law firm founded by his father. Gary had been a pilot nine years. Mark Jamison, age forty-five, the other man killed, owned a trucking company, MJ Transport and Logistics, and was in a relationship with Kevin Robbins. The survivors were Richard Haymaker, thirty-nine, a Charleston stockbroker, and Tom Kale, age forty-seven, also a stockbroker, a fact I'd learned from William. The men were avid golfers. Over the last couple of years, they'd flown to popular golfing destinations in South Carolina and Georgia. The story was vague about the cause of the crash although it hinted that most likely it was the result of a medical crisis with the pilot rather than mechanical. The plane was a 2006 model Cessna 182 Skylane, a fact meaning nothing to me, but would meet Charles's penchant for trivia.

Charles and I were mentioned as residents of Folly Beach who had assisted the passengers out of the aircraft. Tom Kale was quoted as saying, "If those guys weren't there, Richard and I would've been goners." The story ended by referring readers to the newspaper's website for updates, a frequent practice of newspapers, radio, and television stations in this age of instant information.

I turned on the computer, entered the paper's website, to find the story had been updated three hours ago, although all that was new was the coroner's office wouldn't be able to determine cause of death until the toxicology tests were complete which could take several days. An employee of Atlantic Aviation, the company providing fuel and other services at the Charleston Executive Airport, who knew the pilot, said Gary was an excellent pilot, kept his aircraft in peak condition, and with the perfect weather the day of the crash, couldn't imagine anything going wrong unless something happened to Gary.

Another nap filled my afternoon. Apparently, assisting men out of the plane was exhausting for this near septuagenarian. I woke up and realized that hunger must also be a byproduct of my recent activities. I called Charles and we agreed to meet for supper at The Washout, one of Folly's larger restaurants. It was located on Center Street, the center of commerce on the island, and three blocks from Charles's apartment. I carried a few extra pounds—if twenty could be defined as few—on my five-foot-ten-inch frame and knew I needed more exercise than I'd been getting, oh, let's say, the last thirty years. The weather was still pleasant, so I walked the six blocks.

Charles was seated on the outdoor patio and sipping a beer when I arrived. He waved. "Yo, hero, come join me."

He wore black shorts and a maroon long-sleeve T-shirt with a strange looking logo with Erskine Flying Fleet under it.

I slid into the booth and avoided looking at his shirt, in hopes he wouldn't need to tell me about it. His T-shirt collection was only surpassed in quantity by the collection of books filling his tiny apartment.

He tapped the logo. "Flying Fleet, get it? Remind you of when we became heroes?"

I waved for the server and ordered a glass of chardonnay, again, to draw attention away from Charles's shirt.

"Did you know Erskine College is in a place called Due West, South Carolina? Can you believe that?"

Not only didn't I know its location, I didn't know there was an Erskine College.

I mumbled, "Interesting."

"Yep. Been waiting years for a good time to wear it. By the way, did you know a 2006 Cessna 182 Skylane like the one we heroed the guys out of cost more than a quarter million dollars? Used! Like a dozen or so years old. Two-hundred fifty-thousand bucks."

That was two things I learned in the last two minutes.

"You know that how?"

"The guy on the TV said the upside-down plane was a Cessna 182 Skylane. Who wouldn't wonder what one costs? Used my handy-dandy laptop computer to ask Mr. Google what he knew about it. Found all sorts of stuff about the plane, most of it I didn't understand. They had the nerve to call it a light utility aircraft. Sure as heck didn't feel light when we were trying to lift it out of the mud to get the door open." He sighed. "Gary Isles must've had a pot load of money to be flying around in that expensive of a plane. Used."

I nodded, the safest response to most anything Charles says. "The paper said he was a partner in a big downtown Charleston law firm his father founded. He could afford it."

The server, Dennis, according to Charles, returned to the table with my drink and asked if we were ready to order. We each ordered fried seafood baskets, negating the calories burned on the walk over, then continued our—Charles's—discussion about the ill-fated plane. I zoned out when he started telling me about the twenty-six variants of the Cessna 182 since its debut in 1956. I rejoined the conversation when he said he wondered if we knew anyone who knew the two men who lived on Folly other than Tom Kale.

"Don't know about the other two," I said. "William called to tell me he knew Tom Kale. Tom and before that, his wife, Alyssa, were William's stockbrokers."

Charles leaned toward me. "When were you going to tell me?"

My friend considered it a personal affront if I learned something he may have interest in and didn't share it with him immediately. Immediately meant immediately.

"I just did."

"What time did William call?"

"Earlier," I said, hoping it was vague enough.

"Tell me everything he said."

I'd made it through retelling most of my conversation with William when our food arrived.

Charles attacked his flounder like he hadn't eaten all day, which could've been true.

He took a sip of beer, belched, then said, "Did William know Casper?"

It took me a few seconds to remember that Casper was Tom Kale's poodle.

"No."

"Wonder how Richard Haymaker's shoulder is," said Charles, a man who could change subjects on the head of a pin.

"Don't know."

"Think we should call to see?"

"No."

"How're we going to find out what went wrong, to find out how the guys are doing if we—"

My phone rang before Charles could lead me farther down Nosy Street.

Cindy's name appeared on the screen. "Good evening, Chief LaMond."

"If you say so. From my bloodshot eyes, it don't look so good. Of course, I have a job where I'm responsible to every citizen of this fine city, and you're, well, you're worthless and retired so everything looks brighter to you than it does to me."

"Cindy, did you call to remind me of my worthless status?"

"Nah, that was extra, no charge. I called to give a preliminary report on the untimely death of Mr. Gary Isles. The coroner won't issue a full report until the tox screen analysis is back in a few days. What he can say is the deceased pilot's heart appeared to be in excellent shape— excellent for a dead guy."

"So, it wasn't a heart attack?"

"That's what I said, pay attention."

"Is the coroner ruling out natural causes?"

I heard an audible sigh. "Not completely, but close."

I stared at the phone then said, "That mean he was murdered?"

I thought Charles was going to twist his shoulder out of the socket flailing his arms around. He wanted me to put the phone on speaker so he could hear. It was too late.

Cindy said, "Could be," as she hung up.

I hit end call, although it was already ended, then received a glare from my friend, before he said, "Was he?"

"Was he what?"

"Murdered?"

I shared the rest of Cindy's conversation and watched Charles get more agitated. Dennis made the mistake of returning to the table to ask if we needed anything else. I suppose that was what he was asking.

Charles interrupted before Dennis finished the question. "Another beer. Quick."

Dennis looked at me, so I nodded and pointed to my near-empty wineglass. I figured I'd need more before Charles calmed.

"Chris, we've got to figure out who killed those men, honest we do."

"Hold on, Charles. Nobody knows if the crash was anything but an accident. All Cindy said was the pilot appeared in good health. And, my friend, even it was something other than an accident, we have no reason to get involved."

"No reason? You've got to be kidding," Charles said while he waved both arms over his head. "That plane all but knocked on our door screaming help us. We saved two, now we have to help the other two. Got to find the dastardly person that killed them."

There was no arguing with Charles once his mind was

set. I sipped the wine Dennis deposited at the table while Charles was in the middle of his proclamation.

I watched Charles take a gulp of his second beer, then said, "Tell you what, let's take some time away from what happened and see what, if anything we learn in the next couple days."

I'd expected a fight about my suggestion. Charles agreed which proved he was exhausted. I knew I was, both exhausted and hurting from head to toe from our peaceful kayak ride.

Chapter Six

I called Charles three times the next day to be rewarded with voicemail. He'd purchased a cell phone a couple of years back when he and his then girlfriend moved to Nashville. As the old saying goes, should go, you can lead Charles to a cell phone, but you can't make him carry it. On the third try, I left the message that I saw in the paper where Mark Jamison's funeral will be tomorrow. I asked if he wanted to go. Charles had never passed up an opportunity to be nosy, so I knew the answer. My message was a formality.

He returned the call around sunset. As only Charles could do, he asked why I hadn't invited him sooner. As only I can do, I ignored the question and told him what time I'd pick him up. I'm certain somewhere in his mumbled response, he thanked me.

Next, I called Chief LaMond and was rewarded with, "Why in a heifer's hoof print are you harassing me while

I'm having a romantic, candlelight supper with my charming, sexy spouse?"

"Whoops. Sorry, want me to call back?"

"Crap no, why wouldn't I want to be interrupted? Besides, the Chef Beef Boyardee I slaved over for seconds is getting cold. I repeat, what're you harassing me about?"

"I saw where Mark Jamison's funeral is tomorrow. I was wondering if you knew anything more about Gary Isles' autopsy or when his funeral will be."

"And you're wondering this because you're a funeral junkie who doesn't want to miss a chance to smell the chrysanthemums? Oh, wait, I forgot, you're a guy, so you don't know the difference between a chrysanthemum and an Iranian bum."

That kind of comment reminded me why Cindy was one of my favorites. I chuckled, then said, "No. Charles and I were there when the men died, so I wanted to attend to express sympathy to their families."

"That'd be touching, if it wasn't a crock. You want to learn all you can about them in case the accident wasn't an accident. Then, you and your faux-detective friend can start meddling in police business."

In the recesses of his lopsided imagination, Charles thought he was a private detective. No training, no law enforcement experience, no license, no problem. He claimed to have read every private detective novel written making him qualified to carry on the legacy of Philip Marlowe, Sam Spade, and Sherlock Holmes. The frightening thing was that over the years, we'd stumbled on several murders, and through actions resembling Wile E. Coyote more than Sam Spade, we'd caught some killers.

"Cindy, all we want to do is pay our respects."

"And dear hubby sitting here staring at me thinks I look like Jennifer Lawrence."

"Of course not," I said. "You're far prettier."

"Nothing like BS with Beefaroni. No."

"No what?"

"Don't you remember your question? No news on the autopsy. No news on Jamison's funeral. Here's an answer to a question you didn't ask. The NTSB guy unofficially told me at first glance he couldn't see anything wrong with the plane. Nothing other than it was plopped upside down in the marsh. He's talked to the two survivors who said everything appeared normal until the pilot collapsed. Nothing official will be released for months."

"Thanks, Cindy. Now get back to your romantic supper."

"Right. Larry's done got bored and is in the living room watching reruns of *Rehab Addict* on the DIY Channel."

———

The funeral home was off Greenwood Road in North Charleston, some twenty-five miles from Folly. As anyone who knew Charles could've predicted, we arrived thirty minutes before the service. What I wouldn't have predicted was the number of mourners gathered around the entrance to the Colonial style, red-brick building. I recognized Richard Haymaker from the crash but hadn't realized how tall he was. At roughly six-foot-two, he towered over most of the others milling around. He was talking with an attractive blond, who, at five-foot-eleven, was taller than any of the women in the group.

Richard, wearing an expensive-looking, dark-gray suit, navy and white striped tie, and polished dress shoes, looked drastically different than how we'd seen him at the crash site. His arm was in a dark-blue sling, color coordinated with his tie. Charles and I approached the couple. Richard glanced at us and his expression changed from disinterest, to recognition, to a radiant smile.

"You're Chris and, umm—"

"Charles," my friend assisted.

Richard's right arm was in the sling, so he shook with his left hand, an awkward move. "Yes. Sorry I forgot. The other day was quite traumatic."

Charles said, "How's the arm?"

"I'm fortunate, only minor damage. The worst part is keeping it in this stupid sling. Allow me to introduce my wife, Charlene Beth. Charlene, these are the men who saved Tom and me. If they weren't there, we'd have drowned."

Charlene Beth, who'd been standing a step behind her husband, stepped forward, smiled, shook Charles's hand, reached for mine, and said, "Richard hasn't stopped talking about you, about what you did. Thank you so much. You'll never know how much your heroic act means to me."

"Me, too," said Richard, as he put his arm around his wife to pull her close.

She kissed his cheek.

I said, "We're sorry we couldn't have done anything for the other two."

Richard looked at the funeral home entry and lowered his voice. "I feel guilty standing here with such a minor injury, while my friend Mark is in there. So sad."

The group started entering the building so I suggested we should go in.

"Would you join us?" Charlene Beth said as she moved toward the door.

I said, "We don't want to infringe on your privacy."

Charles took a step closer to Richard's wife, and said, "Sure."

Those gathered appeared to be in two groups. There was a smattering of men wearing dress shirts and ties. A couple of the shirts were creased indicating they were right out of their packaging and the men were fidgeting with the knots in their ties as if they were being strangled. My guess was they worked at the trucking company Mark Jamison owned and were uncomfortable. The larger group seemed at home in suits.

We followed Richard and Charlene Beth to the third pew in the chapel while organ music playing a song I didn't recognize wafted through the room. In front of us was an impressive mahogany coffin resting on a cloth-covered bier surrounded by flower arrangements. The row in front of us was empty, but there were three people in the first row. The youngest of the three was in his mid-forties, well-dressed and had his head bowed. Beside him sat a white-haired lady, probably in her late sixties along with a balding gentleman roughly the same age.

Charles, seated beside Charlene Beth, asked if she knew the front-row attendees.

"The younger guy is Kevin Robbins. Mark was gay, you know. Kevin was his spouse. They'd gotten married in Florida a while back. I don't know for certain, but guess the others are Mark's parents."

She leaned close to Richard and said something. He replied, and Charlene Beth turned back to Charles to confirm the identities of the couple as Mark's parents.

The music turned more recognizable with the organ playing "Rock of Ages," followed by a minister eulogizing the life of Mark Jamison, attempting to convince those congregated he's in a better place. The short service ended with "Amazing Grace," and the minister inviting those gathered to join the procession to the cemetery. It was also followed by what I would characterize as a dignified stampede of the trucking company employees heading to the exit. I asked Richard and Charlene Beth if they were going to the cemetery, Richard said they'd said their goodbyes to Mark last evening at the visitation.

"I have to get to a meeting with a potential homebuyer," Charlene Beth added.

We were waiting for those going to the cemetery to leave the funeral home when Charles pointed to a couple at the back of the room. "Isn't that Tom Kale?"

Tom had been seated behind us, so I didn't see him until now. He was in a black suit. His hair was slicked back, and he had a sad expression on his face. There was a woman approximately his age leaning close to Tom.

"Is that his ex?" I asked.

Richard made a grumbling sound and said, "No. She's one of his current flings. Think her name's Nicole, or some cutesy name. His wife, his ex-wife is Alyssa, a nice lady."

I remembered her name from William telling me, and that she'd been his stockbroker before the Kales' divorce. I gathered Nichole wasn't one of Richard's favorite people.

The funeral procession pulled out of the parking lot as Charles and I made it to the car.

Charles watched the black Chrysler hearse turn left on the street, then said, "You know how many funerals we've attended since you moved here?"

I didn't and wasn't ready to start counting. "How many?"

"I was hoping you remembered. It's a bunch."

I shook my head, "Way too many."

Chapter Seven

F olly's Fourth of July fireworks had nothing on the light and sound of the thunderstorm that visited overnight and continued as I was awakened a third time by thunder shaking my cottage. The clock indicated it was a little after sunrise, although all I saw outside was coal-black sky and a torrential downpour illuminated by lightning's blinding bolts of pure energy. Two inches of rainwater covered most of my front yard, so I knew several of the city's lower-elevation areas would be flooded, a regular occurrence because of the island's mostly flat, near sea-level topography. This would be an ideal day to stay home to do, umm, whatever a retired bureaucrat would do. I was selfishly thinking how fortunate it was that the torrential downpour waited a day after Mark Jamison's funeral.

I brewed a pot of coffee then settled in the kitchen to enjoy not having to be anywhere when the phone rang.

"Ready to go kayaking in the marsh?" Charles said, in way too cheery a voice.

"Good morning, Charles," I said, in my ongoing attempt, ongoing failing attempt, to bring civility to telephone conversations.

"Good morning? What window are you looking out? Ain't nothing good about there being enough water out there to float the Ark."

"So, we're not going kayaking?"

"If you turn on that contraption called a television the only kayaking you'll see will be down the middle of the market in Charleston."

Charleston was notorious for flooding during heavy rains especially at high tide. A century or so before I was born, the city infilled creeks and marshes making development possible with flooding an unintended consequence. A dozen or so times since I lived here, the local media would show kayakers paddling through the Historic City Market located fewer than ten miles from my house. It made a great visual, while being a major headache for vendors, shop owners, not to mention tourists who had to wade through foot-deep water to cross the street.

During mornings like today, Folly didn't attract the video crews from television stations or reporters wielding cameras but flooding still could do a lot of damage for the barrier island residents.

Another flash of lightning lit the sky. I said, "Would it be asking too much to ask why you disturbed my peaceful morning coffee if we weren't going kayaking?"

"You're no fun."

I agreed.

"Anyway, I was in the bar at Loggerhead's last night, casually asking around if anyone knew the guys on the plane. Mark Jamison's funeral was fresh on my mind. I was confused how three of them could live on Folly with me only knowing one, plus cute fuzzball Casper."

Charles didn't do anything *casually*, so if he was at one of my favorite restaurants asking around, he was on a mission.

"Did anyone?"

"Glad you asked. Yes and no."

"Meaning?"

"Denver, a guy at the bar, not the city, said his wife was friends with Kelly."

"Kelly?"

"Gary Isles' wife. Keep up. Can I finish?"

I didn't respond so he figured he could. Besides, I couldn't have stopped him.

"Denver's wife, I believe her name's Tessa, told hubby, who told me, Kelly is one pissed-off spouse."

"Why?"

"Gary was a hotshot in that three-name law firm his dad started. Remember that from the newspaper?"

I said I did.

"Pissed-off Kelly worked in the firm when she and Gary got hitched. Had to give up her lucrative career to become a happy homemaker."

"Why'd she have to quit?"

"Denver's an electrician and no expert on law firm etiquette, although he says his wife is an expert on everything."

"And?"

"Chris, it's pouring down outside, you have nowhere to go, so chill. I'll get the story out if you stop interrupting."

Charles was a master interrupter, so I figured he knew one when he heard one. "Proceed."

"Denver's wife told him Kelly told her the three-name law firm was so hoity-toity, only working for the most prestigious businesses and individuals, that their attorneys' spouses weren't permitted to work. They had to look rich, act rich, appear like we were living in the 1930s. I added that last part."

"Thanks for the history lesson. Now what's so important you had to interrupt my morning coffee?"

"Oh, did I forget to mention pissed-off Kelly told Denver's wife she was so unhappy that at times she'd like to bash in his head?"

"You think she had the power to wiggle her nose causing her husband to pass out and crash the plane killing him, Mark, and nearly killing the other passengers because she couldn't work?"

"I don't have it all figured out. That's my working theory. Aren't you glad I called so you could cypher out the details?"

His last statement was punctuated by a rolling thunder vibrating coffee in my mug.

"Did Denver, the person and not the city, tell you anything else?"

"He knew my landlord, said if he wasn't careful, the electrical system in the building could start a fire. Said it hadn't been updated since Tyrannosaurus Rex stomped down Center Street."

"Anything else about the pilot or his wife?"

"No. Isn't that enough to cypher on?"

"Charles, you know there isn't anything saying the crash

was anything other than a tragic accident resulting from the pilot's collapse."

"We'll see. Remember, you heard it here first. Pissed-off Kelly has a motive for bumping off hubby. Heck, she even confessed—sort of—she'd bash in his head. The ground did it for her. You need to tell Cindy."

"Why can't you tell her?"

"She thinks I'm a nut. She trusts you. For some reason, the chief thinks my wonderful, innate, level of inquisitiveness, is a bad thing. As President Jefferson said, 'Good qualities are sometimes misfortunes.'"

It wasn't accurate that Cindy considered Charles a nut, although I knew what he'd meant. He's been known to not quite jump off the deep end but would step in water deeper than normal people should venture. I didn't see the motive he saw. I didn't think Kelly's remark about bashing in her husband's head amounted to a confession. What I knew was unless I shared this with the Chief, Charles would pester me until the end of time, if not beyond.

"Okay," I said.

"Okay, what?"

"I'll tell her."

"Really? I figured you'd call me nosy, crazy, claim my imagination was working overtime. Again."

"All true. I'll tell her anyway."

"You're a pal."

I said, "You're welcome."

I no sooner set the phone on the table, poured my cold coffee out, refilled my Lost Dog Cafe mug, and figured out what I was going to say to Cindy, when it rang again. What did Charles want now?

If he wanted something, I wasn't going to learn it. Cindy said, "Are you out playing in the rain?"

"Good morning, Cindy." One more effort to resurrect phone courtesy.

"What's good about it? You think I'm cuddled in my flannel PJs with cute dolphins frolicking all over them? For your information, I've been out with the fire department since four this morning rescuing a carload of citiodiots from Boston who thought their Chevrolet Impala was a boat and tried to float through eighteen inches of water covering the street out by the County Park."

I stifled a chuckle. "Citiodiots?"

"Idiots from the city, my dear unenlightened friend."

"You called to tell me about the rescue?"

"No. I called to tell you the coroner called while I was watching the Impala wash down the street. I figured I'd tell you what he said before you called to pester me about it."

"He said?"

"Preliminary lab results are back. The late Gary Isles left this earth before his plane returned to earth. It appears a form of cyanide ended his life."

"He was murdered?"

"Yep."

Cindy didn't know much more than she'd already shared. She didn't know how or when Gary had ingested the deadly poison, wasn't sure how long it would've taken from when he ingested it to when death occurred, and most importantly, didn't know who'd poisoned him.

I thanked her for sharing what she did know before she added the coroner released Gary's body to his wife and she was having him cremated and there'd be a private funeral with only immediate family invited. I wondered if it was being held privately as Kelly's snub to Gary's three-name law firm, Chapel, Smyth, & Isles, the firm that made her quit. I managed to slip in Charles's theory in the conversation. The Chief responded in a professional, inquisitive manner. She laughed.

I could tell Charles I'd shared it with the Chief.

Chapter Eight

B y noon, the torrential rains had moved on to soak
Georgetown and I realized I hadn't eaten since late
yesterday. It had also been a few days since I'd
talked to Barbara Deanelli, but even then, it was a brief
conversation letting her know what'd happened in the
marsh. She owned Barb's Books, a used bookstore on
Center Street in the building previously housing Landrum
Gallery. It's no coincidence the now defunct photo gallery
shared the surname I'd been using since birth. Opening a
gallery had long been my dream which became reality after
I retired. It turned out to be more of a nightmare after
losing money each year it'd been open. I gave up on the
dream three years ago and the store stood vacant until it
morphed to a bookstore. Barb and I've dated the last two
years.

To meet my need for nourishment combined with a
conversation with someone other than Charles, I walked two
blocks to Center Street, location of most of Folly's restau-

rants and only used bookstore. The walk was challenging since I had to weave around large puddles, and at one low-lying spot, crossed the street to avoid becoming waterlogged.

Snapper Jack's restaurant was in a multi-level building on the corner facing Folly's only traffic light. The rain had taken its toll on fair-weather vacationers, so the colorful building was three tables shy of empty. The hostess told me to sit anywhere, so I chose a bar-height round table by the closed garage-style door facing Center Street. A server I hadn't seen before greeted me. I ordered a fish sandwich, coleslaw, and water. I plopped my elbows on the table and thought about what Charles had said about Gary Isles' wife, now in the context of Cindy's revelation about the poisoning. Was it possible her anger escalated enough to risk killing three others to get rid of her husband? It seemed unlikely, yet if Gary was poisoned, someone was responsible. Then, my thoughts drifted to wondering if Gary was the intended victim. It could've been any or all the men. Yes, it was terrible two people perished in the craft, and it wouldn't have taken much for it to have been all four.

Food arrived redirecting my thoughts to my stomach. I was hungrier than I thought. More vacationers began venturing out of their dry houses, hotel rooms, or condos. The dining room was filling. Thirty minutes later, I'd finished lunch, walked a block and a half, entered Barb's Books, where I was greeted with a smile from the proprietress. Barb was a couple of years younger than me, at five-foot-ten, the same height. I was on the upper end of average weight for my height, okay, upper, upper end, while Barb was thin. She wore one of several red blouses and because of the marginal outdoor temperature had on tan khaki slacks instead of shorts she often wore.

None of the vacationers who'd ventured out were in the store, so Barb moved from behind the counter to give me a peck on the cheek. Her hazel eyes and endearing smile made the walk to the store worth every step.

"To what do I owe the pleasure of a visit?"

"I haven't seen you in a few days."

Barb nodded. "I suppose it kept you busy saving two men and handling the adulation you've received. Fame is time consuming. Want something to drink?"

"I don't know about fame, but sloshing through the marsh, prying a door open in the mud, and putting up with Charles was exhausting. I still hurt from the rescue. What's on the drink menu?"

I followed Barb to her office in back of the store. When I occupied the building, the back room was more of an above-ground man's cave. The office/storeroom had been furnished with a yard-sale table, mismatched chairs more at home in a condemned trailer park, and a full-sized refrigerator stocked with beer, wine, and an occasional soft drink. It was often the hangout for Charles, and a few other friends who were staying busy solving the problems of the world while gossiping about whatever was happening locally. The current drink menu included wine and bottled water. I chose water so Barb grabbed two bottles from the apartment-size, black refrigerator and set one in front of me on the glass-top desk. Classical music was playing from a portable Bose sound system. Night and day was the only way I could describe the difference in the room since I'd lost money in it for years.

She sat in her black, Herman Miller Aeron Chair and took a sip of water before rolling the high-tech-looking chair to where she could see if anyone entered the store. I recalled sitting at the same spot in my yard-sale chair which wouldn't roll anywhere while hoping someone would enter.

I watched her glance toward the front of the store, and said, "Have you heard anything about the plane crash?"

She jerked her head toward me. "Is that what prompted this visit?"

"No. Just curious."

She squinted then glared at me. Her stare reminded me of an attorney in a courtroom homing in on a hostile witness, a look she'd perfected during years as a successful defense attorney, a profession she'd given up when she moved to Folly. That's a story for another time.

Her expression remained unchanged. "Hmm, curiosity?"

I was saved by the bell—the bell over the front door announcing the arrival of a potential customer.

Barb slid the chair back to the desk, stood to greet whoever entered, and said, "To be continued."

No doubt, I thought. Barb hadn't been on Folly that long, but knew firsthand how I, with a few of my friends, had a penchant for getting involved in police investigations that were none of our business. In fact, she'd been the recipient of our help when someone from her past attempted to have her killed. She benefitted from my involvement but didn't like it. She didn't hesitate sharing her opinion.

Barb was gone several minutes, so I finished my water and walked to the front of the store to see if she was still with a customer.

She smiled. "Chris, you know Virgil?"

Barb was talking to a man in his early forties. He was my height, much thinner than I, with slicked-back, black hair. He wore sunglasses so I couldn't see his eyes.

I said, "I've seen you around town, but we haven't met."

The man smiled, shifted three books to his left hand, shook my hand, and said, "You can't say that again. I'm Virgil Debonnet. Your last name is?"

"Landrum."

"Virgil," Barb said and waved her arm around the room, "Chris had a photo gallery in this space before it became a bookstore."

Virgil reached to shake my hand again. "Cool. I'm an amateur photographer. I used to be in it big time, until, umm, until I wasn't. Had a Leica M camera, three lenses."

I never could've afforded Leica cameras, but knew they were among the best made. The equipment Virgil mentioned would've cost upwards of ten-thousand dollars. I also noticed the frayed cuffs on his long-sleeve, button-down, white dress shirt. He wore it untucked over navy blue chinos.

"Great cameras," I said. "What happened to it?"

"My ex has it." Virgil chuckled. "Doesn't really have the camera. She needed some lucre according to the divorce decree, so I pawned it. But, hey, that's neither here nor there. How come this is a bookstore, not a photo gallery?"

I just met Virgil and thought my answer was neither here nor there, also known as *none of your business*. I said, "I decided to move on."

Barb could tell I was uncomfortable with the direction of the conversation. "Virgil's one of my regulars."

"Regular visitor," he said as he chucked, a second time. "Seldom buy anything. I remember back in the day when I had a floor to ceiling set of bookshelves chock full of classics plus books on everything imaginable. The ceiling was fifteen-feet high. Had one of those ladders on rollers to reach all of them. Ah, the memories."

His mouth smiled, but with the sunglasses covering his eyes, I couldn't tell if he meant it. Do I ask what happened? Charles wouldn't let Virgil's statement go unexplored. That was enough reason for me to let it go.

Before I changed the subject, Virgil's head jerked in my direction. He snapped his fingers. "You're the guy who saved the men from the plane crash?"

I gave him my well-rehearsed comment about being nearby and doing what anyone would've done.

Virgil gave me an exaggerated bow then shook my hand again. "Not often one gets to meet a real-life hero."

When he bowed, I saw he wore scuffed, black Gucci loafers. The top of the shoes looked like they had many miles on them while the soles appeared new.

"Virgil, do you live on Folly?" I asked to move past a discussion about the crash.

"I do."

Dare I ask where?

Barb came to my rescue. "Virgil lives in an apartment a few blocks out East Ashley Avenue."

"Close enough to walk here and pester this sweet lady." He grinned.

I returned his grin. "Do you work over here?"

He laughed and shook his head. "I'm between jobs." He laughed louder. "Been between them a long time."

I said, "What kind of work do you do?"

"I know Charlene Beth Haymaker. She's the wife of Richard, one of the guys you saved."

I didn't detect the answer to my question in there. What I did detect was Virgil avoiding the question.

"Have you known her long?"

"A year or so. She handled a real estate transaction for me. After it was over, she and Richard took me to supper to celebrate. Nice couple. In fact, Richard found the tiny-tiny apartment where I'm currently residing." He glanced at his watch then continued, "It was great that you saved him. Too bad about the guys who didn't make it." He again looked at his watch. "Whoops, gotta be going. Barb, I'll get these the next time I'm in." He handed Barb the books he'd been holding, said it was great meeting me, then waved to us over his shoulder on his way out.

I watched the door close. "What's his deal?"

"He's in three or four times a week. Looks at books, seldom buys any. Occasionally he comes in later in the day, smells like he's spent some time, perhaps a lot of time, in one of the bars. Never causes trouble even if he's been drinking. I get the impression he's bored."

"Know what he did for a living?"

"I figured you caught his non-answer."

I nodded.

Barb looked at the front door. "It's funny. I asked him the same thing the first couple of times he was in. He gave me the same answer he gave you."

"None."

Barb smiled. "I stopped asking, although from a couple of remarks he's made, I get the impression he came from money."

"Remarks like the floor to ceiling set of bookshelves, the fifteen-foot high ceiling in his house?"

"Exactly," Barb said. "He also knows a lot about the stock market and international trade, topics that aren't often discussed by the less-fortunate."

"He now lives in a *tiny-tiny* apartment on East Ashley Avenue. Does he always wear sunglasses?"

"Don't know about always. He's had them on every time he's been in."

"Interesting gentleman," I said. "Before Virgil came in, we were talking about the plane crash."

"The one you're nothing more than curious about?"

I nodded knowing I'd be risking the ire of Barb once I told her what I'd learned from Chief LaMond. Regardless, I'd rather her hear it from me than from someone else.

"Cindy LaMond told me what caused of the pilot's death."

Barb frowned. "Let's hear it."

"The preliminary lab results indicate cyanide poisoning. He was dead before the plane hit the marsh."

Barb took a deep breath and stared at the wood floor. After an awkward pause, she looked up. "Murdered? You're going to stick your nose in the middle of it, aren't you?"

I shrugged and started to halfheartedly deny I would get involved, when my phone rang. I didn't recognize the number, so was going to let it go to voicemail when another customer entered the store.

Barb pointed to the ringing phone. "Go ahead, get it. I've got a real customer."

"Is this Chris Landrum?" asked an unfamiliar voice.

I said it was.

"This is Tom Kale. I don't know if you remember. I was one of the men you and your friend pulled out of the plane."

"Of course, I remember." How many crashes does he think I witness in a normal day, although he may think I remembered the crash but not his name?

"Good. Richard, the other man you saved, and I are putting together a reception to thank you and Charles Fowler for your heroic efforts. To thank you for our lives. Would you be available Saturday evening?"

"Yes, although you don't have to thank us."

"Good. I tried Fowler's number a couple of times and he didn't answer. Think you could get with him to see if he's available?"

I told him I could, then would let him know if Charles was available. I didn't tell him but knew there was a 99.9 percent chance Charles would be free. Tom gave me the address and time then ended by saying we could bring spouses or dates.

Now all I must do is invite Barb without it appearing that I was sticking my nose in the middle of a police matter.

I reached Charles the next morning. As could be predicted, he said nothing could keep him away. Barb said she would go if I promised not to leap off the cliff of curiosity into an amateur investigation of who killed the pilot. I told her I had no intention of getting involved. It didn't appear to completely satisfy her, although enough for her to agree to be my date.

Chapter Nine

T om Kale's house was three miles from the center of town on East Ashley Avenue. The large, two-story, pale yellow elevated structure's front door faced the street, its back yard the Atlantic Ocean. Four vehicles were parked on the oversized driveway. To no surprise, one of them was always-early Charles's Toyota.

Barb leaned toward the windshield and craned her neck to look at the tall structure. "Almost as large as your mansion," she said with tongue firmly planted in cheek.

"My back yard's not flooded," I said with a straight face.

"I see Charles is here."

"Of course. He's been here twenty minutes or so."

Barb continued to gaze at the McMansion. "Thirty minutes early?"

I nodded then walked around to open her door.

Tom Kale greeted us at the front door, carrying a white poodle. He was wearing blue shorts and a yellow polo shirt that contrasted nicely with his mocha colored skin. He looked far better than when I'd seen him at the crash.

"Glad you could make it," he said as we shook hands.

I introduced Barb. Tom said he hadn't made it to the bookstore yet but planned to soon. Barb graciously said she looked forward to it. Tom then introduced Casper, who licked Barb's hand but didn't say anything about wanting to visit the bookstore.

"Let's go to the deck," Tom said. "Your friend Charles and his date are already here."

The house's interior could be featured in *Charleston* magazine. The white-washed plank flooring held a large, off-white cushioned sofa and three light-blue chairs. I didn't have time to look closely, but two large paintings of the dunes appeared to be originals. Tom led us up the inch thick, green tinted, glass stair treads to the top floor.

Our host beamed as he said, "This floating staircase system is what sold me on the house. Amazing, isn't it?"

Barb said, "Amazing."

I nodded instead of saying ostentatious.

The stairs opened to an office with a laptop and two computer monitors on a granite top supported by chrome legs. The desk overlooked the ocean. Each monitor was forty-three inches bragged Tom. I wondered how anyone could get work done with the expansive view of the coast. French doors were beside the window. Several people were on the deck.

Tom motioned out to where Charles was standing beside Laurie Fitzsimmons. Laurie was five-foot-three inches tall, petite, and ten years younger than Charles. He and I met her nine months ago after Anthony, her husband, had been murdered while the couple was treasure hunting at the end of the island. Laurie was a retired drama teacher from Jacksonville, Florida. She and Anthony had moved to Folly weeks before his death and didn't know many people here. After Anthony's death, she latched onto Charles and they'd met to share meals a half-dozen times. According to Charles, they were friends, nothing more.

Barb, Laurie, Charles, and I shared hellos, then Tom said he wanted to introduce Barb and me to the others. He escorted us to Richard Haymaker and his wife, Charlene Beth. I remembered both from Mark Jamison's funeral, but Barb hadn't met them. Richard said it was nice meeting Barb, and Charlene Beth said she'd been in the bookstore a couple of times. Barb didn't appear to remember until Charlene Beth said her two-year-old twins had been with her. She apologized for them making a playroom out of one of the chairs. Barb's face lit up. She said she remembered yet compared to many kids who ventured in, how well-behaved the twins had been. Charlene Beth said yes, that would've been memorable since it was rare. Richard still wore the sling, so I asked how his shoulder was doing. He said the doc told him to wear it a few more days, but the pain was minimal. I told him I was glad. Charlene Beth said she was too. He was being a baby acting helpless. Richard gave her a dirty look but didn't comment.

A college-age woman wearing a white waiter jacket moved beside us and offered a choice of white wine, beer, or sparkling water. Richard and Charlene Beth already had drinks, Barb said white wine. I followed suit. The young lady left, and Richard thanked us for coming. He said this reception was the least he and Tom could do to thank us. I skipped my *we did what anyone would've done* story.

Tom left to greet a newcomer. She was five-foot-five,

marathon-runner thin, with brown hair, and a beautiful smile. She hugged Tom and glanced around the deck.

Charlene Beth leaned close to whisper, "That's Kelly, Gary Isles' widow."

Tom kept his arm around Kelly's waist as he escorted her over.

"Chris, I'd like you to meet Gary's widow, Kelly. Richard and Charlene Beth are Kelly's friends."

From the tone Charlene Beth used when she whispered who Kelly was, I hadn't detected much friendship.

Kelly said, "Chris, I apologize for being late. I was talking to Gary's cousin in Montana." She shrugged. "Time got away. Tom told me what you and your friend did to save his and Richard's life. I only wish Gary was here to say the same."

Tom's arm returned to Kelly's waist. "Chris, Kelly lives three houses down." He pointed east. "If you lean over the balcony, you can see her place."

I took his word for it. By now, Charles and Laurie had joined us. Tom repeated the introductions for their benefit. The caterer returned with our drinks and asked if anyone else needed anything. Tom ordered a glass of wine for Kelly. Richard said he could use another.

Charles turned to Kelly. "Did I overhear that you lived a couple of houses that way?" He pointed the direction Tom had indicated.

Kelly said, "Three houses over. Gary's father owned the house. My husband inherited it when his dad passed away a few years ago."

Tom added, "Gary was an attorney in the firm his father founded."

"I worked there until we married," Kelly said.

Charles moved closer to Kelly. "Why'd you leave?"

Only Charles could get away with asking that kind of question. He'd already learned why from the electrician, so he wasn't asking out of curiosity.

Kelly looked toward the beach before saying, "They have a policy that spouses of members of the firm don't work, female spouses, that is. They're old fashioned. Think it looks bad on the firm if the 'little women' must make money. Damned stupid policy. Anyway, that's why."

Barb said, "That's not unusual in some of the older law firms. It was that way when I was practicing law in Pennsylvania."

Kelly's eyes opened wider. "Oh, I thought you had the bookstore. Do you still practice?"

"No, I retired to the leisurely life of running a bookstore when I moved here."

Few people on Folly knew the circumstances of why Barb had left Pennsylvania and the law. She wanted to keep it that way.

I said, "Tom, you have a lovely house. I think I'm speaking for Charles when I say we appreciate you having this gathering."

The caterer returned with Kelly's drink plus a tray of finger foods. Each of us took a couple of whatever the little things were, and the discussion drifted to the perfect weather. Three seagulls were doing flybys in hopes we would share our bounty.

The conversation remained polite and benign until Richard said, "Kelly, have you heard if poor Gary had a heart attack, or what happened to him?"

She lowered her head. "No, sometimes things just happen."

Charles said, "Could someone have hurt him on purpose?"

Kelly looked at him like she hadn't seen him before. "What do you mean?"

"Oh, I don't know. Like a gunshot, poison, or something."

Charles was fishing since he knew Gary had been poisoned.

Kelly continued to stare at Charles. "Why would you even say something like that?"

Tom moved closer to put his hand on her shoulder.

I made a mental note to ask Cindy if the police had told Kelly about the poison. If they had, why was she acting confused?

"I was wondering," Charles said.

Laurie patted Charles on the arm. "Why don't we talk about something else?" She whispered, "Please."

Her husband's murder was still raw on her nerves. It was clear that Tom and Kelly were uncomfortable with the conversation.

"Tom," I said, "we have a mutual acquaintance. William Hansel has been a friend for several years. He told me you're his stockbroker."

Tom smiled. "Yes, William is a wonderful man. My ex-wife was his broker until she changed firms. I inherited William's portfolio. How do you know him?"

I gave him an abridged version of how we'd become acquainted. The story was interrupted when Richard, who was standing on the other side of the balcony with Charlene Beth, raised his voice and said, "No wonder you're gaining weight. How much more can you stuff in your mouth?"

Charlene Beth looked toward us. Her face turned red.

She slammed her wine glass down on a nearby table, turned, and scampered through the French doors. Richard mumbled a profanity, came over to us, and said, "Charlene Beth isn't feeling well, so we'd better be going. Charles and Chris, thank you again for what you did. I hope to see you soon."

He whispered something to Tom then followed his wife off the deck.

The Haymaker's rapid departure put a damper on the festivities. Tom tried to keep everyone cheered by plying us with drink and a few humorous stories about his clients. I'm certain in stockbroker circles the stories would've been funny, but stories involving words like puts, calls, IPOs, and my favorite, although I had no idea what it meant, Fibonacci retracement, didn't tickle my fancy.

Even Charles, the ultimate trivia collector, began to yawn. I thought it was time for the honored guests to bid farewell. Tom and his neighbor, Kelly, walked the four of us to the door and thanked us for coming. Kelly said she was going to stay to help Tom clean up. I thought that was the role of the caterers and wondered why Kelly felt the need to tell us why she was staying. Charles gave me a sideways glance when she said it, so I knew I'd hear more from him about it.

Chapter Ten

The next morning, I left a message for Chief LaMond to call. After two hours, I wondered if she'd received it. My wondering ended when the phone rang a little before noon.

"You buying lunch?" the Chief asked as a preamble.

"Where and when?"

"The Dog. Now."

"Fifteen minutes," I said.

"Good."

The strange thing was we both understood the conversation. I drove six blocks to the Lost Dog Cafe, a half block off Center Street behind the Folly Beach branch of the Charleston County Public Library sharing a building with the community center. Rain was in the forecast, so I rationalized that as reason for driving instead of walking, the heart-healthy approach, the one I should be taking. Granted, there wasn't a cloud to be seen, yet all it took was the word rain to convince me not to walk.

The Lost Dog Cafe, shortened to the Dog by most, was my favorite breakfast spot. I'd spent more time in the restaurant than in my kitchen, not surprising since unlike my kitchen, there was always food there. It was also the workplace for Amber Lewis, one of my favorite Folly residents. We'd dated when I first moved to Folly. Since then we'd remained friends, something many people couldn't say after a breakup.

Cindy LaMond's Ford F-150 was parked across the street in the parking area reserved for customers and employees in an adjacent building. Parking in a lot marked *For customers only* was one of the perks of being Folly's top law-enforcement official. I would've been towed if I'd tried, so I drove past the restaurant before I found a spot a block away.

Amber greeted me. She just turned fifty, was five-foot-five-inches tall, with auburn hair tied with a rubber band. Her wide smile accented her dimpled cheeks. She pointed to a table in the center of the room where Chief LaMond sipped coffee and stared at her phone. I exchanged a couple of pleasantries with Amber, asked about Jason, her twenty year old son, and said I'd appreciate a glass of water once I joined the Chief.

Cindy looked up from her phone when I pulled out a chair facing her.

Instead of saying something normal like "Good morning, handsome citizen," she said, "Did you know the estimated median household income on Folly is just shy of a hundred grand?"

"Somehow that'd slipped past my demographic database. How and why do you know that?"

"That world-renowned statistician Dr. Google told me."

Amber interrupted the stimulating, meaningless, conversation, when she set a Ball jar of water in front of me and asked if I wanted to order.

Cindy answered for me. "Give him a few minutes to see what the cheapest thing you have on the menu is and put it on my check."

Amber moved to a table behind us and I said, "Okay, that answers where you found that enlightening statistic. How about why?"

"My highly-efficient staff gave me a report this morning where I learned roughly two-thirds of our fine citizens owe the city parking ticket fines. I figured the average resident must earn about four hundred dollars a year and couldn't afford to pay the tickets."

I got over the shock she was buying lunch. I didn't dare mention her vehicle was illegally parked. "Do I detect sarcasm?"

"Absolutely." She smiled. "It's one of my endearing qualities."

"Endearing, I'm not sure, although I agree you do sarcasm well."

Amber returned to ask if I was ready to order.

I said, "Hot dog with kraut."

Cindy interrupted, "That the cheapest thing you have?"

Amber said, "A cup of soup is less."

Cindy sighed. "Give the growing boy the hot dog. He's almost worth it."

"Sometimes," Amber said.

"Enough of the lovefest," I said.

Amber laughed as she left to put in the order.

Cindy watched her go then said, "Where were we?"

"You were bemoaning a pile of unpaid parking tickets."

"Enough of that. Guess where I was this morning?"

"Applying for one of those four-hundred-dollar-a-year jobs?"

"Funny. Although for the hours I spend on this one, it's tempting."

"Cindy, where were you this morning?"

"Thought you'd never ask. I was out in the marsh watching one of those big-ass helicopters picking up the plane that nearly decapitated you. They had to fly the big-ass helicopter in from out of state. Would you believe there aren't any in South Carolina?"

"Not enough marsh plane crashes to justify one?"

"Funny. You know they use them for humongous construction jobs or to replace HVAC units on super-tall buildings."

I ignored her comment. "So, you invited me to lunch to tell me about the plane being moved?"

"No. Guess who was at the plane-raisin'?"

I looked at her and rolled my eyes.

"Okay, you couldn't guess it anyway. Aaron Cole."

I shrugged.

"He's a field investigator from NTSB's office in Atlanta. Seems like an okay guy, a tad stuffy for Folly, but I suppose not everyone can be as wonderful as those of us here. The NTSB on the back of his black T-shirt was about the size of that Hollywood sign in, well, in Hollywood. I bet the guys on the space shuttle could read it. I asked him if I could have one to give Charles. The stuffy part of him said no. He didn't even ask who Charles was."

My second cheapest item on the menu arrived and I took a bite while Cindy was winding down about the field agent's shirt.

"Did he say anything about the crash?"

"Nothing he hadn't said before. It'll be weeks before they issue a final report on the cause. He did say while nothing was official, he hadn't seen anything unusual about the plane other than it was upside down in the marsh, not a normal hangout for airplanes. Since the pilot died of a lethal poison, the cause of the crash seems obvious." She shook her head. "There's one thing that upset the investigator, me too. Someone had been in the plane. Absconded with everything that wasn't attached. Wait, that's not true. They tore the radio out and took the golf clubs, luggage, no telling what else. Aaron looked at me like it was my fault. I told him I couldn't have had someone camping out there twenty-four-seven until he arrived."

"What'd he say?"

"Cross between a growl and a profanity. He finally calmed and said he understood. The bad thing is if there was evidence of how the pilot was poisoned, it was gone."

I nodded. "I'm glad you mentioned poison. When did you tell Gary's widow about what happened?"

"I didn't. Detective Callahan broke the news to her the day I told you."

Detective Michael Callahan is with the Charleston County Sheriff's Office, the office charged with investigating major crimes on Folly. Cindy's force is lean and not equipped with a staff to investigate murders. The Folly Beach Department of Public Safety and the Sheriff's Office cooperate with each other, but occasionally the cooperation is challenging since the Sheriff's Office treats the Folly Beach department like a stepchild, not always forthcoming with information. I'd become acquainted with Detective Callahan four years ago after I stumbled into a murder investigation he was conducting. He had the reputation for being one of the best detectives in the department, so I was glad he caught the case.

"That's interesting," I said.

"Why?"

"Last night, Charles and I were talking with Kelly Isles, Gary's widow. She acted like she didn't know the cause of her husband's death."

"Whoa, nosy one. Why were you two vagrants talking to Ms. Isles?"

I told her about the gathering at Tom Kale's house and who was there.

"Please, please don't tell me the two of you are sticking your nosy noses in police business."

"Of course not. We thought it was kind of Tom and Richard to invite us, so we graciously attended."

"The only part of that I believe is Tom and Richard invited you. With my suspicion noted, you sure Kelly didn't know her husband was poisoned?"

"I couldn't say if she knew or not, although she gave the impression she didn't."

"Makes one wonder, doesn't it?" Cindy took a sip of Diet Coke as she looked around the room. "I'll let Detective Callahan know."

"Good."

"Now I have another question. Why was Gary Isles' widow there?"

"She lives a few houses past Tom Kale's McMansion. She said even though we couldn't save her husband and Mark Jamison, she wanted to thank us for saving the other two. I don't know how friendly Tom had been with Gary, but he seemed quite friendly with Kelly. She stayed at Tom's after everyone else left."

Cindy lowered her head then glanced up at me with her eyes at half-staff. "Think there's something going on between them?"

"All I know is they were a tad too friendly with each other."

"Hmm," Cindy said then took another sip. "I suppose I'd better mention that to Detective Callahan."

"Another good idea."

She nodded. "What's the deal with Charles and widow Laurie?"

"Don't know if there's much of anything. They've gone out to eat a few times. She enjoys his company. He doesn't say much about her."

"Hmm," Cindy repeated.

We finished lunch on lighter notes. Cindy wondered how many photos of dogs adorned the walls. I said there were as many as there were residents of the island. The chief speculated the dogs would pay their parking tickets quicker than many of the human residents. I didn't dispute her analysis before she said she needed to get back to the office to pester her staff.

"And call Detective Callahan to tell him about Kelly and the interesting relationship between Gary's widow and Tom Kale."

She sighed then headed to the door.

Chapter Eleven

I wanted to tell Charles about my conversation with Cindy, and to follow in his footsteps by being nosy about his "date" with Laurie. I left two messages before figuring out he'd probably left the phone in his apartment. Instead of waiting at home for his call, I walked three blocks to Cal's Country Bar and Burgers, commonly called Cal's for a couple of reasons. First, most of us are too lazy to say its full name. Second, the quality of the bar's burgers didn't deserve being included in the name, a fact even its owner doesn't dispute. Fortunately, Cal's is a great country music bar. It's owner, Cal Ballew attributes its success to its vintage look, often confused with old and worn out by those who step through its door the first time.

I stepped through the paint-peeling front door for nowhere near the first time. If I didn't know what year it was, I would've sworn I was sauntering into the 1960s. The walls were painted dark green with other colors peeking through the chipped paint. There were a dozen tables, a long wooden bar along the right side of the room, with a tiny, elevated bandstand along the back wall bookended by restrooms.

A Wurlitzer jukebox, a relic of the 1960s, was on the corner of the bandstand playing George Jones's classic, "He Stopped Loving Her Today." Three tables were occupied, two with couples, the third with four patrons. Empty beer bottles exceeded the number of customers at two of the tables. Behind the bar, illuminated by neon beer advertisements, Cal was multitasking by singing along with George while drying a wineglass.

Cal saw me, waved me over, pointed the wineglass at me. "Knew you'd be coming. Was getting it ready for you. White?"

I'm glad one of us knew I was coming, although he did have the drink right. I'd known Cal eight years, including a year before he'd taken over the bar after its previous owner killed a local attorney and is now residing behind bars, the steel kind. Cal had been a country-music singer before most Americans were born. He'd travelled the South forty-plus years singing at any venue that'd have him while living out of his 1971 Cadillac Eldorado. Folly was his last tour stop and where he made a career change from traveling musician to bar owner. He kept his voice in shape by performing on weekends.

"Haven't seen you in a while," he said, as he handed me the glass then tipped his sweat-stained Stetson my direction.

Cal had lived about a hundred years during the seventy four he'd been on earth. His spine curved forward from leaning over to sing in a microphone nearly every night of his life.

"Missed being here," I said then took a sip.

John Wesley Ryles' haunting version of "Kay" filled the air, as Cal said, "Hear you and Charles saved a couple of guys in that crash out in the marsh. How do you and your shadow manage to be at every disaster? Hell, I hear you were at this one before it was a disaster?"

Cal received my speech on *we did what anyone would have done*. I tried to change the subject as I looked around the room before saying, "Light crowd."

"It'll have to pick up a heap to be light. It'll take more than this to keep the old jukebox spinning ole George, Johnny, or memories from the rest of my buds."

Cal had recorded "End of Your Story," a song he'd penned, which became a regional hit in his home state of Texas while reaching number seventeen on the national country charts. That was the peak of his musical career. In 1962. That didn't stop him from telling anyone who'd listen he'd been friends with Hank Williams Sr, George Jones, Johnny Cash, Patsy Cline, and Willie Nelson. Four of the five are residing in hillbilly heaven and unavailable for confirmation. To my knowledge, the fifth, Willie Nelson, has never been to Folly Beach. True or not, Cal spins some interesting stories about his escapades with the music greats.

Cal wasn't to be distracted. "What caused the plane to crash? Rumors flying around here, pardon the pun, are it ran smack-dab into a squadron of pelicans. After chopping up a couple, the propeller broke. I heard the pilot intentionally crashed it so his wife could collect his life insurance. Oh yeah, I also heard but didn't take it too seriously, it was shot down by a terrorist with one of those handheld surface-to-air missile things. Figure you'd know the skinny since you were there."

Before I shared the "skinny," two people entered.

Charles spotted me and made a beeline to the stool next to me. He wore a navy and light blue Roger Williams University, long-sleeve T-shirt, red shorts, gray tennis shoes, and his canvas Tilley hat. He pointed at his chest. "It's in Rhode Island."

I nodded like I cared.

"Got your message. Instead of calling, figured I'd check out a few bars and would find you. Did you know you're not at Planet Follywood, the Crab Shack, or Rita's?"

Can't slip anything by my friend. I nodded a second time when Cal returned from getting a beer for the other man who entered with Charles. He'd sidled up to the far end of the bar.

Charles knew Cal's beer selection numbered three, so he said he'd have whatever the other guy was having. Cal turned, pulled a bottle of Budweiser from the cooler, set it in front of Charles, leaned across the bar then whispered, "Either of you know who that is?"

Charles and I pivoted toward the stranger who looked to be in his fifties, tall, maybe six-foot-two, overweight, not bad looking except for the long, straggly black beard that could house a family of mice. I told Cal I didn't recall seeing him before. Charles said, "Me either. Why?"

"Something strange about him. He came in last night. Sat at the same spot, sipped on three beers for a couple of hours, didn't say anything except 'another beer' and 'check.' I could be imagining it but had the feeling he was staring at me when I wasn't looking. Strange."

That was all it took for Charles to grab his drink, hop off the stool, walk over to the man, and take a seat.

Cal turned away from Charles and his new friend.

"When's this ole, washed-up, country crooner going to learn to keep his mouth shut around Charles?"

Never, I thought. I knew the rumor about a surface-to-air missile shooting down the plane wasn't true but was certain Charles was a surface-to-surface missile when he wanted to find out something. Sammy Smith was singing "Help Me Make It Through the Night" while I was trying to distract Cal from worrying about what Charles was saying to the stranger. I was partially successful, which didn't stop Cal from glancing over at the newcomer like he thought he was going to pull out a gun and shoot up the place. I was glad when one of the tables of drinkers waved for Cal to bring refills. The group at another table asked for their check.

Charles's new acquaintance patted him on the back before heading to the door. Cal was back in front of me when Charles returned with a smile and message for Cal to put the stranger's beer on my tab. Charles was generous with my money.

Charles ordered another beer then said, "Okay Cal, what do you want to know?"

Cal looked at the door where the stranger had exited. "How about who he is?"

"Name's Junior Richardson, says he's from Arkansas."

Cal said, "Name's really Junior?"

Charles smiled. "Didn't figure he'd show me his driver's license. We'll have to take his word."

I said, "What else?"

"He was passing through. From what he's seen the few days he's been on Folly, said he may settle here. He's been impressed by how laid back everybody is. He thought some of the street names are out of place. Silly him. He didn't think Arctic, Huron, or Erie should be streets in the South."

He wasn't the first to wonder that, so I didn't comment.

Cal said, "Why's he been staring at me?"

Charles took a sip of beer, then stared at the stool Junior vacated. "That's a question I couldn't figure how to slip in the conversation. He seemed like a nice guy. Looks like the kind of person who'd fit in."

I asked, "Did he say what he does for a living?"

"He was vague when I meandered down that path. Garbled something about the food industry, owning restaurants, then threw in retired. If I had to guess, I'd say he does nothing." Charles rubbed his chin. "I'm not done getting the scoop on him."

That, I didn't doubt.

Chapter Twelve

Mel Evans called the next morning. It surprised me since he calls slightly more often than wild kangaroos hop past my house. I'd met Mel, affectionately or not so affectionately known as Mad Mel for reasons obvious to anyone who met him, five or so years ago through a mutual friend, Dude Sloan. Mad Mel had pulled me out of a jam at that time. I, along with Charles, had managed to prove him innocent of murder three years ago. I masked my surprise and asked what I did to deserve a call.

"Haven't seen you in a while. I like to keep contact with a few straight people to reinforce how stupid all of you are."

"Generous of you," I said and chuckled. "Now, what's the real reason?"

"Gotta take a boat load of freakin' left-wing, brain-washed, snivelin', college brats on one of my world-famous marsh tours at fourteen hundred. Checking to see if you were free for lunch."

Mel was a retired Marine who operated a marsh tour

business out of Folly View Marina just off the island. He specialized in taking groups of students, a.k.a. freakin' left-wing, brainwashed, snivelin' college brats, on excursions to remote areas of the marsh so they could drink beer while partying to their hearts' content and bladders' discontent. Unlike other marsh tour operators who specialized in educational excursions, Mel knew as much about the flora and fauna of the marsh as I did about the heart rate of a camel. Mad Mel had found his niche.

We agreed to meet at Rita's at twelve hundred in Mel-speak before he decided he'd talked long enough. He hung up on me. Rude was another of his charming qualities.

To kill time before meeting Mel, I Googled Junior Richardson in what I suspected would be a futile search. As is often the case, Google exceeded being helpful by showing more than twenty-million references to the name. I narrowed it down by adding Arkansas, which proved to be equally unsuccessful. I don't know why I'd hoped to find him. First, I doubted his first name was Junior. Second, even though Charles said he was from Arkansas, he didn't say that's where his restaurants had been, or even if he'd owned restaurants.

I abandoned the Internet search when it was time to head to Rita's. The restaurant was two blocks from the house and sat on a prime spot of Folly real estate across the street from the iconic Edwin S. Taylor Folly Beach Fishing Pier. The temperature was in the upper sixties but with the outdoor seating area in the sun, it would be comfortable. Mel didn't have Charles's proclivity—obsession—for being early, so I figured he wouldn't be here and requested a table on the patio.

I heard the rumble of Mel's retro-styled, black Chevy

Camaro before I spotted it rounding the corner and parking on East Arctic Avenue. Even if I hadn't seen him park, it would've been hard to miss the six-foot-one, burly, tour boat operator as he ambled across the street, holding out his hand to stop a car from hitting him. He was wearing his constant frown along with leather bomber jacket with the sleeves cut off at the shoulder and woodland camo field pants sheared off at the knee. His frown almost broke when he saw me seated at a table at the side of the patio.

"Suppose you're going to whine, scold me for being two minutes late," he said as he removed his camouflaged cap with Semper Fi on the crown and dropped it on the table.

I smiled as he plopped down in the chair. "It's good seeing you, Mel."

He shook his head. "Add salt. You're too damned sweet."

I continued smiling. "How many are you taking out this afternoon?"

"M5 will be cluttered with fifteen freakin' morons."

M5 was shorthand for Mad Mel's Magical Marsh Machine, the name printed in nine-inch-high letters on the side of his twenty-five-foot-long Carolina Skiff.

"You ever thought about being nice to the students, you know, your paying customers?"

"Hell no. What's this I hear about you trying to get your head sliced off by a damned aircraft?"

Good, I'm getting to the reason for the lunch invitation. I gave him my explanation of what we did plus my well rehearsed it wasn't anything different than what anyone else would do.

"Bet he was a freakin' Air Force pilot. Couldn't even land the plane on dry land."

According to Mel, there was only one true branch of the military, the Marines. I told him I didn't know, then he mumbled a couple of more profanities. I added that the pilot had been poisoned, was dead before the plane crashed.

"Excuses, excuses," he mumbled. He waived a server over and ordered a cheeseburger plus two beers. I ordered a fish sandwich and a Diet Coke. Mel looked at me like I'd ordered a glass of Kool-Aid and a Twinkie.

The server left. I said, "By any chance, did you know Mark Jamison, one of the men killed in the crash, or possibly Kevin Robbins?"

Mel waved his fork at me. "Crap, Chris. I'm gay so you think I know every gay person? Hell, I've never met Barry Manilow, Anderson Cooper, Leonardo da Vinci, or most of the other gay dudes and dudettes in the world."

I didn't point out he couldn't have known Leonardo da Vinci. "Mel, I'm asking since they lived in Charleston."

Our drinks arrived.

Mel took a gulp of beer, mumbled something I couldn't understand, then said, "Know both."

"Elaborate."

"Let's see. If the newspaper's correct for a change, Mark Jamison's dead. Kevin Robbins ain't." Mel grinned, or what passed as his effort at a grin. Smirk would be a better description.

I sighed, "Anything else?"

"Met them in Connections. For you narrow-minded straight folks, that's a gay nightclub in town. I talked more with Mark since we both have businesses. Caldwell got to know the other guy better. He's a grocery store pharmacist on the other side of the Cooper River, maybe in Mt. Pleasant."

Caldwell Ramsey is Mel's significant other who made up for Mel's lack of political correctness and civility.

"A pharmacist?"

"Ain't that what I said?"

"Yes. I was thinking ..." I didn't finish the thought.

Mel took another bite. "Spit it out. Thinking what?"

I hadn't realized I'd said it out loud.

"If Kevin Robbins is a pharmacist, he'd know poisons."

"Aha! Don't say it. You're sticking your pasty-white nose where it don't belong."

"Curious, that's all."

Food arrived; Mel took a large bite of burger. With part of the meat oozing out of the side of his mouth, he said, "It's a wonder as much crap as you keep spouting out of that mouth you don't have a flock of flies circling your head. Mark my words, you're playing cop."

He guzzled the rest of his first beer.

"How well did they get along?"

"Do I look like a freakin' head shrink? They talked; they drank. I didn't notice them making google eyes at each other if that's what you mean."

Not exactly, I thought. "Did they argue about anything?"

"Mark was pleasant. He wasted too much time talking about how poor business was, how much little companies struggled. My business is doing just fine, thank you. I ignored most of what he said. If I wanted a lesson in economics, I'd subscribe to *Forbes*."

"Think his trucking business was in trouble?"

"He never said it, but I wouldn't be surprised."

"Anything about Kevin Robbins?"

"Let's see," Mel said then glanced at his watch. "Don't recall hearing him say he was going to poison his lover.

Gotta head out to play nice with the left-wing, brainwashed college brats."

"Nothing else about Mark or Kevin?"

"Caldwell spent more time talking to Kevin. I'll see if he recalls anything. Will let you know."

Mel waved to the server and asked for his check. It was one of the few times whomever my dining partner was hadn't stuck me with paying. There was hope for Mel yet.

He finished his cheeseburger, washed it down with beer, paid, and before leaving the table, said, "Try not to get yourself killed while you're not sticking your damned nose in someone else's business."

Chapter Thirteen

The unseasonably warm weather had headed south, with the temperature now in the low sixties, normal for early-March. It was sunny and the perfect day for a walk, so I grabbed my Nikon, Tilley, and headed a block to Arctic Avenue then toward the Tides, Folly's nine-story hotel standing where Center Street terminated at Arctic Avenue. Each room overlooked the ocean with a spectacular view of sunrise and the Pier. Over the years, I'd become acquainted with several Tides's employees, so I walked through the lobby to see if any were working. A large group was checking out, so members of the staff were scurrying around helping with paperwork and luggage.

I left the hotel to walk to the beach access walkway bisecting the hotel's parking lot and the large Charleston Oceanfront Villa's condo complex where I saw someone I thought was Virgil Debonnet. He was leaning against the wooden railing on the ramp leading from the walkway to the beach. The breeze coming off the ocean was strong. Virgil's hair that had been neatly slicked back when he was in Barb's Books was whipping around the front of his face. I wasn't certain it was Virgil until I recognized the resoled Gucci shoes. He was drinking something from a brown paper bag, something I'd wager wasn't sweet tea.

Virgil was focused on the Pier to our left and didn't notice me moving beside him.

"Hey, Virgil. Nice day, isn't it?"

His head jerked my direction. "Umm, yeah."

His eyes were hidden behind sunglasses and I couldn't tell if he recognized me, so I said, "I'm Chris. We met in Barb's Books."

He nodded. "Oh, sure. Barb tells me you two are an item." He took a drink of whatever he had in the paper bag. "I'd offer you some, but it's illegal drinking this at the beach. Wouldn't want you to get in trouble."

"That's okay."

"Good. I don't have enough to share. Before you get the idea I'm an *arfarfan'arf*, I consume no more than a dozen adult beverages a day." He laughed as he tapped me on the shoulder.

"You're not an arf what?" I asked, channeling the inquisitive mind of Charles.

"*Arfarfan'arf*, my good man, a Victorian term for a drunkard."

I wondered why I'd asked in the first place. "Oh."

"Sorry to wax erudite. Couldn't help it. My ex has a degree in English, not the helpful kind of degree that helps you conjugate verbs, but one that made her act superior to all of us lowlifes who don't speak Victorian."

And there he was speaking Victorian to me. He'd already forgotten his discussion about Barb and me.

"The other day you said you were between jobs. What kind of work did you do?"

"Isn't that a bit forward to be asking someone you don't know and simply found gandering at the deep blue sea?"

"Sorry if I offended you. I was thinking if I heard of anything in your field, I could let you know."

Virgil laughed. "Just teasing. I had a semi-stellar career as a stock market analyst." He looked around the ramp only the two of us occupied. "Truth be told, I made my money the old-fashioned way. I inherited it." He laughed. "Anyway, my father, who art probably in hell, had been part of Charleston's old money. He made a fortune in shipping, boats bringing stuff from the old country to the good old US of A, not UPS." He paused as he looked at a couple walking hand-in-hand on the beach.

"Interesting," I said to let him know I was paying attention.

"He left me one of those stately mansions overlooking the Battery, you know, the ones tourists ogle over, the ones carriage tour guides spend way too many words talking about. Yes sir, life was grand."

To ask, or not to ask. Why not? "What happened?"

Virgil chuckled. "My stock market analytic skills failed to exceed my fortune. Well, that's not all that caused my, let's say, downsizing. Gambling, like with bookies plus junkets to Vegas, also gambling big on stocks, and, oh well, why not say it, an illegal substance or two, led to me, umm, to me standing here with absolutely nowhere to go or anything to do, nor with the resources to do it." He laughed. "Is that a sad story, or what?" He took another drink.

I started to say I was sorry, but sorry for what? Instead I looked at him and nodded like I understood.

"Know why my wife left me?"

I shook my head.

"She said poverty wasn't in her genes. When my platinum American Express card got shredded, she shredded our marriage license. Being smacked in the face by broke was her tipping point. Go figure."

One of the amazing features of Folly was the wide range of residents, and those living here without a residence. It was no accident the island was labeled *The Edge of America*. Homeless men and women coexisted with the wealthy. People who thought Barry Goldwater was a screaming liberal coexisted with people who'd supported Bernie Sanders. While there were constant disagreements about, well, about everything, most of the people on Folly whom I'm acquainted with would defend to their death the rights of those with whom they held strong disagreements.

I'd only met Virgil twice, yet figured he'd fit in quite well. His positive attitude was welcomed and appreciated. I hoped it wasn't a result of what was in the paper bag. He seemed to take his situation in stride, had a much better attitude than I would if I'd lost a fortune.

I told him I was sorry about losing his wife. He said he was sorry that he'd lost someone who'd constantly criticized him for how he'd dressed, who he chose as friends, how terrible he'd treated her silver-spoon-in-the-mouth relatives. He said it didn't take long to realize how little he missed her.

He shook his head and added, *"C'est la vie."*

I wasn't fluent in any foreign language, was moderately fluent in English, and knew he wasn't speaking Victorian, and said, "True."

He nodded at my camera then turned toward the Pier. "Think anyone ever took a photo of it?"

I thought I detected a grin on his face, although it was hard to tell under his sunglasses.

I chuckled. "A zillion, give or take."

"Did I ever tell you about my Leica?"

"You mentioned it when we were at Barb's," I said, wondering how many conversations he thought we'd had.

"Loved that piece of incredible German technology. Did I also tell you I knew the Haymakers? A fine couple, they are."

I was beginning to wonder if my new acquaintance was operating on all cylinders. I was also glad he didn't have enough of his drink to share with me.

"You mentioned that."

"Did I tell you how we met?"

"Yes."

"Ah, I now recall. I told you about them because you saved Richard and that other guy in the plane. So sad about the others. So sad." He bowed his head like he was praying.

I remained silent wondering why he felt the need to talk about the Haymakers.

Virgil lifted his head, glanced at the Pier, then turned to me. "Did I tell you the circumstance of how I met Charlene Beth and Richard? Whoops, just asked that, didn't I?"

"Yes, and yes. It was something about her handling a real estate transaction."

"Ah, I gave you the sanitized version. Suppose that wasn't unusual since I'd only met you seconds earlier." He patted me on the arm. "Now that we're good buddies, I'll share, as that old geezer used to say, the rest of the story."

Good buddies, I thought, then nodded for him to continue.

"Did I mention I had one of those mansions on the Battery?"

Not quite five minutes ago, I thought. "Yes."

"It appears in this country when one becomes unexpectedly broke, even though one's domicile is paid for, there still are taxes to be paid, and those in charge expect them to be paid each year. Who would've guessed? Anyway, not only was I without money, a condition I could've recovered from, if I hadn't been a couple of million dollars on the underside of broke, the house had to cease being in my name, a name I regret had lost its luster."

"Two million dollars in back taxes?" I said.

Virgil shrugged. "Not all taxes. A half-dozen companies thought they should be paid money I owed them."

"That's too bad," I said.

"Not really. I'd been a *zounderkite*, got what I deserved."

"A what?"

"Oh, sorry. Another Victorian word my ex called me on numerous occasions. Means a complete idiot."

"Oh."

"Anyway, it's water under the dam, or is that water over the bridge? Doesn't matter, it's gone, so here I am, happy as a lark, enjoying an adult beverage, talking with a new friend. Umm, did I mention, happy as a lark?"

I said he had.

Virgil shook his head and laughed. "Charlene Beth and Richard took me to the Peninsula Grill, treated me to a magnificent supper to 'celebrate' my freedom from home ownership." He laughed again. "It really was a sympathy meal although they were too kind to put it that way. Did I mention Richard helped me find the apartment I now call home?"

"Yes."

"Did I tell you how lovely Charlene Beth is, how adorable her twins are?"

That was something he hadn't mentioned, and I told him so.

"Well, she is, they are. If I had more money and less integrity, Richard had better look out." He slapped the side of his head. "I'd better stop while I'm ahead. Besides, I'm beginning to repeat myself. Let's end this chat to continue it another time. I would give you a card with my name and phone number, but while my name is unchanged, I left my phone in the apartment. I don't recall the number."

I watched my new "friend" turn, nearly trip over his own feet, then stagger up the walkway to the sidewalk behind the hotel and condo complex. I then took a photo of the Folly Pier. Photo number zillion-and-one.

———

After finishing my Folly-like conversation with Virgil, I headed up Center Street to Barb's Books. I hadn't talked with the lovely store owner since the gathering at Tom Kale's house. I held the door open for a smiling customer who was leaving carrying a bag holding several books.

"Looks like you've had a profitable morning," I said as Barb greeted me with a kiss.

She waved toward a bookshelf along the left wall. "I didn't even know I had three books on pottery. Now I have none." She turned to me. "What brings you in?"

"Thought it was a good day to visit the most fetching bookstore owner on Folly."

Barb rolled her eyes. "Only bookstore owner."

"Most fetching even if there were a hundred bookstores."

"With the bull out of the way, what brings you in?"

"I'm curious about your reaction to Tom Kale's party."

"Wondering when you'd ask. I thought it was nice of him and Richard to have you and Charles over. They didn't have to do anything. Something bother you about it?"

"Not really," I said and asked if she had any coffee in back.

Barb led me to her office where she had a Keurig coffeemaker. We each brewed a cup then she moved to the doorway, so she could see if anyone came in the store.

"I was surprised to see the pilot's wife," Barb said.

"She lives close, so I suppose she wanted to thank us for trying to help the guys in the plane."

Barb slowly nodded. "I get that. What struck me unusual was how she didn't appear too distraught over her husband's death. I also had the impression she was irritated by Gary's law firm's policy against spouses working. As I told her, it's rare but not unheard of, but I see how it'd bother her since she was an attorney who'd worked at the same firm. Don't get me wrong, it's only an impression."

"I didn't catch that, but it seemed she was closer to Tom than a three-houses-away neighbor."

Barb smiled. "I was wondering if you noticed. Curious, isn't it?"

"Speaking of curious," I said. "This morning I had a strange conversation with Virgil Debonnet."

"That's redundant. Where'd you see him?"

"He was on the walkway to the beach beside your condo building."

"Why strange?"

"He was standing there looking at the Pier while drinking something out of a paper bag."

Barb smiled. "Gatorade?"

"Hardly. He started telling me his life history. How he'd been wealthy, had a big house at the Battery, how he'd lost everything because of bad luck and bad choices, about losing his wife, on-and-on. This was only the second time I'd talked with him. Remember, you introduced us? Don't you find it weird he'd be telling all that to someone he'd just met?"

Barb took a sip of coffee and said, "Virgil's a talker. He'd told me everything he shared with you. He doesn't hide much. To be honest, I find his self-deprecating humor refreshing. We all would be much better off if we took ourselves less seriously."

"I agree, although it still struck me as unusual."

Barb laughed. "To quote the guy who's standing in front of me, 'On Folly, unusual is usual.'"

I returned her laugh. "You do listen."

Chapter Fourteen

"I've been thinking," Charles said as we walked up the steps to the elevated, diamond-shaped, upper-level of the Folly Pier.

"Dare I ask?"

Charles had called on my way home from the bookstore to ask if I could meet him on the Pier. I knew not to ask why. He'd tell me when he was ready. I had nothing else to do so I agreed to meet.

"Been thinking about the crash," he said as he sat on a wooden picnic table with a view toward the beach.

I joined him on the table. "What about it?"

"Wondering how we're going to figure out who poisoned Gary." He glanced sideways at me, probably because he expected me to say it was for the police, not us to figure out.

I didn't want to be too predictable. "Why should we get involved?"

He twisted around and faced me head-on. "Have you already forgotten how someone poisoning poor Gary nearly got us decapitated? How much more involved can we be? Yep, we've got to figure it out."

I sighed. When Charles is on a mission, it'd be easier to stop a speeding locomotive with a toothpick. Also, a few things about the crash were bothering me. First, if someone wanted Gary Isles dead, why choose a method that most likely would've killed the other three men?

That must've been on Charles's mind as well when he said, "Think Gary was the person the killer was after?"

"If he was, why kill the others?"

"Exactly. I think one of the passengers was the intended victim. Poisoning Gary and crashing the plane was a clever way of doing it without giving away who was supposed to die."

"It could've been more than one," I said as I looked back at Pier 101, a restaurant on the structure.

Charles said, "Or all four."

"If Gary hadn't taken the extra time to buzz Folly, the plane would've been at a higher altitude when he collapsed. The crash would've killed all of them."

Charles removed his Tilley and ran his hand through his thinning hair. "The killer could've targeted one of the people in the plane, two of them, three of them, or all four."

I agreed.

"See," Charles said, "it's too complicated for the police to figure out. That's why we need to."

Charles logic at its best.

"How do you propose we do that?"

"Coming up with a list of likely suspects would be a good place to start."

"First," I said, "let's eliminate Richard and Tom. They

were fortunate to survive. Who would gain the most by the death of one or more of the group?"

Charles returned his Tilley to his head then leaned back on the bench. "You're always telling me the top motives for killing are love, money, or revenge. So, what about love?"

"Charles, that's impossible to answer unless we know the intended victim. If it was Gary, I suppose Kelly could be guilty. She's probably the beneficiary of his estate. This morning I was talking to Barb who told me she detected resentment at the party when Kelly was telling us about having to leave Gary's law firm."

"Kelly didn't seem too distraught about his death."

"That too," I added. "Yet, it could only be her if Gary was the person the killer was after. Add to that, others we don't know who could've wanted Gary dead."

"Okay, what if it was the gay guy, what's his name?"

"Mark Jamison," I said. "I don't know anything about his relationship with his spouse, Kevin Robbins, but Mel told me that Robbins is a pharmacist. Who better to know poisons?"

"Chris, you're giving me a headache. Too many options, too much information."

I nodded toward Charles. "You're the one who decided we needed to do something."

"Yeah. You're the one who's supposed to talk me out of it."

I smiled.

Charles said, "What do we know about Richard Haymaker?"

"Not much."

"At the party he was on his wife's case about gaining weight."

I smiled. "If every woman who's been told by her husband she's gaining weight killed him, the male population would be cut in half."

"True," Charles said. "Suppose we need to find a better motive to accuse Charlene Beth of sabotaging the plane. What if Tom Kale was the intended victim?"

"We know less about him than the others. He has an ex-wife. William told me she'd been his stockbroker before their divorce. When she left the firm, Tom took over William's portfolio."

Charles looked at the hotel and then at a group of surfers patiently waiting for the perfect wave. "At the party, he seemed mighty friendly with Gary's grieving widow. What if some hanky-panky is going on? That'd be a reason for the widow to want her hubby dead."

"But if she poisoned Gary, the odds were high Tom would've been killed in the crash."

"Picky, picky."

Something came to me that I hadn't thought of. "Virgil Debonnet."

"Huh," Charles said, for good reason.

"I ran into him this morning at one of the walkovers to the beach. Interesting guy. He was telling me Charlene Beth handled the real estate transaction when he sold his house in Charleston. She and Richard had taken him to supper after the closing."

"Dang," Charles interrupted. "You've figured it out. Virgil killed Gary to crash the plane to kill Richard because he had the nerve to feed him."

"May I finish?"

He motioned me to continue.

"Virgil was telling me how lovely he thought Charlene

Beth is, called her twins adorable. He said if he had more money and less integrity, Richard had better look out. It's a stretch, but that could've been a motive."

"About as weak a one as possible. I think Charlene Beth is a fine-looking woman. Think I poisoned Gary?"

"Charles, we're throwing out ideas."

"Good, cause I'll throw that one out."

I conceded he was probably right.

"That covers love," Charles said. "What about money or revenge?"

"I don't know about you, but I don't know enough about the cast of characters to know if there's a reason for any of them wanting revenge. Do you?"

"No. How about money?"

"Kelly would inherit Gary's estate which should be substantial. Charlene Beth would get Richard's. Since Tom was divorced, I don't know what'd happen to his estate."

"What about Mark Jamison?"

"Don't know. Guess he'll get it if they were married."

Charles stood, looked over the railing, then mumbled something I couldn't understand. I moved next to him and asked him to repeat it.

"Remember in the past when you got me stuck in the middle of trying to catch a killer?"

"I'm fairly certain it was the other way around."

"Whatever. My point is there was one dead person— one, not two, not almost three or four. Our only problem was figuring out who killed one, I repeat, one, dead guy. Even then, it was hard. If memory serves me correctly, it nearly got us killed a time or two."

I nodded. "Now, no one knows who the intended victim was. Or intended victims."

"You got it. That's the problem."

"Let me add another unknown to the equation. We know the pilot was poisoned. I don't know much about it, but from what I've heard, cyanide poison is quick acting. If swallowed it can cause almost immediate unconsciousness. How'd he get the cyanide? If he ingested it on the plane, where did it come from. I've also heard it has an almond smell. Wouldn't he have noticed something wrong if he'd drunk something with it in it?"

Charles nodded. "When we rescued the guys, one of them said Gary had a cold. That could've kept him from smelling the poison."

"Yes, I believe it was Richard. That could explain why he didn't notice it. That still doesn't explain what it was in, or if it was in anything. Cyanide can also be inhaled, although if that happened, the others on the plane would've been drugged."

"Either of the guys mention drinks on the plane? I didn't see anything, although we were sort of busy saving people."

I thought for a moment. "No one said anything. I didn't notice a cooler or drink containers on the plane."

Charles said, "Cindy told you someone stole everything before the plane was hauled out of the marsh. It could've been the person who poisoned Gary. If there was evidence on the plane, it would've been smart for the killer to steal it before it could be found."

"True, although that seems remote. It was a few days after the crash before the plane was removed. Cindy or someone from the Sheriff's Office could've found it long before the theft."

Charles pointed at my phone. "Call Cindy. Ask if

anyone from her office, or from the Sheriff's Office, or the NTSB found where the poison came from, or if they asked the survivors if they had any idea."

"Charles, how do you propose I ask her without looking like I'm nosing in her business?"

"You're the smart one. You'll figure it out. Put her on speaker. If I think of anything you should say, I'll use sign language to tell you."

I exhaled. "Sign language?"

"Oh yeah, I forgot. You don't know sign language."

I rolled my eyes. "Neither do you."

"You certainly know how to shoot down a great idea. Okay, I'll whisper wisdom in your ear."

I smiled as two girls about ten years old rushed to the railing, squealed, as they pointed to a couple of dolphins frolicking in the waves near the Pier. Their parents moved beside them, joining their girls watching the graceful aquatic mammals doing their thing.

Charles elbowed me. "Don't get distracted. Remember, you're calling the Chief."

I didn't know what I was going to say yet knew unless I called, I'd suffer more from the mouth of Charles.

Cindy answered on the third ring. "This is Chief Lamond. How may I help you?"

The polite answer told me she was with someone and couldn't talk. I asked her to call when she had a free minute. She said she would then ask for my number, the number she had, the one appearing on her phone's screen.

"What could be more important than talking to you?" Charles asked, sighed, then said he had to make three deliveries for Dude. If Cindy called when he wasn't with me, I should take notes, so I could tell him everything she said.

It was my turn to sigh. I told him I'd let him know. I didn't mention I wouldn't have notes.

Charles barely had time to get off the Pier when Cindy called. "If I promise not to have you arrested for pestering a police chief, will you buy me a beer at the Surf Bar?"

"When?"

"Five minutes."

"I'm on the Pier. It may take me a little longer to get there."

"If you're planning on jumping, go ahead. I'll buy my own beer."

"See you at the Surf Bar."

Chapter Fifteen

The Surf Bar is a popular hangout, especially for locals, and, as implied in its name, surfers and the younger crowd. Cindy is at the average high-end age of the bar's clientele. I'm the grandfather's age of many of its customers. Regardless, most regulars are accepting of any age visitor, more importantly for the Chief, the bar is directly across the street from Folly's Department of Public Safety.

Cindy was at the bar staring at her beer. When I took the stool next to her she held up the beer and said, "Don't worry. They said they'd wait so you could pay."

I thanked her for her allowing me to buy. Before I could order, the bartender set a glass of white wine in front of me. Cindy smiled saying I could pay for my drink as well.

"Rough day?" I said, figuring it must be considering her drink was half gone.

"Once upon a time, many moons ago, traffic didn't get bad until around Memorial Day. Our fine citizens didn't start bitching about how bad it was until, oh, let's say, the holiday weekend." She took another sip and continued, "Then something happened. Perhaps it was global warming, or word got around that Folly was a cool place to hang out, or those same fine citizens who are now bitching were younger and more tolerant, or no telling what else." She shook her head then took another drink.

"And?" I said to break up her monologue.

"Even though horologists tell us it's mid-March, and the meteorologists tell us the average high this time of year is still in the sixties, flocks are already arriving. They're driving, parking everywhere. Car clutter."

I was stuck on the first part of her sentence.

"Horologists?"

"Thought you were smart. They're folks who're obsessed with time, even study it, if you can believe that. True, most of them study time measured by clocks, but the oldie-goldie horologists are still hung up on the calendar." She grinned as she leaned back on the seat.

"I'm impressed."

"Don't be. I saw it in a magazine this afternoon. Been waiting three hours to drop it on somebody."

By now, I'd forgotten what she'd been talking about. I didn't have to remember, she said, "Why the call?"

"Charles and I were talking about—"

Cindy waved her hand in front of me, then waved for the bartender, who was quick to respond.

"Another beer. I'll need it." Cindy turned from the bartender to me. "I'll warn you now. I may retract my offer not to arrest you. Go on."

"We were thinking about the crash, wondering since the pilot was poisoned, how it was administered."

"Um, hum," Cindy responded, saying nothing.

"Do you know how cyanide got in his system?"

She took a sip of her second beer, glared at me, before saying, "Chris, you're incorrigible."

I smiled, hoping to get her to do the same. "Did you read that in the magazine?"

She shook her head. "All the damned cars cramming the island, not even one of them ran over you on your way here."

"So, you know how it got in his system?"

"Chris, if you weren't so nice, on a rare occasion lovable, I wouldn't be letting you bribe me with drink. I'd have my guys pack your stuff up then escort you off island." She looked around to see who was in hearing distance, lowered her voice, and said, "In a rare moment of cooperation, Detective Callahan let me sit in on his interview with Tom Kale. If Callahan's boss, the Sheriff, knew, he'd probably boot Callahan down to corrections officer strip-searching drunks."

She took another sip, so I said, "Learn anything?"

"Kale said Gary had a cooler. He offered each of them a drink when they were ready to take off. Mark Jamison grabbed a bottle of Mountain Dew. Richard and Tom didn't take anything."

"What about Gary?"

"That's where it got interesting. Tom said Gary took a screw-top bottle of an energy drink. Detective Callahan asked if Gary drank from it. Tom said yes, he opened it after they were in the air heading this way. Callahan asked if Tom knew what the drink was. He said he didn't know because he was distracted trying to see Folly and his house."

"How long after he took a drink did he collapse?"

"Tom said it seemed more like seconds rather than minutes. That's consistent with what the coroner said about how fast cyanide works."

I said, "Did anyone else on the plane have access to the cooler before Gary took out his drink?"

"Tom said no since Gary took off as soon as the others arrived."

"I don't suppose he had an idea who would've had access to the cooler before they arrived."

"Nope. Let me tell you what I do know. Fries are good with beer." She once again waved for the bartender, ordered fries, adding for the employee to bring her another beer with the fries.

I told her I didn't need anything else, then turned to Cindy, "If whoever put the poisoned drink in the cooler meant for it to go to Gary to crash the plane, he or she must've known which drink Gary would take. The one Mark chose didn't have poison in it, and probably neither would the ones the guys in the back seat may've selected."

"Correct, Mr. Faux Private Eye. That's why the real detective and I left our interview with Tom and drove out to the rich end of the island. We knocked on Kelly Isles' door and had a pleasant conversation with her."

"I don't suppose she confessed to poisoning her spouse?"

Cindy stared at the bartender like that would speed up the delivery of her fries and third beer. It didn't, so she turned back to me. "Do you think if she confessed, I'd be wasting time sitting here talking about interviewing Tom Kale?"

"Sure, because I'm nice, lovable."

"Correction, I said lovable on rare occasions."

The fries and Cindy's drink arrived before I could

dispute her correction. She grabbed two fries, stuffed them in her mouth, then mumbled, "Dear, sweet, widow Isles invited us in, grabbed a box of Kleenex off a table by the door, before ushering us to the living room where she lowered her head, did a passable job appearing grieved, patted her eyes with a Kleenex, before asking how she could be of assistance."

"Cindy, you said that like you're doubting her sincerity."

"Neither yes nor no. It was over the top, making me suspicious. Detective Callahan expressed sympathy for her loss then asked about the cooler. The widow Kelly said she had no idea what was in it. Her story was Gary always filled it before heading out to play golf. She didn't know he had it on the plane, had no idea who else may've had access to it before taking off."

"Did you believe her?"

"Something about it didn't feel right. I can't put my finger on what."

"What did Callahan think?"

Cindy grabbed two more fries, dipped them in catsup, and studied dollar bills attached to most every surface in the building while she chewed the fries. I took a sip and waited.

"If our fine citizens didn't stick their money all over this place, they could pay their parking fines."

I rolled my eyes. "Callahan, Kelly's story?"

"Guys are swayed by a sob story or a tear, especially if the sobber is attractive," Cindy said. "Callahan said Kelly's story sounded sincere. He pointed out how sad she must be, that her story about the cooler made sense."

"Anything else you can share?"

"Crap, Chris, I shouldn't have shared what I did. Now,

let's either change the subject or let me arrest you for harassing the police chief."

I smiled. We started talking about the weather, how crowded the bar was getting, and I asked how her husband Larry was doing. She finished her third beer, the fries, and said she had to get home to see what TV dinner Larry wanted for supper.

"One more thing, Cindy. Was the cooler in the plane when it was hauled out of the marsh?"

"Gee, Chris, why didn't we professional law enforcement officials think of that?" She shook her head. "It wasn't there. Callahan thinks it was taken by whoever stole the rest of the stuff out of the aircraft."

"And the bottle Gary drank from?"

"Gone."

Convenient, I thought. I didn't share that with the professional law enforcement official who was now standing to head home to heat a TV dinner.

Chapter Sixteen

The phone rang as I was sipping coffee and standing on my screened-in porch watching a line of sleepy commuters drive by on their way to work.

An equally sleepy, barely recognizable voice said, "Good morning, Kentucky. Didn't wake you, did I?"

I couldn't recall talking to Cal this early in the morning since he normally doesn't leave his bar until after midnight. I knew it was him since he referred to me by my state of birth, a habit the crooner occasionally resurrects.

"I was on the porch watching traffic go by. What's up?"

"What're the chances you could mosey over to my apartment?"

"When?"

"Now?"

I'd never been to Cal's apartment. Something was up. Although I'm nowhere near as curious as Charles, Cal had my attention.

"I'll be there in fifteen minutes."

"Super. I also invited Charles. Whoops. He's knocking. See ya."

Cal's place was three blocks from his bar and located in a concrete-block building that had been divided into a duplex about the time of the Revolutionary War. The north side of the building was covered in mildew and looked like it'd been painted green as opposed to the off, way off, white of the other sides. Charles answered the door like he'd invited me and said, "Cal's fixing us breakfast."

The room's furnishings were sparse. There was a brown recliner tilted in its reclined position and listing to one side. It faced a twenty-seven-inch JVC television that I knew from having one years ago weighed as much as a cruise ship. The dark-green carpet was threadbare yet clean. To the left of the television, there was a laminate, three-shelf bookshelf that held two rows of record albums with an empty top shelf.

Cal appeared, saw where I was looking, and said, "Used to have a record player there but it died a while back."

I didn't have time to check-out the rest of the room, which wouldn't take long since the apartment was so tiny it'd make a telephone booth look like the Biltmore House.

Cal straightened his Tammy Wynette, faded-blue T-shirt, before continuing, "Thanks for moseying over." He handed Charles and me a paper plate with a slice of toast slathered with butter and red jam made from some unknown fruit. "Thought I'd better feed you breakfast after screwing up your morning."

I took the *breakfast* as I looked for somewhere to either sit or to set the plate.

Cal followed my gaze. "I'm not used to visitors. Suppose we'd be more comfortable in the kitchen."

The kitchen was tinier, if that was possible, than the living room. A round, vintage, pub-sized Coca Cola table with one chair filled the room.

Cal pointed for us to set our plates on the table. "Best piece of furniture I have. It's a classic." He chuckled. "Like me."

He asked if we wanted something to drink, followed by saying that the choices were beer in the green refrigerator and water.

"Jadeite green," trivia collecting Charles said as he pointed at the refrigerator that also had to be a classic.

"If you say so," Cal said as he made a tipping motion where his Stetson would normally reside. His straggly white hair was Stetsonless.

I declined the beer saying water would be fine.

Cal turned to the dripping sink. "Good, got plenty of it."

What he didn't have was an explanation of why he'd summoned us. Cal rooted through the cabinet, found two glasses, wiped a smudge of something off one, and delivered our water. He started talking about the weather and how slow business was the previous night. He appeared to want to talk about anything but the reason we'd been summoned.

Charles would have none of it. "Cal, good buddy, I appreciate the fine breakfast, chance to visit your abode, but why're we here?"

Cal plopped down in the chair that went with the Coke table while Charles and I rested in the two card table chairs Cal dragged to the kitchen from the back porch.

He took a deep breath, looked in his water glass like he was trying to find the next words, and said, "The guy you met in the bar came back last night."

That didn't narrow it down much, but Charles did when he said, "Junior Richardson from Arkansas?"

Cal pointed his forefinger at Charles and winked. "That's the one. Know what he asked me?"

Charles told him he didn't know. I shook my head.

"The boy was on his second beer then motioned me out from behind the bar, asked me to hop on the stool beside him. There were only two other guys in the place, so I sidled up beside Junior. He then gasted my flabber when he said, 'Cal, know where you were this date fifty-seven years ago?'"

Not a normal question to ask a bartender you hardly knew, I thought. "What'd you say?"

"Looked at him like I'd look at a red stoplight. Told him I couldn't tell you where I was Thursday. Asked what he was talking about."

"Cripes, Cal," Charles muttered. "Spill it. What was he talking about?"

Junior sat up straight, ran his hand through his beard and said I was getting hitched to Jasmine Folkstone." Cal shook his head. "Now that was a blast from the past. Remember a few years back when I told you I'd been married a few times?"

I said I remembered.

"Jasmine was *numero uno*."

Charles leaned toward Cal. "How'd Junior know?"

Cal shook his head, looked at me, then at Charles. "Suppose because he's my son."

Charles jerked back. "He's what? Didn't you tell me you didn't have kids?"

Cal rubbed his hand through his hair getting most of it to go the same direction. "Didn't know I did. Was hitched to Jasmine six months. Got married in sixty-two, the year I had my hit record. She was from Fulton, Arkansas, a town about the size of my bar. Charles, you being a trivia collector will like this. Fulton was named after Robert Fulton the steamboat inventor. Anyway, I'd been on the road a couple of years, figured it was about time to settle down. Met Jasmine, sort of fell in love, got hitched. The problem was there was only one place in Fulton for me to sing. I tried to make it work. Honest to God, I tried."

"And failed," Charles said.

Let Cal tell his story, I wanted to say.

"Yes, Charles, I failed. Jasmine was a nice gal, but I had, what's the word, wanderlust. Settlin' down wasn't my thing. Besides, I had to get to other cities to promote my record. I tried to explain it to Jasmine. I was as successful as grabbin' a beach umbrella and flying it to Uruguay. We didn't depart on kissy-face terms."

I said, "You didn't know she was pregnant?"

"Nope. Last I heard from her was a year later when she found out I was staying in a flea-bag motel near Nashville. Sent me divorce papers to sign. Not a word about a kid, no sir, not a word. Hell, not even a syllable."

I said, "How do you know Junior's telling the truth?"

"That's a fine question, Kentucky. I asked him the same thing. The first hint was when he told me his real name was Calvin Richardson. Claimed his mom named him after his dad. He pulled a wallet out of his britches, slid out a folded, old black-and-white photo of Jasmine holding a baby. The kid didn't have a beard like Junior, but Junior, umm, Calvin, said it was him. When he was old enough to understand, his mom told him his dad was a soldier, that he was killed in Vietnam."

"Cal," Charles said, "a picture doesn't prove you're the dad."

"Same thing I said to him. He said that was true but said he'd take a blood test if I wanted."

Charles said, "What'd you say?"

"I've been around the block a time or two, pretty good at figuring out when someone's lying. I don't doubt Junior, Calvin, is being square with me. Guys, I'm a dad at the ripe young age of seventy-four, yes I am."

"Cal," I said, not wanting to get in a semantic argument about when he became a father, "if Jasmine told him his father died in Vietnam, how'd he learn about you?"

"Jasmine died five years ago, lung cancer. Heck, I remember her chain-smoking Kool menthol cigarettes from the time she had her first cup of coffee until climbing in bed at night. It's a wonder she made it as long as she did. Bless her soul."

Cal stared into space until Charles interrupted his memories. "Junior learned about you?" He made a move-along motion with his hand.

"After Jasmine passed, Calvin Jr. was going through her stuff. He found a promotional picture of me, one of those record companies send to radio stations along with records. Junior said I almost looked handsome back in those days. He also found newspaper clippings about me at shows in Arkansas, some in Texas. The tipping point was when he found his birth certificate. In the space for father, it said Calvin Ballew."

This was coming from so far out in left field that I was at a loss of words. Charles wasn't.

"How'd he find you?"

"Said it wasn't easy. It took him three years of surfing

the Internet, going through old newspaper clippings in Little Rock. The boy even took a trip to Nashville to look through newspaper morgues. He finally found something on the Internet about when I took over the bar a few years back. Persistent fellow, I'll give him that."

"Congratulations, Dad," Charles said. "What's your baby boy want?" He drew a dollar sign in the air with his forefinger. "Money?"

Cal stood and looked out the back door. "Same question I asked, except for the baby boy and money part." He laughed although I didn't see anything funny about his recent discovery.

Charles said, "Well, what'd he say?"

"Look around you. Do I look like I live in a mansion overlooking the ocean? Hell's bells, I have a breathtaking view of a commercial dumpster." His laughter turned to a chuckle. "It ain't a breathtaking view but is breathtaking to my nose. Money. If that's what he's looking for, he's barking up the wrong family tree."

"Cal," I said, then repeated Charles's question, "you asked Junior, umm, Calvin, what he wanted. What'd he say?"

"Said all he wanted was to meet his old man. If it's okay with me, he'd move to Folly."

Cal had returned to his view of the dumpster. Charles said, "What's he do for a living?"

"Said he owned a chain of chicken restaurants in Arkansas. Twern't no KFC, but he made a good living, then sold the chain to track down his fathe—umm, to track me down. He's not starvin' for money if what he said is true."

"You believe him?"

Cal shrugged. "Suppose so. He said the only reason he was here was to get to know me better."

"How do you feel about that?" I asked.

"Strange, odd, weird."

Charles said, "You honestly believe him?"

Cal rubbed his hand through his hair, again, blinked twice, then said, "Yep."

I said, "What happens now?"

"He said he'd stop in tonight, so we could shoot the breeze. That's why I wanted to talk to both of you. Can I handle having a new son, new even if he's fifty something years old?"

Charles nodded. "Teddy Roosevelt said, 'Believe you can and you're halfway there.'"

Chapter Seventeen

C al said how much he appreciated us coming, yawned, then hinted that he needed to get some shuteye before opening the bar. After leaving, we agreed that Cal's well-intended breakfast did little for our stomachs. A trip to the Lost Dog Cafe would meet that need.

The restaurant was near full. The only vacant table was a four-top in the center of the room. Amber was quick to greet us with a mug of coffee and asked if I wanted to order a bowl of fresh fruit parfait. I said her sense of humor was outstanding. She told me the same was becoming true for my stomach. Charles leaned back taking it all in with a smile. I sucked in my stomach and said I'd have French toast. Amber said she'd wasted time asking.

Charles waved a hand in her face. "Yo, Amber, I'm here, too."

She smiled. "Of course, you are. That's why I put that mug in front of you."

He got around to ordering pancakes. Amber left the table mumbling something about Pillsbury Doughboys.

Charles sipped coffee, looked around the room, and said, "Can you believe Papa Cal?"

"I can't think of many things more shocking. He seemed to take it in stride."

"I hope Junior isn't running a scam. Cal can be naïve about things, even if he's in his mid-seventies and according to him, been around the block a time or two."

I didn't have a chance to respond. Virgil Debonnet was standing beside our table alternating between looking at me and the empty chair.

I took the hint asking if he wanted to join us.

"If you don't mind."

Charles said, "Not at all. We'd love to have you."

I thought Charles was being overly friendly to someone he'd never met. Virgil sat and introduced himself to Charles, who said he'd heard lots of good things about Virgil.

"That's nice," Virgil said. "I've also heard a few things about you."

I noted he omitted the word *good*.

Charles asked what Virgil had heard.

"You and Chris have a reputation around here. I've heard from more than one person you are killer-catchers extraordinaire."

Charles smiled like Virgil had crowned him king of Monaco. "I don't know about extraordinary, but in all modesty, I must say we've been successful."

I wanted to move off that subject. "Virgil, any luck finding a job?"

He smiled. "No, but that brings up something I wanted

to talk to both of you about. Word around town is that you're trying to find out who offed the pilot."

"No," I said. "The police have it under control."

Charles interrupted, "Chris, let Virgil talk."

I motioned our guest to continue.

"Chris, do you remember I told you about working with Richard and Charlene Beth on the sale of my house?"

"Yes, plus how Richard helped you find your apartment."

"What I didn't tell you was I know the other survivor's wife, umm, Tom Kale's wife, ex-wife, Alyssa."

I asked, "How do you know her?"

"She's a stockbroker. I ran into her at a couple of social gatherings of people in that business."

Charles leaned closer to Virgil. "Think she poisoned the pilot to kill her ex?"

"That was before the crash. She didn't mention planning on killing him while we were standing around at a cocktail party sipping vino." Virgil chuckled. "I would've remembered her saying she was going to bump off the pilot."

Amber returned with our food and asked Virgil if he wanted anything. He looked at our plates but said water would be all. Charles, generous Charles, told Virgil if he wanted something to eat, I'd buy. He hadn't gotten the last of the sentence out when Virgil interrupted and asked Amber for a menu, studied it, then ordered a breakfast burrito.

I imagined snarling at Charles, but instead said, "Virgil, did Alyssa say anything to indicate she was unhappy with her husband?"

Virgil smiled. "I thought you said you're not trying to catch the killer?"

Charles turned to me. "Yeah, Chris."

I said I was curious, nothing more.

Virgil rubbed his chin. "Now, let's see. She didn't say she wanted him dead. What she said was their divorce was filed a year ago, it was acrimonious, they were still fighting over everything including their poodle. I believe it's named Casper."

"There you go," Charles said. "The ex had a reason for bumping off her husband."

I took a bite of French toast as Virgil picked up his knife and pointed it at Charles, then at me. "Want to know what I was thinking last night?"

I was tempted to say no, but knew it'd be rude. I told him to continue.

"I was thinking several things. For example, I know two spouses of the guys plus one of the men in the plane that tried to be a boat. Then, I was thinking if I saw you two today, I could give you what you detectives call a clue, that being Alyssa Kale had motive for wanting her husband gone, dead gone. Then, I was thinking it'd be nice if I still lived in the mansion overlooking the Battery." He shook his head. "Ignore that thought. Was feeling sorry for myself." He took a deep breath. "That leads to my biggest thought."

His breakfast burrito arrived along with coffee refills for Charles and me. Before he had time to chew the first bite, Charles said, "What was your biggest thought?"

Virgil put his finger to his lips which I figured meant he'd wait until he finished chewing before answering. That proved he had more couth than either Charles or me, or for that matter, most of my friends.

The aroma of bacon was strong as Amber delivered an order to the table beside us.

Virgil glanced at Amber, swallowed, then turned back to us. "I'm between jobs, have time on my hands, so I thought I could join forces with you to find out who killed the pilot and nearly took the life of my friend Richard. We could be the crime-fighting dynamic trio."

Dynamic trio! I felt a headache coming on caused by the man sitting beside me, a man who was eating breakfast I was paying for.

"Interesting idea," Charles said as he poured more syrup on his pancakes. "What makes you think you could help?"

A question asked by Charles, the person who thought he's a private detective because he's read a plethora of detective novels.

"Good question," Virgil said. "It's easy to see why you're a successful detective."

Charles beamed. I turned my head, so Virgil wouldn't see me roll my eyes.

Charles said, "Thanks."

Virgil continued, "I confess I'm nowhere near as good as you, not close by a kilometer. I haven't had formal investigative training, although I've watched every episode in the Masterpiece Theater Mystery series. I've been a fan of NCIS since there was only one of them. And don't forget, I know some of the players involved in the tragic event." He gave a short nod.

Was he waiting for applause?

I said, "Virgil, that's a good thought, but I don't think—"

He waved for me to stop, looked at the nearest table, then whispered, "I forgot to mention, everyone knows Sherlock Holmes was a druggie, something he and I had in common before I cleaned up a while back. That could be a big help to us."

I didn't waste time reminding him Sherlock Holmes was fictional.

Charles said, "That gives us something to think about."

Virgil clapped his hands. "That's all I can hope for. I won't push. With that out of the way, tell me what brought each of you to this enchanting island."

I was glad to change the subject and gave a brief synopsis of my move to Folly, Charles did the same. Virgil shared he found many of the residents to be friendly, much friendlier than his neighbors South of Broad in Charleston. I'd never lived in a mansion overlooking the Battery, so I couldn't compare.

We stayed off the topic of becoming the dynamic trio until Virgil finished his burrito. He said he didn't want to be a *rakefire* and would leave.

Of course, Charles asked what a *rakefire* was and Virgil enlightened us with another lesson in Victorian-speak. For the record, *rakefire* was someone who overstays his welcome.

My headache increased.

Chapter Eighteen

"What a morning," Charles said after Virgil left the restaurant. "We learn Cal's a pop and our dynamic duo can become a trio. Yes sir, what a morning." He took a sip of coffee, clasped his hands behind his head, then leaned back bringing the front legs of his chair off the floor.

"Charles, how many times do I have to tell you we're not a crime-fighting duo, dynamic or otherwise?"

After a slight nod, he said, "Thirty-seven."

I told him it'd exceeded thirty-seven years ago. He agreed it may be true, but for me to look at our track record then added our success rate would be the envy of many honest-to-goodness, real detectives. I reminded him we knew near nothing about Virgil Debonnet, that he could've poisoned Gary Isles.

"Chris, you're always telling me some of my ideas are half-baked, if that baked. Throwing Virgil in the suspect pool is less baked than some of my ideas. What's his motive?

If he did it, why would he be trotting over to us in his Gucci loafers to offer to help us catch him? Your idea doesn't make a lick of sense."

"I don't think he did it. I was pointing out how little we know about the man. With that said, I wouldn't rule him out. He's overly interested in the crash. As he said, he knows three folks directly or indirectly involved with it."

"Using your logic, Chris, we could've poisoned Gary. We know four people involved. That's more than Virgil knows."

"Charles, I should've said Virgil knew three of them before Gary was poisoned. We met the four we know after the crash."

"I'm confused. Are you saying Virgil did it or not?"

"Probably not, although probably leaves a possibility."

I was so intent on explaining myself that I didn't notice Cindy LaMond approach.

She said, "What in holy hamsters are you mumbling about? Probably, possibly, poop."

"We were—"

"I don't want to know," she said. Without any gestures or hints, she took the seat Virgil vacated. "Yes, I'd love for you to buy me coffee."

Amber must have seen Cindy enter. She was quick to see what the Chief needed.

Charles waited for Amber to return with Cindy's coffee, and said, "Do you know Virgil Debonnet?"

"Would that be the Virgil Debonnet who just met me in the parking area, the one who told me I looked as lovely as a Gainsborough painting on this fine March day? Hell, I don't know a Gainsborough from a Gaines-Burger but figured it must not be too bad for him to claim the top-cop looked that way. That the Virgil?"

I said, "Yes."

Cindy nodded slowly. "Most of the people I know are ones I've gotten to know over the years, or ones we arrest, where I get a quick dose of getting to know them. Virgil doesn't fall in either group. He'd gone out of his way to find ways and places to talk to me. I gather he hasn't been on Folly long. If he can be believed, he used to be among the wealthy who have their domestics fold and gently place their underwear in dressers costing more than my annual salary. Because of bad luck and bad habits, he now hangs his tighty-whities outside to dry while he lives in an apartment that's not as big as his walk-in closet from days gone by."

I said, "He told you all that?"

"That and more. He may wear his tighty-whities inside his britches, but he wears his deepest secrets on his sleeve."

Charles said, "Could he be hiding something?"

"Who isn't?" Cindy said. "You thinking about something in particular?"

"Not really," Charles said.

Cindy's focus narrowed. "Hmm. Mind if I don't believe you?"

Charles shrugged.

She took a sip, then said, "The only thing I see a problem with is his drinking. I suspect the only thing that's keeping it from getting out of hand is his state of broke."

I said, "I had that impression."

"Are you going to tell me why you wanted to know about him?"

I smiled. "I met him in Barb's. We've talked a couple of times since then. I thought he was an interesting fellow, so I wondered what you knew about him."

"Now that your vague brush off is out of the way, are you ready for me to tell you why I'm here?"

I said, "I thought it was because we were fascinating, handsome, charming men."

Cindy shook her head. "Add delusional."

"Chief," Charles said, "I want to know."

She turned to Charles. "Thank you. I got a call from Detective Callahan this morning. He'd talked with Aaron Cole, the NTSB investigator. Everything is still unofficial. Seems NTSB folks can't sneeze without waiting six months until an official sneeze report is finished. Anyway, Cole told Callahan there is still no indication anything was mechanically wrong with the plane. That wasn't news. He said it was fortunate any of the passengers survived. The flight to Myrtle Beach takes less than an hour. If the plane had ascended at its normal rate, it could've been at roughly seven-thousand feet when Gary took his last breath. The odds on anyone surviving would have been plus or minus zero. The Folly flyby saved Haymaker and Kale."

That wasn't anything we didn't know or suspected, so why did Cindy come to share that with us? She already said it wasn't because we were fascinating, handsome, or charming.

"Cindy," I said, "did Callahan have anything else?"

"Yesterday, he interviewed Richard Haymaker and Tom Kale."

I said, "Isn't this the second or third time he's interviewed them?"

"Third. We now know the pilot took cyanide and it's a quick-acting poison, so Haymaker and Kale were with him when he ingested it. Remember, I told you Kale said Gary drank from an energy drink."

I nodded.

Charles leaned closer to Cindy. "Don't suppose either of them confessed to killing him?"

Cindy shook her head. "Charles, can you think of one reason either would've had to poison the pilot which would result in a quick trip to dead for all of them?"

"Just asking."

I waited for Charles to give a reason, which he didn't, so I said, "Did Callahan learn anything new from the survivors?"

"No. They were in back of the plane, more intent on seeing their houses than anything going on in front."

Cindy still knew something she wasn't sharing. "Cindy, what else did Callahan tell you?"

"Has anyone told you you're getting as pesky as Charles?"

"There's hope for him," Charles interjected.

Cindy ignored him. "It's a gut reaction on Callahan's part. He said Kale seemed overly concerned about dead Gary's wife, Kelly. He said it was nothing he could take to court."

I said, "Like what?"

"Callahan didn't go into detail, other than Kale's voice got softer when he talked about poor, poor Kelly. Said Kale almost broke into tears when talking about her. Nothing else."

I reminded Cindy how comfortable Tom Kale had been with Kelly at the reception he and Richard had for Charles and me.

Cindy said, "They live close to each other; their husbands were friends."

"True, but I had the impression they were closer than most neighbors."

"That's consistent with Callahan's comment."

I said, "It still doesn't make sense either is responsible. Tom could've been as dead as Gary, and Kelly would've lost Tom and her husband. Cindy, she knew Tom was going with the group, didn't she?"

"Yes."

Charles said, "Did Callahan say anything else?"

"Yes, Charles. He said if I run into nosy, busybody, troublemaking Charles Fowler, to cuff him and throw him in the clink."

Charles's mouth opened wide and he took a deep breath. "He didn't say that."

"He should have," Cindy said, stood, and headed to the exit.

Chapter Nineteen

"**I**s this the Chris Landrum who tried to balance a damned airplane on his head while he was cavorting with dolphins in the marsh?" boomed the loud voice of Bob Howard soon after I made the mistake of answering the phone before inserting earplugs.

One of my first memories when I arrived on Folly Beach eleven years ago was meeting Bob, then a realtor with Island Realty, which, as he was prone to say, was *the second largest of the three very small island Realty firms*. If you picture the ideal realtor, Bob would be absent. He was loud, boorish, profane, opinionated, politically incorrect, and dressed street-person chic. Despite traits that would be the antithesis of anything found in a realtor handbook, Bob had been successful for decades. He and his wife, Betty, lived in one of the more prestigious sections of Charleston.

Bob had helped me find a vacation rental, then an inconsiderate killer torched the rental with me in it, Bob found the house I now call home and for reasons way more complicated than I can articulate, we'd become friends.

"That's old news, Bob. Did you crawl out of a cave?"

"Betty and I just got back from a damned cruise to some freakin' backward islands in the middle of nowhere."

"Sounds like you had a wonderful time."

"Damned right I did. Betty told me so. Enough about my trip to ecstasy, or whatever the damned islands were called. What happened to you and your shadow?"

I gave him the abridged version of our fateful kayak trip plus a little about what I'd learned since the crash.

"Let me guess," Bob growled. "You nearly got your head chopped off, so you and your quarter-wit friend feel a lunar pull making it your calling to catch whoever killed two men and nearly killed their golfing buddies."

"Bob, it's in the able hands of the Sheriff's Office with the assistance of the Folly Beach Department of Public Safety."

"So, there's no need for me to tell you how I know the spouse of one of the survivors?"

"Who?"

Bob laughed. "Gotta get to Al's. If you stop by for a cheeseburger, I might have time to share the skinny on … whoops, guess you'll have to wait."

A year and a half ago, Al Washington, a close friend of Bob experienced near-fatal health issues and sold Bob his bar. He knew as much about running the business as I did about conjugating the verb to belch in Hungarian, but his friend needed him, so Bob was there for him.

I parked in front of Al's. Bob's purple PT Cruiser convertible, the vehicle he'd had since I met him, was taking up two spaces in front of me. He'd told me he takes two spaces so no stupid, terrible driver would accidentally scratch his classic mode of transportation. A few years back, I told him taking two spaces was a trait of a stupid, terrible driver. My observation was met with a gaggle of profanities, so I never mentioned it again.

The first person I saw when I entered the paint-peeling concrete block building Al's shared with a Laundromat was the former owner seated on a wobbly, wooden chair beside the door. Heart problems and arthritic knees limited mobility for the eighty-two-year-old but didn't stop him from appearing each day to serve as greeter.

Al saw me and pushed up from the chair, smiled showing his coffee-stained teeth, and wrapped his bone-thin arms around me.

"Mr. Chris, it's good to see you. We've missed you around here."

I told him it'd been too long and asked how he was doing.

From the jukebox, Vern Gosdin was singing "Chiseled in Stone" as Al started to answer. Both Vern and Al were drowned out by Bob yelling, "Old fossil, stop pestering the poor boy. Let him get over here and spend money."

Two tables of diners glared at Bob. He motioned for them to mind their own business then pointed to the seat opposite the new owner. His polite way of saying he'd loved to have me join him.

In addition to Bob not knowing anything about a restaurant other than spending many hours in them stuffing his face, he was marshmallow white. That wasn't a big deal most of the time but considering Al and roughly ninety-nine percent of his customers were African American, it rose to significant proportions. Bob prided himself as being an equal-opportunity offender, so tensions were occasionally elevated. While he wouldn't admit it, that was one reason Bob had encouraged Al to remain involved in the restaurant.

"Shut your trap, you old tub of lard," Al responded.

The other diners didn't give Al a standing ovation but didn't hide their laughter.

Country crooner Vern Gosdin was followed by The Supremes with "Where Did Our Love Go."

I sat across from Bob in the booth that everyone knew was his because he'd attached a brass plate on it that read *Bob's booth. WARNING: Sit at your own risk.* He held his chubby hands over his ears while mumbling something about that damned music being the death of him. For years as an outward sign of the two men's friendship, and to the consternation of his other customers, Al had salted his jukebox with Bob's country favorites.

Bob, at six-foot-tall carrying the weight of someone a foot taller, barely folded into the booth. He was in his normal attire of a Hawaiian flowery shirt and black shorts he wore because he said black made him look slim. He looked as slim as a rhino, an observation I'd keep to myself.

"Who ran the restaurant while you were on your luxury cruise?"

Bob pointed toward the kitchen. "What's his name back there and old fart Al chipped in managing to keep the place from burning down from a grease fire."

Lawrence was Al's cook. Bob knew his name as well as he knew his own. Given the choice of a compliment or an insult, Bob always leaned negative.

"I see it survived."

"Don't tell him I said it, what's his name does a fantastic job. I'm thrilled to have him."

Okay, he doesn't always lean negative.

"Bob, you said you know one of the—"

Bob interrupted and yelled in the direction of the kitchen, "Get this scrawny honkie a cheeseburger and a glass of our finest jug wine."

I waited to see if he would yell anything else. He didn't, and I said, "You said—"

"Alyssa Kale," Bob interrupted, again. "The person you were taking too long to ask about."

"You know her?"

"Isn't that why you're here?"

"That, getting the best cheeseburger in the country, and to see you and Al."

"Yeah, right," he scoffed. "Alyssa is my stockbroker. I inherited her after Jordon had the audacity to up and die instead of managing my portfolio."

"What do you know about her, other than she had to have thick skin to put up with you?"

"You want to know this because you are not, with a capital N and O and T, getting involved in what happened to the plane?"

"It's because I met her husband so was curious about his wife."

"Ex-wife," Bob said. "She was quick to point that out during our first meeting. She's about as opposite from her predecessor as can be. He was laid back, would shoot the breeze as much as shoot stocks, had an awesome body like mine."

I couldn't help interrupting. "Awesome body?"

"Do I detect doubt?"

"Of course not, Bob. How is Alyssa different from Jordon?"

"Let's see. He's white, she's black; he had an ample body like mine, hers is petite; he's laid back, she's wound tighter than a girdle on a four-hundred-pound woman; oh yeah, he's dead, she's not. That's not what you really wanted to know. The main thing I got from her is she's two steps past royally pissed at her ex."

"Why?"

"I didn't ask. I was more concerned if she was recommending I sell my Apple stock than her pissed level with Tom Kale. Tell you what, if you want I'll set up a face to face with her and say something like, 'Alyssa, tell me why I should sell a hundred shares of Microsoft and why you poisoned the pilot.'"

"You're always thinking, Bob. Not a bad idea, although I doubt it'll work. Did she say anything else about her ex?"

He shook his head. "I'm not as good a detective as you and your fractional-wit sidekick."

Lawrence delivered my cheeseburger and wine, Patsy Cline's haunting voiced filled the room singing "I Fall to Pieces," and three customers at the next table moaned in unison.

"Bob, while we're talking about the crash, do you know Charlene Beth Haymaker?"

"By reputation and rumor," Bob said, as I took a bite of the cheeseburger.

I wiped catsup off my lip then said, "Elaborate."

He spelled *NOT* with his forefinger on the table as he said, "Getting involved."

I got the message. It didn't stop me from repeating, "Elaborate on reputation and rumor."

"Charlene Beth is one of the new wave of realtors. That's one of the reasons I retired from that life, why I started living the dream of running a dilapidated, dying bar. Charlene Beth." Bob hesitated, and said, "Have I told you how much I hate people who use two first names?"

"I've heard seven hundred other things you bitch about. That's a new one."

"Add it to the list. Wouldn't Charlene do? How about Beth, a perfectly acceptable name? Why clutter up speaking by using two names when one will do?"

I pointed to Bob's phone. "Call her and ask?"

Bob tilted his head. "You being a smart ass?"

"I am. With your most recent pet peeve out of the way, new wave of realtor?"

"They do everything on the Internet." He picked up his smartphone. "If someone took this away, they'd be dead in the water. They're showing out-of-town clients homes with live chat thingies. They walk through a house, talk about every damn room while they point their damned phone camera at it. The client asks questions. Hell, some of their clients buy a house without stepping through the door. After that, all the paperwork is done in bits and bytes. Robots will be doing all of it before the sun sets. Chris, it ain't right."

I figured that qualified as the reputation part of Bob's comment about Charlene Beth. I said, "Rumor?"

"The word in Realty circles is she's having an affair with Walter Middleton Gibbs."

"Who's he?"

"Who's he? Chris, I continue to be shocked by your ignorance. Walter's old, old, old money. His ancestors were in Charleston so long ago the town was named Chuckie."

I smiled, hoping that was a joke. "Think the rumor's true?"

"Hell if I know. If it is, and if you were not not trying to figure out who poisoned the pilot, two-named Haymaker could be what you detectives call a suspect. She could've bumped off the pilot to crash the plane killing her loving husband."

I ignored his comment about me being a detective. "Know anything else about her?"

"Not a thing."

I figured Bob had shared all he knew about Alyssa Kale and Charlene Beth Haymaker, so I leaned closer to him. "How's Al?"

Bob lowered his head. "I'm afraid he's as good as he's going to get. On the positive side, that's a hell of a lot better than he was when I bought this trillion dollars in debt dump. I worry about him." Bob raised his head, looked at Al, then in a voice about the level of an Indy 500 race car, yelled, "Old man, get your scrawny, ancient ass over here!"

The customers who'd moaned at Patsy Cline's singing turned to Bob and looked ready to leap over the table to show him where he could take his far-from-scrawny rear.

The equal opportunity offender smiled at them as he yelled for Lawrence to take them another round. On the house. Bob never apologized with words but with deeds.

Al arrived at the table after what appeared to be a painful walk across the room. He sat beside me and for the next hour Bob and Al shared insults, humorous stories about Bob's encounters with customers, Al's family, and some of the best cheeseburgers known to man.

I left Al's with a full stomach plus a head full of questions about who poisoned Gary Isles. This was the second time that I'd heard about Tom and Alyssa Kale's divorce. William had said it was highly contested. Bob was less civil in his description by saying Alyssa was highly pissed with her ex. Contested divorces weren't uncommon, but the vast majority didn't end in one spouse killing the other. Was this the exception?

Then what about the rumor that Charlene Beth was having an affair with one of Charleston's leading citizens? If true, could she have orchestrated the crash? Of course, she could have, although if everyone who has had an affair killed their spouse, we wouldn't have to be worrying about overpopulation.

All I knew for certain was someone killed Gary Isles which led to the death of Mark Jamison.

Chapter Twenty

The next two days were uneventful. I spent them doing the routine, aka boring, activities of living alone. The highlight, or to me, lowlight, was my bimonthly trip to the Harris Teeter which I looked forward to as much as I would look forward to prepping for a colonoscopy the same day I was having a root canal. Most of my often-meager grocery shopping took place next door at Bert's Market instead of traveling the extra two and a half miles to the large, chain store. The grocery shopping safari combined with a day of cleaning floors helped keep my mind off the crash.

That streak ended when I answered the phone to the aristocratic voice of Virgil Debonnet saying, "Is that you, Christopher?"

I admitted it was while wondering how he got my number.

"Good, this is Virgil Debonnet. I hope you don't mind me calling. Mary, the lovely young lass at Bert's, gave me your number. I told her we were friends and I misplaced the way to get in touch with you. Folks in Bert's are better than Google. They know everyone and everything while selling you a headache remedy at the same time. A true blessing. Anyway, I bet you wonder why I'm calling."

Definitely, I thought. "It entered my mind."

"I've acquired some information that'll help you, your fellow detective friend, and me as we search for the dastardly person who poisoned the pilot of that ill-fated aircraft. Let's get together so you can hear what I've learned. We can plan our next move."

I was curious enough to ignore his comment about my "fellow detective friend," or about the three of us searching. "I suppose. Have you tried to contact Charles?"

"No. Mary didn't know his number. Could you see if he's available?"

"If he is, where and when do you want to meet?"

"Umm, my finances are a bit tight this month, so I'd rather not meet at a restaurant. How about gathering at the end of the walking pier adjacent to the little park by the bridge? I don't know its name. It's where they have outdoor art shows."

"The Folly River Park. When?"

"Sooner the better. We don't want a killer roaming the streets longer than necessary. How about this afternoon if you all can fit it into your schedule?"

"I'll call him then let you know."

Virgil gave me his number then added he'd be on pins and needles waiting for my answer. I wondered how he would've said that in Victorian.

Ten minutes later, I'd called Charles, and got Virgil off pins and needles when I told him we'd be there.

I arrived at the park at two-thirty since I knew Charles would arrive early. He didn't disappoint. He was standing at the railing overlooking the Folly River as I made my way out the narrow foot pier. Charles was wearing dark-green shorts, a Tilley hat, tennis shoes looking like they'd survived a long hike in pluff mud, and a long-sleeve, green T-shirt with Johnson State on the front below a strange-looking, cartoonish creature.

"What's so all-fired important that Virgil took me away from reading a biography of Calvin Coolidge?"

I smiled and thought how little it would've taken for me to stop reading the biography. "Don't know. We'll have to wait and see."

We didn't wait long. Virgil headed toward us with a smile on his face and Gucci shoes on his feet. In between, he wore a short sleeve, wrinkled button-down white dress shirt, and gray dress slacks thinning in the knees.

He pointed at Charles's T-shirt. "That a weasel?"

"It's a Mustelidae, same family but not a weasel. It's a badger, the mascot of Johnson State College in Vermont."

"Oh," Virgil said, a common reaction to Charles's T-shirts. He turned to me, "Thanks for pulling this meeting together."

We sat side by side on the wood bench and watched traffic cross the river.

"Virgil, Chris told me you have something to help us catch the person who killed the pilot."

Virgil took off his sunglasses momentarily and wiped his brow. It was the first time I'd seen his green eyes. He returned the glasses to his face. "After we agreed to work together on catching the killer, I sort of accidentally ran into Richard Haymaker and Tom Kale."

I saw my reflection in his sunglasses as I said, "Sort of accidentally?"

"I'd been looking all over for the survivors or their significant others. The extent of my detecting is rather limited since my only means of transportation is an old scooter I bought from a guy working at the Tides. Did I tell you I used to have a Jaguar, the car, not the animal?"

"No," Charles said.

"Anyway, back to the subject, do you know how many times I went in restaurants, stores, up and down Center Street hoping one of them would appear?"

That was the kind of question Charles lived for. He said, "Nineteen?"

"Shoot, I don't know. Could be. It was a lot. It finally paid off two days ago when I saw Tom getting gas at Circle K. I walked up to him and said, 'Are you Tom Kale?' He kept pumping gas as he looked around to see if I was part of a band of roaming marauders fixing to steal his money or his car. He didn't see any but looked at me like I was a stranger."

Charles said, "Had you met him?"

"Nope, I was a stranger. I covered by saying I'd heard he was one of the crash survivors. The person who told me described him. Told him I wanted to say hi. Wanted to say how glad I was he was among the living."

Charles said, "How'd he respond?"

"Said he was fortunate. I asked if he'd heard how come the plane crashed. Course I knew the answer."

Charles gave what I knew was a nod of frustration. "Kale said?"

"He hemmed, hawed, and looked at the pump like he wanted it to spew petrol faster so he could get out of there."

Virgil hesitated, looked at Charles, and said, "Then he said Gary, the pilot, was poisoned. I acted shocked. 'Wow, who would've poisoned him?' Tom looked at me, said he didn't know. I think he was fibbing."

I asked, "Why?"

"His eyes got all shifty, he wouldn't make eye contact. Isn't that a sign of lying?"

"Not necessarily," I said. "Did he say anything that seemed out of place?"

"He jumped right to saying how bad he felt for Gary's wife, Kelly. Now you can take this with a grain of salt, heck, maybe a shaker full, but the way he said her name, I took it they were closer than friends, if you know what I mean."

That's consistent with what I felt after seeing Tom and Kelly together at Tom's reception.

Charles swiped a bug away from his face then said, "Do you think Tom and Kelly are having a thing?"

"Charles, I've already told Chris this, but one of the reason's I'm living in an apartment the size of a wasp nest instead of a mansion is because I managed to lose a Fort Knox load of money gambling. For that reason, I'll refrain from saying if I was a betting man, I'd put money on it."

I said, "Does that mean you think Kelly poisoned Gary so they could be together?"

"Wouldn't rule it out."

I would. If Kelly poisoned Gary, there would've been an excellent chance Tom would've been killed in the crash. I pointed that out to Virgil.

"That's something to think about," he said as he once again removed his sunglasses while wiping his brow. He returned the glasses to his face before continuing, "There's something else. Not only did I accidentally on purpose run into Tom, I saw Richard Haymaker in Bert's. I already knew him, so I didn't have to use the ruse I used on Tom. He was buying milk for the twins. He said they were driving Charlene Beth crazy. He wondered if he should get some tranquilizer to put in the milk to calm the kids and his wife's nerves. He was joking. Anyway, he asked how I liked the apartment, liked living on Folly. I told him the apartment was good, Folly was fine, blah, blah, blah. It didn't get interesting until we started talking about the crash. Know what he said?"

We said no.

"Get this, Richard told me Gary was poisoned, no news there, but he said the poison was in Gary's drink, that someone must've put it there before Gary put the cooler on the plane. Here's where it gets interesting. He said the cooler had been in the hangar at the airport and he knew several people were in there."

"How'd Richard know that?" I asked. "My understanding is he, Mark, and Tom arrived late, with Gary and the cooler already onboard."

"Richard told me Gary told him it was busy that morning, that he was surprised to see someone he thought he recognized in the lot."

"Who?"

"Didn't say. He started talking to the air traffic controller." He shook his head. "Gary didn't say anything else about it before he dropped dead."

I said, "Did Richard say if he saw anyone familiar when he arrived?"

"Holy moly, I'm going to be a good detective," Virgil said, before fist bumping me. "That's the same question I asked him. Near word for word."

Charles looked at Virgil like he was ready to fist bump him in the head. "Did he?"

Virgil said, "Did he what?"

Before Charles went for Virgil's throat, I said, "Did Richard say he recognized anybody at the airport."

"No."

That was an indication Virgil was becoming as good a detective as Charles.

"Learn anything else?" I asked.

"To be as good a detective as you two, I'll have to learn how to be sneaky asking questions. You know, so the other person doesn't know what I'm doing. Don't think I'm there yet."

Charles frowned at Virgil. "Did you learn anything else or not?"

"That's all," he said. "Knew you'd want to hear about my conversations with both survivors. What's our next step?"

For him to step off the pier into the river was my first thought. I held my tongue, thanked him for sharing what he'd learned. I also hinted I'd tell Chief LaMond, although I had no idea what he'd said worth sharing.

"That's a good start. Give me a holler if you think of anything else I can do to help catch the killer."

I said I would, leaving out when hell freezes over.

"I've taken up enough of your time." Virgil started walking away. He stopped, pivoted, then said, "I've been thinking. Nobody knows who the killer wanted dead. If Gary or Mark weren't the target, it's Richard or Tom."

"Yes," Charles said, showing more interest than irritation with Virgil.

"So," Virgil said, "seems somebody desperate enough to

crash an entire airplane to kill someone is mighty desperate. If the person he or she wanted dead is Richard or Tom, they'll try again." He put his hand up to eye level, palm facing Charles and me. "That's only my theory. I'm not a great detective like you."

That was about the only thing Virgil had said that made sense, that is, until he got to the part about us being great detectives. I told him I agreed that Richard or Tom could be in danger.

"When you're talking with the Chief, you better ought to let her know." He walked away.

Chapter Twenty-One

We remained on the pier. Charles appeared more fascinated with a fishing boat as it passed under the bridge than talking. He hadn't spoken for fifteen minutes, rare for my friend, so I asked what was bothering him.

Charles shook his head like I'd awakened him from a trance then looked in the direction that Virgil had gone. "Here I am, a detective, now look what happens. I've been so caught up in how Richard and Tom survived the crash I didn't consider one or both could be in danger. Then Virgil comes along, figures it out."

During my many decades on this earth, I'd never been able to explain how televisions get a picture into my living room, how we can be heated by a sun that's 92.96 million miles away, or why God created mosquitos. I have also never been able to explain to Charles he is not, never has been, never will be a private detective. Like my other unexplainables, I'd stopped trying.

"Charles, Virgil could be right. There's no way to know if anyone else is in danger. Virgil was stating the obvious, something we knew."

He slowly shook his head. "That's my point, Chris. I didn't think about it. How stupid can I be?"

I didn't want to say anything that'd send my friend further down the rabbit hole. Heather, his long-term girl-friend, left Folly a year ago leaving Charles a note asking him not to try to find her. He'd planned to propose the next day. Since then, he's been moody, more negative, less inclined to find the good in everyone, something that'd been one of his most enduring qualities.

"Charles, it may not have been something you'd given a lot of thought to, but we knew it was a possibility."

He looked at the deck. "If you say so."

"Charles, I'm going to let Cindy know what Virgil said about someone being at the airport Gary recognized. Want me to call her now or later?"

He nodded toward the pocket holding my phone.

"Hi, Chief. How are you this lovely day?"

"It's not bad for a change. What are you going to say to ruin it?"

"I'm with Charles—"

"That's the perfect recipe for ruining my day."

I put the phone on speaker and said, "Two things. First we were wondering if you or Detective Callahan learned anything new about the crash?"

"Yes. What's the second thing?"

Charles leaned close to the phone and said, "Whoa, Chief. Yes what?"

"Hello to you too, Charles. I'm glad you haven't lost your hearing in old age. Where are you?"

I told her. She said for us to stay put, she'd see us in ten minutes. I took it as a sign she had more to share, not that she was excited about seeing us.

A handful of minutes later, the Chief's pickup pulled in a parking space at the edge of the park.

Before she made her way to the table we'd moved to, Charles said, "What've you learned?"

She sighed. "Move over. Let these tired but much younger than your legs get a break."

Charles scooted while repeating his question.

"You didn't hear this from me. Callahan told me Tom Kale has a two-million-dollar life insurance policy."

Charles whistled.

"Hubby better not ever get that big a policy," Cindy said. "I'd bump him off in a heartbeat. Whoops, that's the second thing you didn't hear from me."

Cindy and Larry are the happiest married couple I know. She was teasing, I hoped.

"Cindy," I said. "Tom was divorced so who's the beneficiary?"

"Excellent question. He hasn't changed the beneficiary. It's still his ex, Alyssa."

Charles shook his head. "That's a humongous motive for her to poison the pilot."

"Guys, we have motives out the ear." She raised her forefinger. "Gary Isles' wife has a burr up her butt about him not letting her work. He had big bucks, most likely a large policy." She raised another finger. "Richard's wife Charlene Beth … Have I told you how people with double first names irritate me?"

I told her how Bob Howard had the same problem.

"Then, never mind. I don't want you to confuse me with

your realtor friend. Anyway, Charlene Beth doesn't seem torn up about Gary and Mark being killed. When I was talking to her she tried to look lovey-dovey, cooing about how great it was Richard survived. She was as sincere as a used car salesman. Granted, that ain't much of a motive, but in my eyes it's a glimmer of one. Then add Alyssa Kale's two-million-dollar motive." She shook her head. "Mark Jamison is the only person on the plane who didn't have someone with a motive to kill him, or someone we didn't know about."

"Let me add something to Charlene Beth's possible motive." I shared what Bob Howard had told me about the rumor that Charlene Beth was having an affair.

"Interesting, I'll share that with Callahan," she said. "One of these days I'll give you a Deputy Dog detective badge."

Charles waved his hand in Cindy's face. "Me, too?"

She put her hand over her face and mumbled. "Why not?"

"What next, Chief?" I asked.

"Crap on a cupcake, Chris. We don't even know the intended victim."

I'd nearly forgotten the main thing I wanted to tell her.

"You know anything about Virgil Debonnet you didn't share with me in the Dog?"

Cindy looked at me like I was trying to trick her. "Other than he's the millionaire who slipped to a dollaraire?"

I said, "Anything else?"

"Not much. He's not been arrested. He's not been in any trouble I'm aware of. He does strike me as odd. If I was rich, yes, I'm dreaming, and lost it all, I'd be a holy terror, mad at the world, sucky miserable. Not Virgil. He's nonchalant about his new state of poverty. I wouldn't say he's happy about it, but he ain't outwardly pissed. Odd."

I agreed.

She said, "What about him?"

I shared what he'd told us about the pilot seeing a familiar person at the airport and Gary was the only one of the four on the plane who had access to the cooler.

"How is it you know Virgil enough to be sharing information about the plane and its passengers?"

I told her how he'd approached me saying he wanted to be a detective, how he could join Charles and me to find out who killed the pilot.

Cindy frowned. "Odd and delusional."

A voice from Cindy's radio disrupted our conversation. "Chief, we've got a 10-57 in the three-hundred block of East Huron. We're rolling police and fire."

Cindy keyed her mic. "Donna, speak English. You know I'll never learn all those codes."

"Sorry, Chief. Hit-and-run. Car versus pedestrian. That's all I know."

Cindy thanked the dispatcher for the translation then told us she had to go.

Charles yelled to her as she headed to her vehicle. "Let us know what happened."

"Big N. Big O."

He turned to me. "Should we follow her?"

"You want to jog after her truck?"

Sirens began filling the air. The three-hundred block of East Huron was four long blocks from our location. After considerable back and forth, I agreed we could walk that way to see what happened. Besides, I couldn't have convinced my friend not to go, and the walk would do me good.

Chapter Twenty-Two

E ast Huron is a narrow residential street a block
from houses backing up to the Folly River. Many of
the structures predated Hurricane Hugo that
devastated the island in 1989. There were no sidewalks, so
we moved off the road three times to allow emergency vehicles to pass. A patrol car had the road blocked at the inter-
section of Third Street East and Officer Allen Spencer was
detouring traffic onto the perpendicular street. I'd known
Allen since I arrived on Folly. He was new to the force at the
time, so we had several conversations about Folly's character
and characters.

I asked what happened.

"Don't know much. I was third on the scene, asked to
stop traffic. Apparently, a man was walking east on Huron
and struck from behind."

"What's his condition?"

"Bad, I think."

To echo that opinion, a Charleston County ambulance,

siren screaming, pulled up behind the cruiser. Allen rushed to move his car so the emergency vehicle could head to the hospital. We waited for the officer to once again block the road. East Huron was a lightly travelled street, so Allen had little to do except talk.

"Anybody see it happen?" I asked.

"Don't know. Our guys are canvassing the houses to see if anyone saw anything."

"The driver skedaddled?" Charles said.

Allen nodded.

I pointed in the direction of the multiple emergency vehicles. "The Chief back there?"

"Yes, but if I were you, I'd stay clear. You know how she gets at scenes where bad stuff happened."

"Good point, Allen. I'll get with her later."

A car pulled up to the cruiser. The driver said he lived two houses down and needed to get home. That was well before the scene of the incident, so Allen moved his car to let the resident through. Charles and I headed toward the center of town where I would turn left to go home. Charles stopped before going the other direction to his apartment. He said, "So when are you going to call Cindy?"

I told him I didn't know but it wouldn't be until much later to give her time to do her thing at the scene.

"Okay," Charles said, "Call me in an hour with what she told you."

Only Charles would interpret "much later" as an hour. I limited my response to, "Okay."

———

I didn't have to call Cindy since she called at seven-thirty that evening. It was the third call I'd received. As anyone who knows him could've guessed, the first two were from Charles wanting to know why I was taking so long to call the Chief.

"Good evening, Cindy."

"You're not going to believe this," she said as a nonsensical, although typical opening by my friends.

"Try me."

"Know who got hit?"

I'd been home since leaving Charles, so I hadn't heard anything about the hit and run. "Who?"

"Who were we talking about when I got the call?"

I drew a blank, then it struck me. "Virgil."

"Bingo."

"Is he alive?"

"Barely."

"What happened?"

"He was walking out East Huron, then he was flying through the air over East Huron, vehicle propelled. Don't ask, we don't know what kind of vehicle, nor do we know who was driving."

"Nobody saw it happen?"

"I suppose the driver did. No one else we've found. None of the residents were outside, no other cars were driving by. Crap, there wasn't even a nosy grandma sitting in a rocking chair staring out her window like you see on television shows. All we know from seeing the condition of Mr. Debonnet is that somewhere there's a vehicle with a serious dent in its front end."

"Could you tell if it was an accident or if he was hit on purpose?"

"It looks like he was on the edge of the road, so I wouldn't rule out intentional."

"You said he was barely alive. What'd that mean?"

"The EMTs who hauled him off said he was breathing, but from the number of broken bones, suspected internal injuries. His age plus apparent good physical condition could help him, although I wouldn't put money on it." Cindy paused, and I heard someone speaking in the background. She returned to the phone. "Larry's here so I have to play housewife. As you know, I'm as good at that as I am at wrestling alligators."

"One more thing," I said. "Does anyone know Virgil is in the hospital?"

"Other than the person who sent him flying?"

"Yes."

"Don't think so. He had a wallet on him, but no next of kin or emergency contact was listed. You told me he knew the Haymakers, so I contacted Charlene Beth."

"And?"

"She checked her records but couldn't find contact information on his ex-spouse. She thinks the ex moved back to Boston, or some other snooty city, but didn't know anything else."

"Will you call me if you learn anything about his condition?"

"Chris, you know I live to keep you informed."

She was being sarcastic. I thanked her anyway.

Now to call Charles.

Chapter Twenty-Three

I spent the next two days working on taxes, an annual event where I'm traumatized by how much money the government wants, no, demands, this aging, retired, non-producing member of society to send them simply for existing. To show how traumatizing the exercise is, I stopped twice to clean the house which, next to swimming with the sharks, is one of my least favorite activities. Charles had been surprisingly quiet. Since I called him after my talk with Cindy, I hadn't heard from him.

The person I did hear from with two calls was Cal, more calls than I'd received from him in the last five years. He vacillated between being thrilled having his middle-aged son in his life and overwhelmed by having Junior here. Cal needed a willing ear to listen to his varied emotions and reactions. I'd become that ear.

I spent little time thinking about the plane crash because if I had I'd have been lost in a maze of confusion. Who was the intended victim? Without knowing that, how could anyone determine who poisoned the pilot? Then, if Richard or Tom, the two survivors, had been the person the killer was wanting dead, was one or both in danger? Finally, how did Virgil fit into the equation? Or, did he? Was his near-death experience a result of talking to Richard or Tom? Or, was it simply a tragic accident caused by someone not paying attention then panicking after hitting him?

A call from Cindy didn't answer any of the questions although it was encouraging about Virgil. His condition had improved. Unless something unexpected occurred, he'd live. She reported he had more broken bones than if he'd fallen from a satellite, an exaggeration I suspected. He was lucid enough to tell her he'd been minding his business while strolling down the road when clobbered. He saw nothing except his life flashing before his eyes. She ended by telling me not to visit him, especially to keep my buddy Charles from invading the hospital. I assured her I'd wait until she said it was okay to visit. I wisely didn't comment on my ability to stop Charles.

Another day passed, then I received a hushed call. "Chris, this is Cal, Sorry to whisper. Can you hear me?"

"Yes. Why are you whispering?"

"Don't want Junior hearing. He's poking around somewhere."

"What's up?"

"Think you can stop by the bar this afternoon around two?"

Let's see, finish my taxes, do more cleaning, or visit Cal's?

"I'll be there."

The weather was nice, so I walked. I was a few minutes

early when I saw Junior leaving through the side door. I waited until he was out of sight before going in.

Johnny Cash's version of "Ring of Fire" was playing, the lone customer was leaning on the bar staring at a half empty bottle of Budweiser. Cal was at the jukebox punching numbers. I smiled at his sartorial splendor. He wore his Stetson, a green and red striped polo shirt, and blue jogging shorts. He saw me, pointed to the table farthest from the bar, and asked the customer if he needed anything. The customer looked content staring at his beer as he told Cal he'd yell if he needed another.

Cal plopped down on the chair opposite me so hard I was afraid it'd collapse. It didn't, so I said, "You okay?"

From the jukebox, another Cal, Cal Smith, started telling a story about being a "Country Bumpkin."

He glanced at the customer and leaned closer to me. "No."

That much I could tell. "What's wrong?"

"Junior."

"What about him?"

"Don't get me wrong, pard, it's wonderful having him around. I'm still adjusting to having an offspring. Junior found himself an apartment, so he didn't have to bunk in my hole in the wall. If he had, one of us would be dead by now."

I still hadn't heard what was wrong. "What's the problem?"

Cal waved his arm around the room. "Remember when I took over this place?"

How could I forget? He'd been performing here when it was GB's. The owner, Gregory Brile, then rudely murdered a local attorney resulting in an all-expense paid, thirty-year, vacation in prison. Cal, who knew as much about running a bar as a housefly knows about driving a Mack truck, took over, stumbled through learning pains, and now managed running a profitable business.

"Sure."

He sniffed. "Take a whiff."

I followed his lead.

He smiled. "Smell stale beer and burgers?"

I said I did.

"See the classic, raveling carpet? How about these table and chairs? Do they ever have stories to tell." He patted the back of the chair next to him. "How about that old Wurlitzer? Listen to old George moaning about how 'She Thinks I Still Care.'"

Somewhere in there was a reason for me being here. Unlike Charles, I waited for Cal to share what it was.

"Chris, my friend, this here is the quinty, umm, what's the word?"

I guessed, "Quintessential?"

"Yeah, that's it. Cal's is the quintessential country music bar, yes, it is."

"Let me guess," I said. "Junior owned a chain of restaurants. He knows more than a thing or two about the restaurant and bar business." Cal nodded so I figured I was on the right track. "He thinks you ought to change some things."

Cal looked at the ceiling then back at me. "Some? Hell, he wants what those TV shows call a total makeover." He turned and pointed toward the tiny kitchen. "He wants to knock out a wall, enlarge the kitchen, expand the menu. Chris, can you see us selling chicken cordon bleu or steak with bacon on it?"

I choked back a smile. "No."

"That's right. He wants me to mosey over to the bank, borrow money, buy new tables and chairs." He shook the tabletop. "Get this, he wants me to start selling craft beer. I don't even know what it is."

"What'd you tell him?"

"Here's the biggy," Cal said, ignoring my question. "Junior wants me to put some new songs on the jukebox. By new he don't mean old songs that ain't on the jukebox, but that country crap youngsters listen to nowadays. Can you believe that?"

If Cal hadn't heard a song before 1980, it wasn't on his Wurlitzer.

I tried again. "What'd you tell him?"

"Chris, the only thing we agreed on was the walls could use some paint."

The paint-chipped walls hadn't received attention in twenty years. They were dirty, coated with aromas of food, and dried beer.

"It's good you could agree on that. What about the other stuff?"

"Told him I'd ponder it. Didn't tell him I'd pondered it for about three seconds after he brought it up. Rejected the hell out of them. Haven't worked up the nerve to tell him. He's my kid so I don't want to discourage him."

"Cal, he's not a little boy, he's in his fifties. This is your place. The quicker you get it over with the better."

"I know. Needed someone I trust to tell me. Thanks, pard." Cal snapped his fingers. "I'm being inhospitable. Let me get you a glass of wine. I think I could use a Bud myself. I'm plum out of craft beer."

He smiled, a good sign I thought, as Roger Miller sang "When Two Worlds Collide."

Cal slid another Budweiser in front of his customer at the bar before returning with my wine and his non-craft beer.

"Figured out who snuffed Gary Isles?"

I would've rather talked more about Junior than the plane crash.

"No."

"Want to know what I heard?"

I channeled Charles. "Sure."

"I hear Tom Kale's ex, Alice, is pissed that her ex survived."

"Her name's Alyssa," I said, continuing to channel Charles. "Who said that?"

"Denton, a semi regular. He has a few, quite a few, bucks. He's heavy in the stock market. Seems that Alice, umm, Alyssa is his broker. He was talking to her the other day. He told her he was glad Tom survived. Know what she told him?"

I didn't.

"She said, 'I guess.'"

"That's not enthusiastic but doesn't mean she's pissed."

"Denton said it was how she said it. He was surprised. Anyway, I figured you'd want to know since no matter how many times you claim it ain't so, you're trying to figure it out."

I took a gulp of wine, changed the subject, and didn't give another thought to the plane crash until Cal said something about a group of locals who'd wandered in recently who were becoming regulars. I didn't recognize the names until he said Virgil.

I stopped him mid-sentence. "Virgil Debonnet?"

"I'm not big on last names. There've been a few times I

couldn't remember mine. If he's to be believed, he was rich, now he ain't. I figured you'd know him or knew about him since you know about all the bad stuff that happens here. He's the guy smacked by the car."

"That's Virgil Debonnet. What do you know about him?"

"Just told you."

"I meant anything other than he used to be rich and was victim of a hit-and-run?"

Cal took a sip of beer, looked to see if his bar customer needed anything, then said, "Now that I think about it, there is something you might be interested in. The night before he was hit, he was here talking to a gaggle of guys. I heard him say something like he was figuring out who caused the plane crash." Cal paused then nodded like that was all.

And Cal didn't think that was important enough to mention first?

"Did he say he was figuring out who caused it or was trying to figure out who?"

"Ain't that the same thing?"

"Not exactly. If he said he was figuring it out, he may have a good idea who it was."

Cal removed his Stetson and scratched the back of his head. "I don't know anything about them puny differences. Besides, I was behind the bar trying to get a customer to pay his tab. I wasn't concentrating on everything Virgil said."

"Remember who he was talking to?"

"Nope. It was that group of new customers."

"Remember anything else he said?"

"No, but he must've been saying something funny. Guys around him kept laughing, patting him on the back. One of them picked up his tab. I hope he gets okay. I like customers who make people laugh, make people feel good." He rubbed his chin. "Could be because I'm a fossil, but it seems folks used to have a better time in the old days. Now everybody's all serious, uptight, griping about everything. Gripe, gripe, gripe."

Four men entered the bar and Cal said, "Gotta get back to work. Thanks for kicking my butt into action. I'll tell Junior I love him, but to get his nose out of my business."

I wished him luck.

I left Cal's with Eddy Arnold singing "Make the World Go Away."

Chapter Twenty-Four

F ive more days passed before Cindy let me know Virgil had improved enough to have visitors. Fifteen minutes and a phone call to Charles later, he and I were on our way to the hospital on the outskirts of downtown Charleston. A helpful nurse told us where we could find our new friend but encouraged us to limit our visit. She shared he was doing much better than when he arrived but wasn't ready to run a marathon. A glance in his room told me he not only wasn't ready to run a marathon but wasn't ready to sit without the aid of a forklift. *Mummy* was the word that came to mind. Except for a few square inches of actual Virgil, his body was wrapped in either gauze or a plaster cast. His left leg was elevated and held in place by a gadget suspended from a stainless-steel bracket. I barely recognized him, not just because of the white covering, but because he wasn't wearing sunglasses. He was in a double room in the bed closest to the door. The curtain was pulled so I couldn't see if he had a roommate.

Virgil's eyes were closed. I moved closer to the bed and whispered, "Virgil, you awake?"

He blinked several times, probably because of the non-sunglasses unfiltered light. He said, "Hey, Chris, how're you doing?"

An interesting question considering his condition. "Fine." I tilted my head, something I doubted Virgil could do, toward Charles. "You remember Charles, don't you?"

Virgil's head didn't move, but his eyes shifted in Charles's direction. "Hi, Charles. What brings you two to this cheery place?"

I told him we'd come to see him, he said he was honored, and for us to pull up chairs. There was one chair on Virgil's side of the curtain, so I motioned for Charles to sit. Virgil told me to grab a chair from the other side of the room, adding the man over there hasn't had a visitor for days. The chair was going to waste.

I maneuvered the chair to Virgil's side of the room then asked how he was doing.

He smiled. "Know how many places itch every day, places you can't scratch because of this clunky cast?"

I knew what he meant and nodded. Charles, the collector of all things trivia and unimportant, said, "How many?"

"A bunch."

I hoped that was good enough for Charles. In case it wasn't, I asked Virgil if he knew how much longer he'd be in the hospital.

"The docs said I was better than I look with all this crap wrapped around me. They also said I was lucky. I asked how much worse I could look if I wasn't lucky. One of them, think he's from India, gave me a lengthy answer in medical gobbledygook. I understood two of the hundreds of words he spewed. A doc from around these parts tapped on the cast on my leg and said that if I was worse, I'd be all spiffed-out in a suit, resting in a coffin. That I understood."

"Virgil," Charles said, "I believe I heard Chris ask how much longer you'd be here?"

"If I knew, I wouldn't have hopped over to talking about what the docs said. My friend, I don't know."

I remembered Cindy had said he hadn't remembered anything about being hit. That was more than a week ago when he'd told her. Was more coming back to him?

"Virgil, tell us what happened."

He blinked a couple more times. "Can't tell you much. I remember talking to you in that park, then heading out Huron. I haven't been on Folly long, but long enough to know many roads are narrow, there aren't many sidewalks. To be safe, I walked as far on the edge of the road as possible. Ha, see how much good that did? Anyway, speeders can be a problem. I'd heard that more than one person had been killed walking along the streets."

Charles interrupted, "That's true. Chris was with someone who—"

"Charles," I said, interrupting the interrupter, "let Virgil finish."

"Sorry. Go ahead, Virgil."

"I'm afraid I can't add much. The car, truck, bus, boat, train, whatever hit me from behind. I never heard it coming. Smack! The next thing I remember was waking up somewhere in this building with lights the size of searchlights glaring down at me."

"You're fortunate to be alive," I said, stating the obvious. "Do you think the vehicle hit you on purpose?"

"Don't know. I was on the side of the road so whoever it was had to be drunk, texting, or falling asleep and weaved over to where I was. I heard he didn't have the courtesy to stop."

"Or intentionally ran you down," Charles added.

Virgil hesitated, then said, "Why? I don't know many folks on Folly. I'm not having an affair with anyone's wife. I'm not working for the IRS, not working at all, for that matter. Hell, I think I'm a pretty nice fellow."

A pretty nice fellow who's been asking questions about the plane crash, I thought. "Virgil," I said, "Cal told me you were in his bar talking to a group of men about how you either were figuring out or had figured out who poisoned the pilot. What was that about?"

"Don't remember saying anything like that. Heck, I don't even remember being in Cal's. My memory is sort of fuzzy these days. Think it's the drugs they're pumping in me."

I said, "Do you remember much that was said when you talked with Richard and Tom? In other words, could they have thought you were questioning them about the crash?"

"You mean like I suspected one of them of the poisoning?"

I nodded.

"Nah, that's what I was trying to figure out, but I was sneaky about how I was beating around that bush. They wouldn't have figured it out."

I wasn't sure about that. "Had you talked to anyone else about the crash?"

"Chris, I may be drip-drip, getting drugs, drip-drip into my body, and may not be catching what you're hinting at.

Are you saying one of them tried to kill me because I was getting close to learning who killed the pilot?"

"Yes."

"Wow, umm, wow. That's scary."

"Virgil," I said, "it's a thought. It could also have been nothing more than an accident."

He laughed, something I couldn't imagine doing if I was in his condition. "Suppose I should be happy if someone did all this by accident."

Charles smiled. "You bet."

"Virgil," I said, "we'd better be going. The nurse told us to keep our visit short." I stood; Charles followed suit.

"Oh," Virgil said, "speaking of the crash, I nearly forgot, the day before I got smacked, I ran into Kelly, you know, Gary's wife, at Bert's. One of the clerks pointed her out. She was buying a package of bologna. I sidled up to her and told her how sorry I was about her loss. She gave me a funny look like she didn't know who I was. Natural, I suppose, since she didn't know who I was. I introduced myself then told her again how sorry I was."

"That was nice of you," I said, wondering how he remembered that but not his conversation in Cal's.

"Yeah, I told her it was terrible about what happened, that I was working on helping find out who poisoned her husband. I figured that'd give her hope."

I figuratively rolled my eyes. If Virgil had been that obvious with Richard, Tom, or others, it was becoming clear his accident was no accident.

I asked, "What did she say?"

"She smiled and said that was nice. She asked me to remind her what my name was then wanted to know if I lived on Folly. I told her. She said she was glad to meet me. I think I cheered her up."

And if she happened to be the person who poisoned her husband, he'd given her a reason to run him down.

We told him we were glad he was doing better. On our way to the door, Virgil said, "Before you go, would you check and see if my Guccis are with my clothes? We've been together for a lot of shoe leather."

They were. He exhaled a sigh of relief.

Chapter Twenty-Five

C aldwell Ramsey called the next morning to ask if I could meet him for lunch at Planet Follywood. It was the first time he'd invited me to lunch, so I was intrigued enough to say, "What time?"

Planet Follywood was one of the island's more established restaurants. In addition to good food, it was known by many as the restaurant with a large, painted mural covering an exterior wall with images of famous entertainers ranging from Elvis, Marilyn Monroe, Sammy Davis Jr., to John Wayne. I walked to the Center Street restaurant and was pleased to see Caldwell seated at a table along the side of the room. He wasn't hard to spot since he was six foot six-inches tall and African American, both traits in short supply on Folly.

He saw me enter, stood, and said, "Chris, glad you could make it."

Caldwell was in his mid-fifties, trim, his short, black hair had patches of gray sprinkled in. He'd played basketball for

Clemson in the eighties and looked like he could still compete.

"Thanks for the invitation. Why didn't Mel come with you?"

Caldwell laughed. "He told me he's sick of talking to you, that he'd rather watch soaps."

I chuckled knowing that wasn't true. "Tell him I said the same."

"Good. With the love messages out of the way, let me tell you why I asked you to lunch. I was nearby meeting a couple wanting to open a bar. They wanted my advice on what kind of acts they should hire to play weekends."

Caldwell was a music promoter and worked with several bars and concert venues.

"It's not on Folly, is it? There are enough bars here."

"No, it's three miles up Folly Road. Besides, I don't know if they have the capital to pull it off. Anyway, that's not why I called."

A server appeared to ask if we wanted drinks. Caldwell said beer, I chose iced tea.

He watched her go then said, "Mel told me you were asking about Mark Jamison's significant other."

"Kevin Robbins."

"Yes. I would've gotten back with you sooner, but I was in Atlanta at an event planners' meeting for a week after the plane crash. To be honest, I was so busy when I got back, I forgot Mel wanted me to talk to you. Sorry."

Caldwell was as opposite Mel as two men can be. The word sorry wouldn't leave Mel's mouth unless he was threatened with severe bodily harm. Even then, it would be surrounded by profanities.

"That's okay. Mel said you knew Kevin fairly well."

"Wouldn't go that far. We spent several hours together at Connections, a bar in Charleston. Mel kept getting into pity-party discussions with Mark bemoaning how bad business was. Mark owned a trucking company. When they went on a tirade about poor business, I was left talking to Kevin. I never saw or talked to him outside the bar. Mel said you were butting in police business. He didn't say it that politely."

"That I figured, but I'm not butting in. I'm curious about what happened."

"I doubt I can offer anything helpful."

"Did Kevin and Mark get along?"

Our drinks arrived. Caldwell ordered a chef salad, one reason for his trim physique; I asked for the American burger, a reason for my not-so-trim physique.

Caldwell asked me to repeat the question.

I said, "Did they have problems you heard about?"

"I don't know if it was a problem as such. Kevin makes good money as a pharmacist. Whenever Mark started talking about the trials and tribulations of his trucking business, Kevin would throw in something about how Mark should find something to do that had a steady paycheck. He wasn't mean when he said it, but if I heard it once, I heard it a dozen times. I don't know about Mark, but I would've been pissed listening to it over and over."

"How did Mark react?"

"He changed the subject. That's when he and Mel huddled and griped to each other leaving me with Kevin."

"Was Kevin covering most of their expenses?"

"I don't know about their living expenses, they have a house north of the city, but he always picked up the tab in Connections."

"Could Kevin have been angry enough with Mark to poison the pilot hoping the crash would kill Mark?"

Caldwell looked toward the exit then down in his beer before saying, "I've given a lot of thought about it since Mel said you were asking. Kevin's a pharmacist, so he'd know how to poison the pilot. He was often irritated with Mark. I don't know if this means anything or not, one night after a few drinks they were carping about something when Mark said something like, 'You'd be better off with me dead.'"

"What'd he mean?"

"Nothing was said then. I remember another night they were talking about something called a key man insurance policy he had through the company. I don't know if that's what he meant."

From working in a human resources department, I knew a key man policy was often taken on top-level executives by a company listing the business as beneficiary in case something happened to the valued, or key employee. In this case, the trucking company, MJ Transport, would get the proceeds from the policy.

"Caldwell, do you happen to know what happens to the trucking company now that Mark's gone?"

"Kevin would get it since they were legally married. I know they'd worked with an attorney on all that stuff because one night Kevin complained about paying the lawyer. Chris, do you think that was enough to kill an innocent man over?" He glanced in his beer. "It could've been three innocent men?"

"Don't know."

Food arrived, and Caldwell suggested we talk about something more pleasant. I switched to asking him about business. He shared a couple of humorous stories, one about a band from California a competing promoter had scheduled for a couple of Charleston venues and how the band had flown to Charleston, West Virginia, instead. After the promoter finally caught up with them, the lead singer said all he knew about Charleston was it's a dance. He didn't know the difference between Charleston, West Virginia and our city. The venue's owner is now booking acts through Caldwell.

I asked how Mel was doing. Caldwell said he was as bad-tempered, cranky, and boorish as ever.

"So, he's doing fine."

"Couldn't be better. In fact, I'm meeting him after lunch. We're going shopping."

"He need more camo pants?"

Caldwell laughed. Woodland camp field pants were to Mel as shorts were to most everyone on Folly in the summer. "I think twenty-three of them is enough. No, he lost his Semper Fi cap to a brisk wind on the marsh the other day."

"Good luck finding one like it," I said, then saw Charles waving for me at the entry. I told Caldwell I'd be back and walked over to Charles.

He looked at Caldwell, turned to me. "How much longer are you going to be?"

"Not much. Why?"

Charles tapped his temple with his forefinger. "My head's about to explode about the plane crash. Figured we needed to talk it out. Tell you what, I'll be on the Pier. Head that way when you're done."

Charles hadn't come in and interjected himself in my conversation with Caldwell, so I knew his head was truly spinning. I said I'd see him at the Pier.

Chapter Twenty-Six

I found Charles on the far end of the Folly Pier leaning
back on a wood bench shaded by the diamond-shaped
second level of the iconic structure. His Tilley was
pulled down over his eyes. His head exploding hadn't kept
him from napping. I joined him on the bench and watched
three fishermen tending to their fishing gear while carrying
on an animated conversation.

Charles jerked his head up knocking his Tilley to the
deck. He picked it up, returned it to his head. "Woah, how
long have you been here?"

"Not long. Enjoy your nap?"

"Pondering, not sleeping."

"If you say so. Tell me about your head exploding."

He glanced at the fishermen then at the deck. "Chris,
remember the last few times we've helped the cops?"

"Of course."

"What'd they have in common?"

I smiled. "Other than nearly getting me killed?"

"Something more important."

"I thought that was important."

He rubbed his chin. "Other than that, what did they have in common?"

"You tell me."

"Everyone knew who the killer kilt."

I nodded. "Now we have two dead bodies, four potential victims."

He used his Tilley like a fan and waved it in his face. "Chris, how in red, white, and blue blazes are we supposed to learn who the killer is if we don't know who was supposed to be killed?"

I didn't offer we'd already talked about that plus we weren't supposed to help catch anyone. Another reason I didn't tell him was because I hated to admit it, but I agreed. We were there when the crash occurred. It came close to adding us to the list of bodies. Now Virgil was nearly killed. Granted, he's not a close friend, but someone who's latched onto us, who's taken an interest in the crash. I also reminded myself he was a suspect until he was run down.

"Charles, I suppose the most logical intended victim was the pilot, Gary Isles. It was his cooler the poisoned drink was in. Regardless of the results of the crash, Gary wouldn't have survived."

"If it was him, the best suspect would be his wife, so what would've been Kelly's motive?"

"It's possible that she resented him for having to leave the law firm because of its rule about wives of their attorneys working there. I know it'd irritate me. Or, it simply could've been for his life insurance."

"Yeah," Charles said, "another thing, and it's mere speculation on my part, but remember how close she was with Tom Kale at the party they had for us?"

"Sure, but they were neighbors, well, almost neighbors, and she'd lost her husband. Maybe Tom is a sensitive guy who wanted to comfort widow Kelly."

"My gut tells me it's more."

I said, "Charles, we've been over this. If she and Tom were having an affair, why would she have poisoned her husband when she knew Tom would be in the plane?"

"True." Charles nodded his head left, then right. "Okay, let's say Kelly did it because she resented not being able to work for the snooty law firm or for the insurance. Why would she endanger the lives of three others if all she wanted to do was to bump off her husband?"

"It seems unlikely. She would've had numerous chances to kill him over the years. I'm leaning toward eliminating Gary as the intended victim."

Charles said, "One down, three to go. My head's still exploding. What about the other guy who didn't survive?"

"Mark Jamison," I said. "Let me tell you what Caldwell shared." I proceeded to give him the highlights of the luncheon conversation.

Charles glared at me. "Why didn't you say that before you started talking about Gary Isles, before letting me go off on a tangent about him being the intended victim?"

"Charles, have you ever stood in a field and tried to stop a charging buffalo?"

"Can't say I have. Why?"

"If I started with telling you what Caldwell said, you'd be like that buffalo. I wouldn't have a chance to slow you much less stop you long enough to talk about the other possible killers."

"I'm confused. Are you saying that because Mark's spouse, Kevin, had an excellent motive for wanting Mark dead, Kelly didn't do it?"

"No," I shook my head. "I'd put Kevin near the top of the list, but not there alone. If I told you what Caldwell said, I was afraid it'd cloud our, your thinking."

"You don't give me much credit." He sighed. "You're right though. I suppose you want to talk about the others on the plane as the possible target."

"Yes. Let's take Richard Haymaker next. Who could've wanted him dead?"

"His wife."

I said yes before telling him what Bob Howard had told me about Charlene Beth, how much he hated double first names, about her alleged affair with Walter Middleton Gibbs.

Charles grinned then said, "So you think she tried to kill her husband because Bob Howard has a thing against double first names?"

I rolled my eyes. "If she's having an affair, she may've wanted her spouse out of the way."

"Okay, so let's add Charlene Beth to the list. What about Leroy Jethro Gibbs, the guy she's supposed to be having the affair with?"

"It's Walter Middleton Gibbs. Leroy Jethro Gibbs is a character on *NCIS*."

"Whatever. It's a three-word, snooty-sounding name. Can we add him to the list?"

"It's your list. Let's talk about Tom Kale. Who'd have a motive to want him dead?"

"The only person I know of is his stockbroker ex-wife,

Alyssa. Didn't you say she didn't seem too happy he survived?"

"Yes. Their divorce was highly contested, with the financial part still not finalized."

"A dead Tom Kale would finalize it. Sounds like motive to me."

"No argument there," I said. "Let me throw something else out. What if the killer is Virgil?"

"The Virgil who's in the hospital looking like a mummy with his appendages propped up in the air?"

"Yes."

"You think he poisoned the pilot, killed two people, then ran himself down to make it look like someone wanted him dead?"

"No. What if his accident was simply that, having nothing to do with the plane crash? It's bothered me how he's wiggled his way into our lives wanting to help catch the killer. Why would he do that?"

Charles hesitated, then said, "To learn what we know about the murder; to know if we're getting close to him as a suspect?"

"Yes. What other reason would he have to get involved?"

"He finds me charming, personable, an outstanding detective. He wants to learn from the best."

That earned a second eye roll. "I'll stick to my first reason. He wants to see what we know."

"For sake of argument, I'll add him to the list. Anyone else?"

"Our problem is we know little about the passengers. There could be, and probably are, others who had a motive for poisoning the pilot."

Charles blinked twice and put his forefinger in the air.

"So, our suspects are Kelly Isles, Kevin Robbins, Charlene Beth, Walter Middleton, not Leroy Jethro, Gibbs, Alyssa Kale, and Virgil Debonnet. Oh yeah, to make it so much easier for us to figure out, add countless others we don't know about. That cover it?"

I nodded.

"That's four potential victims, five counting Virgil, six suspects we know about, plus a cast of thousands of others. See why my head's exploding?"

"Yes," I realized I shared that condition.

What I couldn't say was how we were going to learn the identity of the intended victim. Unless we did that, there was little chance of learning who poisoned the pilot.

We sat and stared at the breaking waves for thirty more minutes before deciding that there were no answers coming to us. We'd be better off in air-conditioned comfort.

Chapter Twenty-Seven

Charles headed to his apartment and I was on the way home when I received a call from a number I didn't recognize. I was tempted to let it roll to voicemail until I realized it may be Virgil.

Wrong.

"Chris, this is Tom Kale. Did I catch you at an inconvenient time?"

I told him no. I didn't share that his civil, thoughtful question was out of character for any of my friends.

"Could I impose on you to stop by the house?"

"When?"

"Within the hour if possible. I must attend a meeting in Mt. Pleasant and will need to leave in a couple hours."

I asked if fifteen minutes would be too soon. He said no.

A black Range Rover with temporary tags was parked in Tom's drive. I parked behind the impressive vehicle and Tom greeted me with a smile with Casper cradled in his arms. The stockbroker wore gray dress slacks and a white, button-down dress shirt. I felt underdressed in my tan shorts and orange polo shirt, yet despite my appearance he motioned me in as I made cooing sounds while Casper licked my cheek.

"Let's go to my office."

I followed him up the stairs as he remarked how the floating staircase was the main reason he bought the house. He'd told me the same thing the day of the reception. He pointed for me to be seated in front of one of the computer monitors, set Casper on the floor, then took a seat at the other monitor. I was again impressed by the expansive view of the coast, and curious about why I'd been invited.

"Thanks for coming," he said, not giving anything away.

I remained silent. It was his show.

"Chris, I've heard some disturbing news." He glanced out the window as his smile turned sour. He gripped the arm of the chair then turned to me. "It's come to my attention you and some of your friends have been nosing into the cause of the crash." He glared at me. "I find that inappropriate."

"Tom, Charles and I have—"

Tom waved his hand in my face. "I'm not finished." His grip on the chair with his other hand tightened. He continued giving me a menacing look. "You've accused my ex-wife of poisoning Gary in an effort to kill me." He slammed his other hand down on the chair arm. His mood change and action startled me. I remained silent. He continued, "That's ludicrous." He took a deep breath. "Then your friend Debonnet starts harassing my acquaintances spewing accusations about me and of all people Gary's widow. Where in the hell do you all get off butting in, sullying Alyssa and my name?"

I was shocked. He reminded me of one of those creatures in the movies that morphs from a friendly, cuddly animal to a fanged demon devouring its prey.

"Tom, I don't know what you've heard. I'm not doing anything to cause harm to you or your ex-wife. When my friend Charles and I learned Gary had been poisoned we were curious about what'd happened. You may not know, but I'm friends with Chief LaMond. I talked to her about the investigation."

I didn't think it was possible, but his glare turned more menacing. I continued, "I'm sorry if you think we're overstepping. I would've thought you'd be anxious for whomever poisoned Gary to be caught. Two people were killed. You and Richard are fortunate to be alive."

He wiped his hand over the granite desktop like he was removing dust and looked out the window before turning back to me. "Don't play me for an idiot. I've heard how you and your friends interfere with police investigations. What happened out in the marsh is none of your business. Period."

He pounded the arm of the chair once more, stood, and jerked open the door to the patio. I remained in my chair as he walked to the outdoor railing. I was about to join him when he pivoted and returned.

I wanted him to get it out of his system, so I remained silent as his glare returned. He continued where he'd left off, "What about your friend Debonnet who's going around telling everyone he's working as an assistant detective for you and your buddy? What in the hell is an assistant detective? Why is whatever happened his business?"

"Tom, Virgil is a new acquaintance who offered to talk to some people to see what they knew about the crash. He told us he'd dealt with your ex. He may've said something to her."

He stomped his foot on the floor. "He said something to Alyssa, crap. He nearly pounced on her, accusing her of killing Gary and Mark." He shook his head. "Alyssa and I have had a challenging time settling our divorce. She doesn't need someone harassing her."

I was floored by his level of anger. What's with him defending Alyssa? From what I'd heard, their divorce was contentious. Did he have something to hide? Did he know she had something to hide?

I took a deep breath to calm my voice. "Tom, when that plane nearly killed Charles and me, it became our business. We've done nothing more than ask questions. As for Virgil, I hardly know him. We've talked maybe four times. He did express interest in the crash. Since he'd worked with Alyssa, he said he was going to talk to her. Nothing more."

"That's not what—"

My turn to interrupt. "Are you aware that someone tried to kill Virgil?"

His scowl softened. "When? How?"

He was either surprised or a good actor. I shared the details of the hit-and-run. Tom asked if Virgil was going to be okay. I told him the doctors thought so. Tom loosened his grip on the chair.

He said, "That's too bad. It still didn't give him the right to pester Alyssa."

He looked at his watch and I knew he'd have to leave soon. "Tom, I understand how you may be displeased about the way Alyssa has been treated, but aren't you concerned about who poisoned Gary, killed Mark, and if it hadn't been for luck, killed you and Richard?"

He rubbed his hand across his face as he looked at the floor. "Sure I am. It doesn't make sense." He stared at me. "I may be overreacting about you and your friends. I suppose I must take my frustration out on someone." He shrugged. "That was you."

A meager apology. "We all know Gary did, but there was a good chance all of you would have perished in the crash. If Gary wasn't the intended victim, do you have a guess who it could've been?"

He didn't answer for several seconds. Finally, in a lower, less hostile tone, he said, "That's all I've thought about since you dragged us out of the wreck. My first thought was it was me. I know Alyssa can be, well, can be vindictive, or hard to get along with, but for the life of me, I can't see her doing something like that." He bit his lower lip. "I've known Richard for years, socialized with him and Charlene Beth at conventions. Richard is liked by all. I can't see anyone wanting him dead." He paused then looked out the window.

"What about Mark?"

"Chris, I don't know if I should say it or not."

"What?"

"If I had to guess who the target was, I'd say Mark."

"Why?"

"Don't hold me to this. I didn't know him as well as I knew the other guys. I didn't know much about his friends or his personal life. What I knew was on several of the golf trips he talked about arguments with Kevin."

"His spouse?"

Tom nodded.

"Arguments about?"

"He didn't talk much about the details. I got bits and pieces from his talks with the other guys. Mark owns, owned, a trucking company. It's had good times but like most small businesses hit rough spots. Recently there were more bad than good. Kevin is a pharmacist. He apparently makes a good living and was always pestering Mark to give up on the company and get a job with a steady income."

"You think Kevin poisoned Gary to crash the plane and kill Mark?"

"Yes."

"Why would he want him dead?"

"Insurance."

I knew what he was talking about but was curious about his version. "Life insurance?"

"Sort of. The last time we golfed, Mark was telling Richard he had a key man policy. That's where if something happened to Mark, the company would get the insurance." He hesitated and looked out the window, before turning back to me. "I hate to say this, and I may not have heard all of it correctly. I'm almost certain I heard him say that he was afraid of Kevin; said the taking out the policy may be the death of him."

"Who was he talking to?"

"Gary."

That eliminated a way to verify it. I hesitated to see if Tom was going to add anything. He didn't, so I said, "Do you think he feared Kevin?"

"Yes, but that doesn't mean he killed him."

"It doesn't. Didn't you, Mark, and Richard ride to the airport together?"

"Yes, Gary was already there. We were late. He was perturbed about us not getting there when we said we would. Why?"

"My understanding is the poison was in Gary's drink, a

drink he got out of his cooler. How would Kevin have inserted the poison in the drink?"

"Don't know. All I know is the cooler was in the plane when we climbed aboard."

"Did you see anything or anyone who struck you as suspicious when you got to the airport?"

"Like what?"

"Anything. Someone you recognized, familiar car in the lot. Richard mentioned Gary told him he was surprised to see a familiar person in the lot while he was waiting for you to arrive."

Tom scratched his cheek and said, "Not really. You might ask Warren. He was there."

"Warren?"

"Warren Marshall. He's an airplane groupie. He hangs around the airport. In and out of the hangars, in the waiting room. I think he's mildly autistic. Nice guy."

"Describe him."

"White, in his fifties, thin, always smiling, probably knows more about planes than the engineers over at Boeing." Tom looked at his watch again. "Sorry, I need to run."

He walked me to the door, before saying, "Sorry I snapped at you. This whole thing has me upset." He shook my hand with a firm, overly firm, grip and hesitated before saying, "I'm not sorry I told you and your friends to lay off Alyssa. She didn't do it."

I told him I understood how he would be upset. What I didn't say was Alyssa would be off limits.

Chapter Twenty-Eight

With nothing on my agenda and a glimmer of a clue provided by Tom Kale, I called Charles.

"Ready to go?" I asked when he answered. This was the kind of greeting I often received when he called.

"Where?"

"Airport."

There was a slight pause before he said, "We flying to Tahiti?"

"Wrong airport, the Charleston Executive Airport."

"Ah, it's beginning to make sense. That's where the lucky two, unlucky two golfers took off."

"Pick you up in a half hour."

I hung up knowing the exhilarating feeling my friends must have when they did that to me.

Charles was standing in front of his apartment when I pulled in his parking area. He was wearing tan shorts, his Tilley, and a long-sleeve, navy blue T-shirt with Air Force

Academy in white on the chest with Fighting Falcons down the sleeve.

The Charleston Executive Airport was fewer than five miles from Folly as the crow or plane flies, but because the pesky Stono River blocked vehicular traffic between Folly and the airport, we had to drive to Maybank Highway to cross the waterway. That added ten miles to the trip which Charles filled by asking me seven ways what I expected to learn at the airport. I answered each inquiry with a two word answer. *Don't know*. I shared what I'd learned from Tom about a regular at the airport who might've seen something.

I didn't think it was a good sign the turnoff to the airport was immediately past a cemetery. That was after we passed a sign for the Cottage Aroma Bella Day Spa, when Charles said, "Think we should stop and get some spa treatments?"

"We got a mud bath in the marsh when the plane attacked us. That's enough for me."

"Just asking."

It didn't warrant a response.

The rest of the way looked more like farmland than an airport as we drove to a large parking lot in front of the single story Atlantic Aviation building. There must be a lull in activity. A handful of vehicles were in the lot. Ten single-engine aircraft and four private jets were neatly parked on the large concrete pad behind the building.

The waiting room had an earth-tone colored tile floor covering most of the surface. A carpeted seating area was off to the left with a sofa and three chairs. Two men were in deep conversation on the sofa. They glanced our way.

"Can I help you?" said the older of the two.

I would've bet the answer to my first question was the fifty-something year old man seated beside him wearing a red plaid, long-sleeve shirt, and jeans. "We're looking for Warren Marshall."

The man who asked if he could help said, "You've come to the right place." He nodded toward the other man.

I stuck out my hand to shake the hand of the man in plaid. "Warren, I'm Chris and this is my friend Charles."

The man stood. "Oh, hi. I'm Warren."

"Nice to meet you," I said. "Do you have a few minutes?"

"Sure, Brady and I were talking planes. Do you have a plane, Chris?"

"No."

He turned to Charles and pointed at his T-shirt. "Cool shirt. You go to the Air Force Academy?"

"Afraid not, Warren."

Warren frowned. "Oh. You have a plane?"

"Can't say I do," Charles said. "I'd like to. Do you have one?"

That was the first I'd heard of Charles's desire for an airplane. I suspected it was his effort to bond with Warren.

"No. Sad, but no."

The older gentleman interrupted to tell us he needed to get back to work. He headed out the door at the side of the room.

Warren watched him go. "Brady's a nice man. He gets to work with planes all the time." He then turned to us. "You really wanted to talk to me?"

"We do," I said. "Let's have a seat."

"Okay." He sat then turned to Charles. "Charles, what kind of plane do you want?"

"I'm not certain, Warren."

Not certain, I thought. It was more like not even approximate. I sat back to watch Charles get off the topic.

Warren smiled. "I know three for sale. Charles, I could get you the number of the owners. One's cool. It's a Gulfstream G550. 2013 model. They're asking thirty-five million, but I bet you could get it for less."

Charles gulped. "Warren, that's a bit more than I'm thinking about spending."

Warren smiled again. "It is steep. There's a Malibu Mirage sitting out there. Only $876,000. Great plane."

Charles returned Warren's smile and said, "That's closer to what I was thinking."

Around $875,000 from being in his price range, I thought, and decided it was time to move on from Warren trying to broker an airplane deal.

"Warren, do you spend a lot of time here?"

"Yes, mostly in the hangars. That's where I got to know several pilots, got to know their planes. You could say I'm an airplane addict." He chuckled. "Chris, you said you don't have a plane. That right?"

I nodded.

"So, why are you here?"

"We're friends with some of the guys who were in that unfortunate plane crash near Folly Beach." I said and guessed, "Someone said you were here when they took off."

Warren closed his eyes before giving a slight nod. "Cessna 182 Skylane, 2006 model, all-metal, mostly aluminum alloy, built in Wichita, Kansas."

He was right about being an airplane addict. "That's the one."

Warren shook his head. "It was terrible what happened.

Mr. Isles was one of my favorite pilots. We talked a lot about planes."

"It was terrible," I said. "Was he here often with his wife?"

"Mrs. Isles was with him sometimes. She didn't like flying. I remember a while back where he nearly had to drag her on the plane." Warren chuckled. "I thought she was about to punch him in the nose. She's not as nice as Mr. Isles."

Interesting, I thought. "Warren, did they argue other times?"

"Don't recall arguing. She didn't look like a happy person. Why?"

"Interested, that's all."

Warren turned to Charles. "Sure would like to show you the planes that're for sale. I know you'd like them."

Charles smiled. "Maybe another time."

I said, "Warren, did you see the other guys get in the plane with Gary?"

"Let's see, I was over at the hangar where Mr. Isles was prepping the plane." Warren chuckled. "Mr. Isles was sort of pissed, whoops, sorry, he was angry because the others were late. He said they were going up to Myrtle to play golf. Mr. Isles thought they'd be late for their game, or whatever you call playing golf."

Charles leaned closer to Warren. "Did you see anyone with him?"

"People were coming and going on the other side of the hangar, but I didn't see anybody talking to Mr. Isles. To tell the truth, I didn't like the language he was using when talking about the guys who weren't there. I went outside to talk to Mr. Jamison. He was getting ready to take off in his

Piper PA-46 Malibu. It was built by Piper Aircraft, down in Vero Beach, Florida." He snapped his fingers. "Charles, I think Mr. Jamison might be interested in selling it. Want me to call him?"

"Not now, Warren. Tell you what, I'll let you know if I want to meet him."

I glared at Charles and turned to Warren. "Got another question, Warren. Did you happen to see Gary, umm, Mr. Isles' drink cooler the day of the crash?"

Warren looked at the floor and toward the door. "Didn't see it, but Mr. Isles was standing by his plane. He remembered he left it in his car and went to get it. He asked me to watch his plane while he was gone." Warren smiled. "Didn't have to watch it too hard. It wasn't going to fly away without Mr. Isles."

I said, "You were there when he returned with the cooler?"

"Sure. I was watching his plane."

"Did he say anything?"

"Now that you mention it, he did say something about seeing someone he thought he knew in the parking lot."

"Thought he knew, or someone he knew?" Charles asked.

"Don't know. It was more like he saw someone. That person reminded him of someone."

That was a confusing clarification. "Did he say who he thought it was?"

"If he did, I didn't get it. It must not be a regular here because he seemed surprised seeing, or think he saw, some-one. Something like that."

I said, "Warren, did you see the other guys arrive?"

"No, I was with Mr. Jamison. Charles, sure you don't

want me to call him? He's a nice fellow. I know he'd give you a good deal."

Charles thanked him then declined.

"Okay. Let me know if you change your mind."

"Mr. Isles' buddies?" I said to get Warren back on the runway.

"Oh yeah, Mr. Isles and his golfing buddies. Like I told you, I didn't see them get here but I saw them take off. That's all."

I said, "Warren, can you think of anything else about that day?"

"Let's see. It was a pretty day. And, oh yeah, Mr. Lionel landed in his Learjet 45. Mr. Lionel is a UPS pilot. He got his own Learjet from his father who passed last year. The Learjet 45 is supposed to be a competitor in the super-light business jet category, a rival to the Cessna Citation Excel/XLS. I personally don't think it's as good as the Cessna. Anyway, Mr. Lionel lets me go aboard and sit in his seat. Of course, he won't let me fly it."

"Warren," I interrupted. "Do you remember anything else about Mr. Isles or his passengers?"

"No sir, afraid not."

"We appreciate your time." Charles and I stood to leave.

"Stop by anytime. If I'm not in here, I'll be down at the hangar, the one closest to here."

We headed to the door when Warren said, "I think it was a woman."

"Who was?" I said.

"The person Mr. Isles may've known."

"Why do you think it was a woman?"

"I could have it wrong, but I think he said spouse."

"Anything else?" I asked.

"Nope. Oh yeah, Charles, if you want me to introduce you to Mr. Jamison, his plane would be perfect for you."

Charles once again said he'd let Warren know. We headed to the car.

Charles patted me on the arm. "Want to go in with me on buying the Malibu Mirage? I could pull together a couple hundred dollars, you'd only have to pony-up the other $875,800."

I met his proposal with silence.

Chapter Twenty-Nine

We decided three things on the way home. First, if we combined our worldly resources, we'd fall well more than three-quarters-of-a-million dollars shy of buying the Malibu Mirage, regardless how good a deal Mr. Jamison would give us. We'd have to live without an airplane. Second, Warren was less than helpful when it came to identifying the person, but he verified that someone other than Gary Isles would've had access to the cooler, someone who could've poisoned Gary's energy drink. Third, we were hungry. More importantly, we needed an adult beverage. Cal's was our next stop.

Not many others felt the same need. It was early afternoon and Cal's was five customers shy of empty, that was counting Charles and me. Cal was standing behind the bar wearing his Stetson, an orange Folly Beach T-shirt, looking bored or irritated.

He leaned on the bar and motioned us over. "Finally, friendly faces. First drink's on me if you'll sit a spell."

That was a nice gesture, although the phrase there's no such thing as a free drink popped in my head.

Charles smiled. "Cal, old buddy, that's mighty generous. What kind of deal you offering if we want a burger with the drink?"

"Michigan, old buddy," Cal said as he tipped his Stetson toward Charles, "add fries to that and I'll throw in all the catsup you can slather on."

The drink was all we were getting out of Cal. I told him it was a great offer and for him to fix each of us a burger, fries, beer for Charles, white wine for me.

"Fine choice, Kentucky. I appreciate your support and presence for a couple of hours this afternoon."

I hadn't thought "sit a spell" would take that long. What I did think was Cal had something to tell us. It became clearer when he pointed to a table on the far side of the room. "Why don't you head over there. I'll take your order to my executive chef."

Charles tilted his head, looked at Cal, and mouthed, "Executive chef?"

Cal nodded, again pointed to the table where he wanted us to sit a spell then walked the short distance to the kitchen entrance.

"Chris," Charles said as he plopped down in the chair, "Now what? I'm at a loss. How're we going to figure out who poisoned Gary?"

I was about to share I was equally lost when Cal arrived with our drinks. Instead of heading back to the bar, he pulled a chair from the adjoining table, sat, and set his Stetson on the table.

Charles repeated what he'd mouthed to Cal earlier, "Executive chef?"

"Junior said he'd be glad to help out his old man. He added calling him anything less than executive chef would be an insult to his expertise, or something along those lines. I didn't have to buy him business cards or one of those expensive chef coats with his name and title sewed on it, so he could call himself whatever he wanted."

I looked toward the door to the kitchen. "Did you have your talk about the changes he'd hit you with?"

"Sort of, pard."

Charles said, "Sort of?"

Cal rubbed his chin. "Let's see, I told him I wasn't comfortable borrowing money to expand the kitchen." Cal nodded like he was finished.

I asked, "What'd he say?"

"I was being shortsighted, not looking at the long-term profitability of the establishment. Told him I was approaching three-quarters of a century on this here earth, my long term was next weekend."

This time Charles said, "What'd he say?"

"He used ten big words to say I was a foolish old man. I told him that was my point. I was an old man. He added a couple more ways of saying it as he stormed out."

A loud bell dinged from the kitchen.

"That's the executive chef telling me your food's ready." Cal pushed the chair back and headed toward the sound.

Charles watched him go. "We here two hours yet?"

I watched Cal return with our burgers, fries, and two bottles of catsup. He set them in front of us then headed to the customers waving for their check.

I didn't realize how hungry I was until I took the first bite. I also didn't realize how much better the burger tasted prepared by an executive chef than from others I'd eaten in Cal's fixed by Cal or his part-time cook. Charles must've agreed since his only comment after taking two bites was, "Yummy."

The other customers exited as Cal returned.

I said, "I gather Junior came back after your tiff over expanding the kitchen."

"You gather right." Cal again looked toward the kitchen. "Surprised the heck out of me when he came back the next day apologizing for his outburst." Cal smiled. "He reminded me of me when I was his age. My temper got me in more fixes than a toad frog in a gaggle of geese. That's ancient history. He was sorry, said he'd be glad to help me out. We could discuss his other ideas later. Later ain't got here yet."

"Discuss what later?" Junior said as he stepped behind Cal's chair. The executive chef wore a black-and-white checked chef's baseball cap, black slacks, and a short-sleeve, white chef's coat with *C. Richardson, Executive Chef, Best Burgers* on the breast.

Cal jumped at the sound of his son. "Hey, Junior. Let me introduce you to two of my best friends, Chris and Charles."

Charles interrupted the introductions, and said, "Junior, we met one of the first times you were in here. We were at the bar."

"I remember. Think you were with him, Chris."

Charles smiled like he'd been recognized by the Governor of South Carolina. I told him he was right about me being with Charles.

Junior pulled another chair to the table. Sat uninvited, and said, "Glad you're here. How're the burgers?"

Charles said, "Yummy," I added, "Fine." The last thing I wanted to say in Cal's presence was that they were the best we'd had here.

Junior smiled. "Great. Now that you're here and are good buddies with Dad, let me bounce a couple of ideas off you to get a customer's perspective."

"Junior," Cal interrupted. "The guys may want to eat in peace."

That'd never stopped Cal from interrupting our eating.

"That's okay, Cal," Charles said like a shark circling a pool of fish preparing for lunch. "We've got time."

"Wonderful," Junior said. "Dad, gee, it sounds strange saying that word. Anyway, he and I've been talking about changes we could make in the restaurant."

I looked at Cal when Junior said *we*. Cal's expression slipped from nervous to frustration, to irritation.

Junior didn't notice or decided to plow ahead regardless. "Things like fixing the place up, getting new equipment in the kitchen, new tables and chairs, expanding our menu and drink offerings. What do you think?"

Charles went first. "Interesting ideas." He turned to me. "What do you think, Chris?"

Thanks, friend. I took a sip of wine then said, "Junior, I agree with Charles. The ideas are interesting. Maybe you could work with Cal and figure out ways to make some of them happen." I hesitated as I thought about what to say next. "During the decade or so I've been on Folly, restaurants have come and gone, some switched ownership, a few opened, closed, reopened with different concepts. I'm sure your Dad's told you this used to be a rock-and-roll bar so it's not immune to change."

Junior interrupted, "See Dad, Chris agrees we should change."

"Junior," I said, "that's not what I'm saying."

Junior stared at me; his eyes narrowed. "What're you saying?"

"Some minor changes might not be bad." I waved my hand around the room. "Cal's is a classic country-music bar. Your Dad's customers come for drinks, mainly beer as you can see, a good burger, and the feel, smell, charm of a calmer, friendlier, better time. If they want a modern bar, or one playing today's music, or somewhere to buy a margarita, there are excellent choices on Folly." I patted Cal on the back. "Nowhere else on earth can they find someone like your Dad. Junior, he's a country legend. Cal's is great the way it is."

Cal rubbed his fingers along the Stetson's brim and grinned. "Thanks, pard."

Junior glanced at his Dad and turned toward Charles and me. "I asked for your opinion, so I should've been ready to listen to whatever you said."

"I'm not saying changes can't be made. Is the kitchen large enough for you to fix burgers and fries? That's all customers want to eat here. They can get limitless choices elsewhere."

"I guess."

"Junior," I continued, "these tables and chairs might not look like much, but they've held up a long time. They have a lot of life left in them."

"Been in here since the Civil War," Charles said. He hated to be left out of a conversation.

"Son," Cal said, "these guys ain't gangin' up on you. They speak for most of my customers. Sure, I could make a herd of changes, a few more folks might mosey in, but that's expensive. I do agree about the old place needing a coat of paint. I have enough cash stocked away to do that."

Junior nodded. "That's great, Dad. One more thing, let me share something I've learned from being in the restaurant business. Most customers are creatures of habit when it comes to their drinks. I'll concede that liquor and some of the fancier drinks may not work, but when it comes to beer, I think expanding the selection could help."

"No craft beers," Cal said. He didn't know what they were, yet he was firm about not adding any.

Junior sighed, "Okay, but why not add Coors, Michelob, or Busch?"

"Suppose we could do that. It won't break us."

I zoned out of the fascinating topic of beer brands and focused on something Junior had said about customers being creatures of habit when it came to drinks. Was that true of the men in the plane? Gary's poison was in his energy drink. Hadn't Cindy said that Mark had a Mountain Dew? What drinks were in the cooler for Richard and Tom? If neither drank energy drinks, then the killer knew what Gary would be drinking.

"Chris, where are you?" Charles said and shook my arm. "Don't you think that's a great idea?"

"Umm, sure," I said, having no idea what the idea was.

"Then it's decided," Charles said. "Chris and I'll be here Monday morning to help you paint."

That'll teach me to agree without knowing what I'm agreeing with. I hate painting.

Two customers came in, told Cal they wanted burgers and beer so Junior and Cal left to do their thing. I looked over at Charles and said, "Tom or Richard?"

Instead of asking what I was talking about, Charles tapped his beer bottle on the table, smiled. "You're getting gooder and gooder sounding like me. I'm proud of you."

It also felt *gooder* and *gooder* returning the kind of statements he'd made countless times. "Well, which one?"

"Tell you what. Give me a hint about what you're talking about, then I'll answer."

"Which one of them are we going to ask what other drinks were in the cooler. We know Gary had an energy drink; Mark had a Mountain Dew."

Charles scratched his temple. "Why is that important?"

I reminded him what Junior had said about customers being creatures of habit before adding, "If the only energy drink was Gary's, the killer knew who'd drink it. If there was more than one energy drink in the cooler, one of the other guys could've been poisoned. If Tom or Richard had taken a sip and collapsed, Gary might not have consumed any. Three of them would be alive today."

"Richard."

"Why?"

"Because Tom's pissed at you for nosing in police business. Might as well get Richard pissed too."

Not the best logic, but it made sense. We decided that since tomorrow was Saturday, he might be home. A casual visit to see how he was doing, might not arouse too much suspicion. We hoped.

Chapter Thirty

Richard's house, located on the marsh side of the island, wasn't as large as the other two Folly residents' homes. He answered the door and if he was surprised to see us standing on his elevated front porch, it didn't show. He wore blue shorts and a white T-shirt with a photo on it of the USS Yorktown, the decommissioned World War II aircraft carrier that serves as a museum ship at Patriots Point in Charleston Harbor.

"Cool shirt," Charles said instead of something traditional like hi or hello.

Richard looked down at the shirt like he didn't know what he had on. "Oh, yeah, thanks. I like yours, too."

Charles had on a long-sleeve University of Hawaii T-shirt. Richard didn't comment on my green polo shirt promoting nothing.

Now that Charles and Richard had bonded, it was time to move the T-shirt discussion to the rearview mirror. "Hope we're not interrupting anything. You have a few minutes?"

Richard stepped aside and invited us in. He was more gracious than I would've been seeing us at the door. He said he'd brewed a pot of coffee and asked if we wanted a cup. Charles answered for both of us when he said we'd love some. We followed Richard to the kitchen. The house was relatively new. The kitchen was filled with black appliances, concrete countertops, and a window with an impressive view of the marsh and a narrow walking pier leading from the yard to the Folly River. The host handed each of us a mug as he asked if we wanted to join him out back.

The view from the oversized deck was more spectacular than the one from the kitchen. The bridge off-island was to our left, to the right we could see the river weaving its way through the marsh. Instead of appreciating the magnificent view, it reminded me of the fateful day we'd met Richard. I shuttered at the thought. I also wondered why Richard hadn't expressed curiosity about why we were here.

He wasn't wearing the sling, so I asked, "How's your arm?"

He waved it over his head. "Almost good as new."

I said, "Great. It could've been much worse."

Charles sipped his coffee, looked around the deck, then nodded at two colorful, plastic toys in the corner. "Richard, it's mighty quiet. Don't you have twins?"

Richard laughed. "Two-year-old twins. They make a jet-ski sound like a feather hitting the floor."

Charles's head bobbed. "I know what you mean."

Words spoken by a man who'd never been around kids, much less twins.

Richard said, "It's quiet because Charlene Beth took them out on the boat a little while ago. They like to look for dolphins in the marsh. I like the silence. It's win-win for all of us." He took a sip, set his mug on the arm rest, and said, "I don't suppose you stopped by to ask about the kids."

I took a deep breath. "Richard, this may seem like a strange question. Do you remember what drinks were in the cooler Gary had on the plane?"

His hand gripping the mug began shaking. He looked toward the marsh then back at me. "Why in heaven's name would you ask that?"

"The police know Gary was poisoned by something in his drink, so I was wondering how the person who put it there knew Gary would be the one drinking it."

"Why aren't the police asking instead of you?"

Great question. "I'm sure they're following up on everything. The drinks were something I've been thinking about. I understand if you're uncomfortable talking about it."

I was preparing to be evicted. Instead, Richard said, "We've been going on these golfing trips a few years now. We know each other's good and bad habits, what foods each like, what drinks. To answer your question, it was a small cooler, only held four or five drinks. Gary was hung up on energy drinks. We teased him that if he had any more energy, he could flap his wings and fly to Myrtle Beach without a plane. Anyway, that was his preferred drink. Mountain Dew was Mark's. I often joked saying it tasted like rotten oranges." Richard hesitated as he rubbed the bridge of his nose. "I won't be teasing him again."

I said, "We're sorry to be dredging up bad memories."

"That's okay. It's always on my mind."

Charles leaned closer to Richard. "What about you and Tom?"

Richard looked at him like he didn't understand the question, then said, "Oh, our drinks. I always have Diet

Coke. Tom's another story. We picked on him nearly every trip because he never knew what to order when we were on the course. One time he'd want Pepsi, the next time root beer, sometimes energy drinks. I don't know what he had in the cooler. Gary was such a nice guy, such a gracious host, I'd wager he called Tom to ask what he wanted."

"You don't know what was in the cooler for him?"

"I didn't look. If it's that important, I suggest you ask Tom. Does that help?"

I said it did without adding *almost* before changing the subject. I didn't want him thinking too much about what I'd asked. We talked about the weather, the topic most people talk about while sitting on the deck on a beautiful spring morning. Charles, who'd never owned a share of any stock, asked about recent market fluctuations. He was rewarded with a lecture about international influences on the United States market. All I understood were the words China and steel.

Richard ran out of words to confuse me, so I said, "Richard, we've taken enough of your time. Thanks for the coffee."

He stood. "Sure you don't want to stay to hear how loud twins can be."

We declined.

———

"What did we learn other than twins are loud?" Charles asked as we pulled out of Richard's drive.

"Richard is a more gracious host than I'd be if two strangers knocked on my door. We came close to learning that Gary was the intended poison victim."

"Until Richard said Tom may've had an energy drink in the cooler. If he did, it could've been Tom who was supposed to die."

"Yes, though that doesn't make sense. What would've been the advantage of poisoning Tom on the plane?"

"Because they were in the air, they couldn't get help, no chance of saving his life."

"Charles, my understanding is there wouldn't have been anything they could've done to help him if he'd ingested arsenic."

"Maybe the killer didn't know that. If he did, I suppose there's no advantage for poisoning him in the air. So, are we going to do what Richard suggested?"

"Ask Tom what drink he wanted?"

Charles rolled his eyes. "No, go back to see how loud the twins are."

"When do you want to visit Tom?" I asked, certain what the answer would be.

"Now."

Charles hadn't disappointed. I wasn't as enthusiastic about dropping in on Tom as I was interrupting Richard's morning. I'd left Tom's house on civil terms after the last visit but remembered the hostility he'd showed before we declared peace. Charles was right, so I headed out East Ashley Avenue to Tom's oceanfront abode.

The Range Rover was in the drive, so I figured he was home. I rang the doorbell then paced in front of the door.

Charles said, "Ring it again. His car's here."

I did and could hear the chimes in the house. Then I heard Casper barking on the other side of the door. Still, no Tom.

Charles, who has as much patience as Richard's twins, said, "Again."

"Charles, he isn't deaf. He must not be here."

I turned to leave, had taken three steps off the porch when the door flew open. Tom stared at us. He was wearing a long-sleeve white shirt with the sleeves rolled up to his elbows, dress slacks, and was barefoot.

Casper was cradled in his arm appearing to smile at us. Tom's glare was anything but friendly.

"What now?" the homeowner said.

"Hi, Tom," I said, putting on the friendliest face I could under the circumstances. "We were talking to Richard Haymaker a little while ago. He said we could stop by to ask a question."

Tom rubbed Casper's head as he continued to scowl at us. He said, "You saying Richard told you to come out here?"

It was sort of what he'd said.

I started to repeat my opening when a familiar voice coming from behind Tom said, "Tom, who is it?"

Tom pulled the door partially closed, turned, and said, "It's nothing. I'll be right there."

Charles was doing everything but standing on one foot while leaning through the partially opened door to see who was behind it. He needn't have, the door swung open and Kelly Isles was standing behind Tom. She was wearing a colorful sundress and barefoot like Tom.

She said, "Oh, Tom, it's Charles and, umm ..."

"Chris," I prompted.

"Yes, Chris. Tom, don't be rude. Invite them in."

He looked at Kelly, then back at us. "Sure, come in."

I didn't detect a glimmer of hospitality, but it didn't stop us from following him.

Kelly gave each of us a sisterly hug then asked if we wanted something to drink. Tom stood back, didn't say anything, as he continued rubbing Casper's head.

"Thanks for asking," I said. "We're okay."

"Water would be nice," Charles said, ignoring my answer.

We followed Kelly to the kitchen. Tom brought up the rear after he set Casper down.

Kelly opened the refrigerator and said, "Sure water's all you want. We have beer, energy drinks, root beer, white wine. Anything else to offer your guests, Tom?"

"No," he said, slamming the door on other options.

"Kelly, water will be fine," I said, hoping Charles would let it go.

Kelly handed us a bottle of water. Tom pushed the refrigerator door closed before saying, "What's the question?"

This wouldn't be an appropriate time to start a conversation about the weather or anything else strangers talked about during uncomfortable times.

"We were wondering about the drinks in the cooler on the plane. Do you remember what Gary put in it for you?"

"You what? You came here, bothering us to ask that?"

I said, "Yes."

"You couldn't have called with that stupid question?"

Charles took a sip of water then said, "We could've called, but we were heading to the old Coast Guard property to take photos of the Morris Island Lighthouse. Lo and behold, we were driving by your house when Chris suggested we stop."

Not a bad reason, I thought, although this was the first I was hearing it.

Tom's hostility lessened a tad. He said, "Phones work out there."

"I apologize for the interruption," I said. "We won't take up more of your time."

"Don't be silly," Kelly said as if she hadn't noticed Tom's irritation. "We weren't doing anything, were we Tom?"

He smiled at Kelly and turned to me. "Why were you wondering what drink Gary had for me?"

I was trying to figure the best way to ask with Gary's widow staring at me, when Charles said, "Richard said it was either root beer or an energy drink. If it was the energy drink, there's the possibility the poison could've been for you."

I was looking at Tom but heard Kelly gasp.

Tom shook his head. "If it hadn't been for the two of you, all four of us would be dead. Why would anyone have targeted only me? Please don't start pointing fingers again at Alyssa. I thought I cleared that up your last visit."

"Tom," Kelly interrupted as she put her hand on his arm, "all they're trying to do is see if you were the person someone tried to kill instead of ..." She hesitated then looked at the floor. "Sorry, instead of Gary."

Tom put his arm around her waist. He scowled at me. "See what you've done. You happy?"

"Tom," I said, "nothing about this is happy. It was a tragedy. Two lives were lost. All we want to do is find out what happened. Hopefully we can help the police bring whoever is responsible for poisoning Gary to justice. Isn't that what you want?"

Tears were rolling down Kelly's cheek and Tom kept his arm around her. The silence was deafening.

Charles did one of the things he does best when he said, "How old's Casper?"

Only he could get away with that transition, that distraction.

Kelly wiped her cheek then bent to lift Casper. "A year old next week. He's a cutie, isn't he?" She smiled for the first time since we'd entered the kitchen.

Tom looked at Casper in Kelly's arms, and said, "Root beer."

It took me a few seconds to realize he was answering the question that brought us here.

All eyes, all except Casper's whose eyes were still on Kelly, turned to Tom who continued, "Gary called the night before asking what I wanted. It didn't matter to me. Hell, I never understood why we had to have drinks on the short flight. It was a big deal to Gary. He said everyone else was easy, he didn't have to call them since he knew their preferences."

I nodded. "Did anyone else know what you told him?"

"I don't know, well, umm, Kelly, did you know?"

She stroked Casper's head, glanced at Charles and me, then looked at Tom. "I heard him on the phone. We were sort of unhappy with each other at the time. The only reason I was in hearing range was that I was on my way to the deck. I didn't hear anything about drinks. I remember him telling you when you were leaving."

Charles leaned over and patted Casper's head before saying, "Did you hear Gary talking to any of the other guys, maybe to tell them the time they were heading out?"

"No. I took a walk on the beach. It was a great night.

Pleasant temperature, nice sea breeze. I was out there an hour or so."

Tom had been watching the exchange as well as his watch. "Guys," he said, "I don't mean to sound rude, but I promised Kelly I'd go with her to the Charleston Crab House for a late lunch. We need to be heading out."

Kelly smiled. "Casper likes to ride in my boat and will be happy in it while we eat on the restaurant's deck."

The restaurant was on Wappoo Creek and one of the nicer casual dining spots in the area. I again apologized for interrupting their day then told them to have a good lunch. Charles had to give Casper a good-bye kiss on his way to the door. Kelly thanked us for stopping by. Tom didn't second it.

After we were safely back in the car headed toward town, I asked Charles the same question he'd asked me after we left Richard's house. "What did we learn?"

"Casper's got a big birthday coming up. Umm, Tom and Kelly are mighty close for her being a recent widow. Both barefoot. How about how she said *we* have beer in the refrigerator, rather than saying *he* has. If she was an actress auditioning for the part of grieving widow, she wouldn't get it."

"That's true, but—"

"Whoa, I'm not done. What's with Tom defending his ex? If I were her and knew my hubby was playing footsie with a neighbor, I'd give serious thought to killing him, even if I had to bring down a plane of golfers to do it."

I glanced over at him. "May I speak now?"

"If you must."

"His ex has more reasons to want him dead than Kelly has, especially if Tom and Kelly had something going before the crash. On the other hand, if Tom and Kelly weren't seeing each other, she could've had other reasons to poison her husband. She was unhappy about not being able to practice law. You heard her say she and Gary were *sort of unhappy* with each other the night before the crash. It could've been far worse than unhappy. She could've easily known what drinks were in the cooler. She, of all people, had the best opportunity to poison him."

"Chris, how are we going to prove any of this?"

I shrugged.

Chapter Thirty-One

The routine events of life overshadowed thoughts about the murder the next few days, that is except Monday when I'd let Charles commit me to painting Cal's. We'd spent three hours finishing one wall. Cal decided we could attack the other walls another day. I decided to listen more closely to what Charles was committing me to. The next three days, Charles helped a local contractor with a room addition on the west end of the island. My friend wasn't good at building anything other than rapport with people and canines but provided the contractor an extra set of hands to haul lumber and other materials. I thought a few times about returning to Cal's to see how the owner and his son were coexisting, yet that was as far as my good intentions went. I started thinking about the crash more than a few times but knew I didn't know enough to draw conclusions. I called Chief LaMond once to see if she knew anything new about the investigation. She was consumed with a rash of break-ins and didn't take time to insult me for calling, so I knew not to bother her further.

Heavy raindrops bouncing off my tin roof woke me a little after sunrise. I barely had time to pad my way to the kitchen to start a pot of coffee when the phone rang. Virgil's name appeared on the screen; his voice came from the speaker. "Did you forget about your assistant detective chilling out in a lumpy hospital bed?"

"Good morning, Virgil. How're you feeling?"

"Like the bonds have been removed from my body. Like birds are singing to welcome me back to the world of the living. Like my detective partners deserted me."

That'll teach me to ask. "You've not been deserted. I've been busy, so has Charles." I hoped he didn't ask busy doing what.

I looked out the window and saw a steady stream of water cascading off the roof, so I figured Charles wouldn't be working with the contractor. "Are you up for visitors?"

"Oh Lord, my prayers are answered."

I took that as yes. I said I'd call Charles to see if he's up to a trip to the hospital. Virgil thanked me three times before I got off the phone.

Charles didn't surprise me when he said he'd work it in his schedule, yet did surprise, no, shocked me when he asked what time I wanted him to pick me up. I could count on one hand the number of times he'd offered to drive. I said ten o'clock and was ready when he arrived at nine-thirty.

"Why'd Virgil call?" Charles asked before we were out of the drive.

I told him I didn't know although he sounded lonely. I left out the words *assistant detective*. I also questioned the wisdom of driving to the hospital in a rainstorm after

Charles slammed on the brakes twice and swerved around puddles the size of lakes covering the road. The jog from the parking lot to the entry added to my questioning the visit. We were soaked as we headed to the floor where Virgil had set up temporary residence.

Our new friend looked drastically different than the last time I'd seen him. He'd shed his mummy look; the only cast remaining was on his lower leg. He was also seated in a chair beside the bed. He greeted us with a smile as he slowly stood, grabbed the crutches leaning against the chair, and balanced himself on them.

He looked at his visitors. "You look like soaked cats. Forget to disrobe before taking a shower?"

Charles looked down at his blue and white Duke University long-sleeve T-shirt like he didn't know it was wet. "Virgil, old buddy, it's storming out there."

"Great," Virgil said, "my detective partners don't have enough sense to come in out of the rain." He laughed which prevented me from smacking him with my soaked Tilley.

I pointed at the crutches. "Are you able to get around?"

"Get around, you bet. They've got me entered in the hundred-yard dash tomorrow." He laughed louder. "Come on, let's go to the waiting room. I could use a change of scenery."

Virgil wasn't ready for a hundred-yard dash but managed to maneuver us through the corridors to a vacant waiting area where he took a chair. Charles and I sat on the sofa opposite him.

"How much longer are you going to be here?" Charles asked as Virgil dropped his crutches beside the chair.

"A few more days. I asked if I could move in perma-nently since it's a lot nicer than my apartment. A cute little nurse gives me sponge baths. Food ain't bad either." He sighed and shook his head. "They said they'd love to have me, but the tightwads at the insurance company frowned on paying my rent." His smile disappeared. "Enough about that. What've I missed in the real world? Caught the killer?"

I summarized what new had happened, a summary that didn't take long since it consisted of nothing had happened.

"Sounds like you need me back on the job," he said as he scratched his leg under the top of the cast.

I smiled instead of commenting. Charles wasn't as vague, when he said, "Virgil, it looks like the cops need all the help they can get."

"My thoughts exactly," Virgil said like he'd won a victory. "I've been thinking on it." He laughed. "That's about all I have to do. The docs haven't asked me to help them operate on anybody. Heck, I even offered to help housekeeping mop the floors. They said I'd be too slow. Can you believe that?"

I was afraid to ask what he'd been thinking. I didn't have to.

He continued, "I'm about ninety-five percent certain Tom's ex, Alyssa, poisoned the pilot. It's a crying shame. The only thing the pilot did wrong was fly the guys to the golf course. He and Mark Jamison didn't deserve to die because Tom's ex was pissed."

"Virgil," I said, "what makes you so certain?"

"I told you all of this when we broke bread together in the Dog. She was fighting him about dividing up their money, she wanted custody of Casper. Tom still has that adorable poodle, so Alyssa wasn't winning that battle."

Did Virgil think Alyssa caused two deaths over the dog? I said, "Virgil, those could be reasons, but from what we

215

know, the other three spouses have the same number or more reasons. That doesn't count suspects we don't know."

He held his hand up like he was either asking permission to go to the restroom or wanting me to stop. I guessed the second reason. "What?"

"I'm still a novice at this detective stuff, not pros like you two. That's my best thinking."

Charles looked around the empty room then moved closer to Virgil. "Those are good thoughts, my friend. Did you and your wife have a boat?"

Virgil didn't appear as confused as I was about Charles's off the wall, or off the water, question.

"Did we ever," he said shaking his head. "Had a forty eight foot Ocean Yachts Super Sport. Loved that boat. Cruised at twenty-six knots—"

Charles interrupted, "Chris, a knot's about 1.151 miles per hour."

I said, "Thanks, Mr. Trivia. Virgil, go on."

"Slept six in three staterooms, two heads. Master stateroom had a queen berth, color TV, stereo system. Should've seen the main salon. Entertainment center, Corian countertop, large L shaped sofa, intelligent 1-5 SAT TV." He shook his head a second time. "Loved it."

Charles, please don't ask about the SAT TV. We could be here all day.

"Virgil, it sounds great."

"It is. It was. I lost it three months before I lost the house." He smiled. "Got to keep the fifteen-foot jon boat. The only head it had was when I pissed over the side."

Charles said, "Sorry to hear that."

Virgil glanced down at the crutches before turning to Charles. "Why'd you ask about the boat?"

I was wondering when he would get curious. I knew I was.

"No reason," Charles said. "Thought you must've had one. Is the jon boat at your apartment?"

Virgil laughed, not quite the reaction to Charles's question I anticipated.

"I can see me hitching a trailer to my scooter to haul a fifteen-foot boat to the river. Nah, gave it to someone I know who lives backed up to the marsh. He can get some use out of it."

"That's too bad," Charles said.

"Not really, but I can borrow it whenever I want." He rubbed his thigh and grimaced. "Guys, this has been fun. Think I need to get back to my luxurious bed so I can stretch out my leg."

We followed him to his room at about half the speed, maybe one knot, we took to get to the waiting area.

Before we left, he said, "Guys, would it be asking too much if I could hitch a ride with one of you back to my apartment when they evict me?"

Charles smiled. "Holler and it'll be done."

"Much appreciated. Oh yeah, one more thing. Could you take a gander in my apartment to make sure everything's okay? Wouldn't want the mice to invite their friends to move in while I'm gone."

Charles said, "It'll be done."

On the elevator ride to the lobby, I said, "What's with the question about a boat?"

"I was curious about what kind of countertops he had in the salon."

"Funny. Need I ask again?"

"No. It was something you'd said before about Virgil

217

asking so many questions about what the cops knew about the crash. You were hinting he may've been responsible, so he could get closer to Charlene Beth. It's a weak reason, but it still counts. Someone took the cooler plus the other stuff out of the plane, someone needing a boat to get there."

I nodded. "So now we know Virgil has access to one."

"Yessiree."

"And remember, Kelly Isles was taking Tom out on her boat. Charlene Beth had the twins out on their boat when we visited Richard. Add to that, there're places where you can rent boats near Folly. Finally, imagine how many boats in the area are owned by private parties."

Charles rubbed his chin. "Yeah, so how are we going to find out if Kevin Robbins and Alyssa Kale have boats." He snapped his fingers. "We could head to Mt. Pleasant, saunter up to Kevin Robbins's pharmacy counter, then say something like 'I've got a cough. What do you recommend and, oh yeah, do you have a boat?'"

"That's an idea. A stupid one. The fact is everyone we consider to be a suspect either has, or could easily get, access to a boat."

Charles pulled onto Folly Road and said, "You're no fun. I think you might be right about Virgil. He's too interested in the killing. Too interested in sucking up to us to see what we know." He scratched his cheek. "Besides, he's too happy, seems content with his situation. How would you feel if you had a mansion, a big-ole boat with Corian countertops, then poof, it was gone? Yep, the boy's too happy to have all that bad stuff happen to him."

I didn't agree or disagree. We made the rest of the trip in silence and pulled in front of Virgil's apartment building, a one story, concrete block structure with five parking spaces for the four units. Virgil's scooter was parked in front of a faded green wooden door with a rusting, six-inch high number 2 beside it.

"Not quite a mansion overlooking the Battery," Charles said in a rare understatement.

Chapter Thirty-Two

The lockset was so loose I had to hold it in place to turn the key.

Charles stood back and said, "We didn't need a key. I could've picked it with my elbow."

The door swung inward, and we were accosted by heat that'd built up. The first thing I did was check the thermostat. It'd been switched off, most likely to save money, so I left it off and looked around. Other than being hot enough to bake cookies, everything seemed okay, to my surprise, neat and tidy. I headed to the kitchen, Charles to the bedroom. Everything in the kitchen was neat. A box of corn flakes was beside a clean, empty bowl on the table that wasn't much larger than a dinner plate.

Everything appeared in order so I turned and headed back to the living room when Charles said, "You might want to stop in the bedroom."

He was staring at the twelve-inch, clunky, tube television

on the dresser. More accurately, he was staring at a six by nine inch piece of paper taped to the TV screen. Neatly typed on the paper was a note that read, *Mind your own business or the next time you won't be so lucky.*

Charles said, "I'm taking Virgil off my suspect list." He was saying something else, but I didn't understand what. I was busy punching in the Folly Beach Department of Public Safety's number on my phone.

I'd told the dispatcher it wasn't an emergency, so I wasn't surprised when it took several minutes before a patrol car pulled into Virgil's parking lot. Officer Trula Bishop stepped out, adjusted her duty belt, checked out the surroundings, then came over to Charles and me. We'd moved outside so we wouldn't disturb anything more than we already had.

"Mr. Chris," Bishop said, "what've you stumbled into now?"

I'd known Officer Bishop for a few years. She'd always been helpful and friendly.

I explained how we'd been asked by Virgil Debonnet, the apartment's hospitalized resident, to check to see if everything was okay. We led her to the bedroom where I pointed to the message on the television.

She read the note, then said, "Would that be the Virgil Debonnet who had the unfortunate contact with a motorized vehicle a while back?"

As we headed back outside, I said it was. She asked if we knew what the note was referring to or who might've put it there. I shared how Virgil had taken an unusual interest in the plane crash, that he'd known the Haymakers and had talked to one of the other survivors since the crash. I omitted Virgil's self-proclaimed assistant private detective title.

Our conversation was interrupted when Chief LaMond pulled in the lot beside the patrol car. She shook her head as she approached.

"Lovely afternoon, Chief," Charles said.

She glowered at him like he'd called her a slimy slug. "I was peacefully sitting in my luxurious office dreaming about vacationing in the South of France when I heard about a call from one of my senior citizens, a guy named Landrum, who could use the services of my fine public safety department. Knowing how much trouble the caller often causes, I took a break from daydreaming to see what trouble he'd blundered into this time. So, yes, Charles, it is a lovely afternoon. I'm anxious to see how you, along with that geezer, standing beside you are once again going to ruin it."

The geezer wasn't Officer Bishop. I shared with Cindy the same information I'd given Bishop. Instead of griping about us being there or nosing where we shouldn't be nosing, Cindy asked how Virgil was recuperating as we headed to the bedroom. Charles shared Virgil's current condition as she stared at the note.

Charles finished his medical update. Cindy turned to me. "What do you think Virgil did to deserve this?"

"He's been asking around about the plane crash. I know little about him, so it may have to do with something other than the crash."

The Chief turned back to the note. "You don't believe that, do you?"

"Not for a second," Charles answered for me.

Cindy sighed, as she turned to Bishop. "Officer, give a

holler to Detective Callahan, key him in, see if he wants to send over crime-scene techs. I doubt they'll find anything, but you never know. Don't tell him who found the note. He'll have a fit if he learns these two snoops are involved." Before she turned to walk out the door, she said, "Also throw the riffraff out of the apartment then wait for whoever shows up from Charleston."

Officer Bishop chuckled and said, "Riffraff, you heard the boss lady. Disappear."

We headed to the car, happy to get out of the hot apartment. There were a dozen people standing on the other side of the police vehicles. I wasn't surprised since police activity was a spectator sport on the island drawing locals and visitors. What did surprise me was seeing Junior Richardson in the group.

He waved at us as Charles motioned him over saying, "Hey, Junior, what're you doing here?"

He pointed to the door two apartments down from Virgil's. "I live there. It's not the Ritz, but it'll do until I find a house to buy. What's going on? Nothing's happened to Virgil did it? Isn't he still in the hospital?"

I didn't know which question to answer first. Charles didn't have qualms. He started telling Junior the chain of events leading us to standing here. Some of the looky-loos began inching closer to listen, so I suggested we take our conversation to air-conditioned comfort in Charles's car. We moved to the car where Charles assured Junior that Virgil was recovering nicely, that the police were at his residence because of a note.

"Good," Junior said. "He's a nice guy."

I said, "How well do you know him?"

"Not that well. We talked a few times since we're both

new to Folly and are having, let's say, an interesting time adjusting to island life."

"He say anything about having enemies?" I asked.

Junior looked at Virgil's door. "Like someone who would want to run him over?"

Charles said, "That'd qualify."

"Not that I've heard. He was always in a good mood. Frankly, if I'd lost everything like he had, I'd be madder than a one-wing parakeet. Not Virgil. He's a nice guy who didn't deserve everything bad that's happened."

"Junior," I said, "someone has it in for him. Do you recall anything he said that could help the police figure out what's going on?"

"Help the police, or help you? Dad says you're disaster magnets, like playing detective. Said you're good at it."

"Yes," Charles said, "we're—"

I interrupted before he went into his story about being a private detective, "That was the Chief who just left. We're friends so if you know something to help learn who's endangering Virgil, we'll tell her."

I hoped I sounded more convincing to Junior than I had to myself.

Junior adjusted the air-conditioner vent and nodded. "Let's see. The last time I talked with him was, well actually, it was the night before he was hit." Junior smiled. "We were laughing about how he'd been rich, how I'd owned several restaurants. Now we're living in this building that's more fit for chickens than for a king. I found it funny because I was here temporarily. I don't know why Virgil found it funny, except that he acted like a burden had been lifted off his shoulder after losing his wealth. Admirable, yet weird."

Interesting, but not what I had in mind. "Junior, did he say anything about looking into the plane crash?"

"He spent time talking about the people he talked with about it. I don't remember any names since I didn't know who he was talking about. As far as I know, unless some of them are customers in Dad's place, I didn't know them."

Charles said, "Remember anything about them?"

"The ones he mentioned were gals."

"How do you know?" I asked.

"Because he kept saying she this, she that."

Virgil had talked to Kelly Isles, Alyssa Kale, and of course, had spent more time with Charlene Beth, so that hadn't told me anything new.

I said, "Anything else?"

"It did worry me a little at the time, worry that proved to be well-founded."

"Worried about what?" Charles said.

"He told me he asked each of them a bunch of questions about the crash and how they thought the pilot was poisoned. It sounded like he was playing cop. If I happened to be the killer and someone kept asking me questions like that, I'd be worried."

Charles said, "Don't suppose he told you who he thought it was, did he?"

"Charles, I'm no detective. If Virgil told me who he thought did it, don't you think I would've started with that?"

After Virgil told me he talked to the wives and the ex-wife about the crash, it entered my mind he may've raised too much suspicion by nosing around—enough suspicion to get him in trouble. I felt that more strongly now after what Junior shared.

"Junior," I said, "have you seen anyone going in or hanging around Virgil's apartment since he was hurt?"

He scratched his chin then shook his head. "Don't think so. We get a lot of people walking by. With my odd hours at Dad's place, I keep the blinds closed so I can sleep during the day. I don't see who's here. If you want, I'll ask around."

I told him that could be helpful. Officer Bishop tapped on the window with a notebook. Charles lowered the window. She looked at Junior. "Sir, do you live around here?"

Junior said he did as he pointed toward his door. Officer Bishop asked if he could step out of the car to answer a couple of questions. He exited and stood beside the officer. Charles, being Charles, left his window down so he could eavesdrop. Bishop asked Junior his name and phone number, before asking if he'd seen anything unusual around Virgil's door or if he'd seen anyone enter. Charles tapped me on the shoulder and smiled because it was the same question I'd asked.

Junior gave her the same answer he'd given me. She asked if any of the other residents were standing in the group watching us. Junior looked at the group and said one of the two remaining residents was there. She got the name, thanked Junior, leaned on Charles's windowsill, and said, "Guys, the crime scene techs can't get here for a couple hours. The Chief told me to lock the apartment. She also asked me to get Virgil's key and drop it at the office for the techs to pick up."

I handed her the key. She said she'd get it back to me when the techs were done. She left to talk to the apartment dweller standing outside. Junior said he had to get to Cal's, that it was nice talking to us.

That left Charles and me with one fewer suspect and a stronger case the murderer might be one of the three women. How to prove which one, if in fact it was one of them, was anyone's guess. I was also left with the realization that if Virgil was run over because he was asking questions, where did that leave Charles and me since we'd been doing the same thing?

Chapter Thirty-Three

I was getting ready for bed when the phone rang. I let it go to voicemail since friends knew not to call this late and the screen read *Unknown*. If it was important, not a robocall, the caller would leave a message. Thirty seconds later, the phone dinged indicating a message. Two clicks later, I heard, "Chris, this is Junior, you know, Cal's son. I talked to the neighbor in my building who wasn't there when the hubbub happened today. She told me things I figure you'd want to know." There was commotion in the background and Junior said, "Cool it, Dad. I'm working on it. Umm, Chris, I'll tell you some other time." The message ended.

It was a little after ten o'clock and I didn't have anything to do or anywhere to be in the morning, so why not walk to Cal's? A couple of reasons came to mind; both related to me being lazy. Besides, the walk would do me good, or so I was trying to convince myself. It must have worked, since I entered Cal's fifteen minutes later. I was met by the comforting smell of frying hamburgers and the sounds of Patsy Cline singing "Sweet Dreams." Roughly twenty customers were enjoying the music, conversation, and beer.

Junior was at the grill flipping a burger, Cal was behind the bar pulling two beers from the cooler. He turned to set the drinks on the bar in front of two men dressed in starched shirts and dress slacks, which most likely meant that they were staying at the Tides. Cal wore his ever-present Stetson, a yellow golf shirt, and even though I couldn't see below his waist, I'd guess shorts.

I took the stool two seats from the men. Cal glanced my way, did a double take, then looked at his watch.

"Lordy, Chris, what brings you out in the middle of the night? Sleepwalking?"

I assured him I was awake.

He said, "Vino?"

"Vino?"

Cal shook his head. "I'm practicing being a classy-joint owner. Junior's influence." He tilted his head toward the kitchen.

I said yes to his drink suggestion, then added, "How's it going with you two?"

He walked to the cooler to grab the wine bottle, poured my vino, set it in front of me, and said, "Much better. Much better until this afternoon."

I took a sip while waiting for him to continue. He didn't, so I asked what happened.

He looked to make sure Junior wasn't near. "You'll never guess what the youngster ordered to make burgers with. Never in a million years."

"Sawdust?" I said, to let him know I was paying attention.

"Near as bad. He ordered bison burgers, then to top it off, ordered veggie burgers, and turkey burgers, yes, turkey burgers. Can you believe that?"

More quickly than I could believe sawdust. "Why'd he do that?"

"Said it'd draw the healthy crowd."

"What'd you say?"

He again looked toward the kitchen. "Told him it ain't Thanksgiving, told him where he could stuff his turkey burgers. Then reminded him veggie burgers ain't really burgers, they're, umm, well, they're vegetables. Finally, I had to point out one of the most important facts of life."

"What might that be?" I asked, enjoying Cal's tirade more than I should have.

"Beer guzzlers can't tell the difference in the taste between a good ole' beef burger and a potted plant. We ain't going to spend a penny more than we have to for the meat we slap on the bun." He shook his head. "Chris, I don't hold out much hope for this to work. Every day something pops up that causes a ruckus. I'm trying, I'd love it to work, but—"

"What ruckus?" Junior said as he slipped behind his dad. The front of his white chef coat was stained, sweat rolled down his cheek.

Cal glanced over his shoulder at his son. "Was telling Chris about the unruly customers a couple of nights ago. Thought I was going to have to call the cops."

"Right," Junior said, not buying it.

Patsy Cline was singing her version of "Faded Love," and a table of four waved for Cal's attention. He headed their way and Junior said, "Get my message?"

I nodded. He motioned me to follow him to the kitchen.

There were two burgers, hopefully beef burgers, on the grill so Junior flipped them before saying, "I talked to Rebecca. She stopped for a drink after work."

"Rebecca?"

"Rebecca Holland. She's the woman who lives next to Virgil who wasn't home today when the police were there. Remember, I said I'd see if she knew anything about the note-leaver at your friend's apartment."

"Did she?"

"Hold on," Virgil said as he slid the burgers on the bun, plated them, and headed to a table on the other side of the room.

He returned with four empty beer bottles and dropped them in a large trash container by the door. Cal was still with the other customers. Junior said, "Yep."

"Yep, what?" I said.

"Yep, Rebecca saw something, actually she heard something more than seeing it."

I was determined to wait him out.

He scraped the grill then said, "Rebecca heard noises coming from Virgil's apartment two days ago. The building's so cheap the walls are as thin as wrapping paper, not the good stuff but the paper you get at dollar stores. She said she didn't think anything of it until she was in bed that night when she remembered Virgil was in the hospital. It couldn't have been him."

"Is that it?"

"Maybe, maybe not."

"Explain."

"Rebecca said while she was in bed, she started putting two and two together. She remembered seeing a woman walking away from the building a few minutes after she heard the noises from Virgil's."

"Did she know who it was?"

Junior lowered his head. "If she's to be believed, no. Rebecca only saw the back of her. Said she had a sweatshirt with a hood pulled over her head. She thought the person was young, could've been tall, not thin or fat."

"What do you mean by if she can be believed?"

"Nothing," Junior said sharply.

I started to pursue it, but figured he'd said all he was going to about it. Instead, I said, "How'd Rebecca know the person was young?"

Junior smiled. "I asked her that. She said young people walk different than old folks. Faster, more confident."

I watched Cal heading back to the bar. Rebecca was right.

"Did she say if the woman was black or white?" I asked, thinking of Tom Kale's ex-wife, Alyssa.

"Didn't mention one way or the other."

"Anything else about her?"

Junior put two more patties on the grill before saying, "Not really. Rebecca said she wasn't paying attention since folks are around there all the time. She didn't put any of it together until she was in bed."

"Did she tell the police?"

"Nope. She wasn't there when the cop lady talked to us. Nobody came back to question her."

"I'll share this with Chief LaMond. She'll want someone to talk to Rebecca."

"Sounds like a plan."

"What's the plan?" Cal said as he stuck his head in the kitchen.

Junior smiled. "Chris was telling me the health inspector was going to shut us down. That way, you could sell the building to McDonald's, so they could tear it down, build a Mickey D's."

Cal said, "Funny."

Junior thought it was. He was laughing as he patted his dad on the back. Cal started to respond when my phone rang for the second time during my no-call hours. It was Bob Howard.

With his booming voice, he said, "Didn't wake you up, did I?"

"No. In fact I'm at Cal's."

"Well, crap. I was going to get a kick out of shaking you out of your sugar-sweet dreams. What in the hell are you doing out this time of night?"

"What are you doing calling this time of night?"

"I already said. To irritate you."

"That the only reason?"

"Hell no. Got some gossip you'll be interested in."

"What?"

"Not tonight. You're probably sleepwalking and won't remember it when you wake up. Head to Al's around lunchtime tomorrow. Bring your shadow, as if I could stop him from showing up. Thy rumor will be disclosed while you're savoring the best cheeseburger in the universe."

He'd hung up before I could let him know I'd either be there or not. He knew me well. It'd take a natural disaster for me not to show.

Chapter Thirty-Four

I t took Charles fewer than ten seconds to say he'd go, and that included him asking where, when, and of course, why. I answered two of the three questions before we'd pulled out of his lot. The answer to the remaining question would have to wait until Bob told us why I'd been summoned.

Traffic was heavy, so it took twice as long to get to Al's than normal. That wasn't bad, since it gave me time to call Chief LaMond to share what Junior said Rebecca Holland told him about the noise from Virgil's apartment, then seeing a woman walking away. Cindy asked for the description and huffed and puffed while I told her the mysterious woman was young, could've been tall, not thin, not fat, black or white.

"Hot damn," the Chief said, "I'll put out an APB. My guys won't have trouble snagging someone with that description. A few dozen."

The phone was on speaker. Charles leaned close to it and said, "I have confidence in you, Chief."

There was a moment of silence before Cindy said, "Chris, your voice has turned stupid."

"Charles is with me."

"Duh," the Chief said in police-speak. "Chris, not you Charles, did Junior happen to say anything that can be the least bit useful?"

"No."

"Anything beyond that spot-on description?" Charles added.

We ignored him. "Chief," I said, "has Detective Callahan learned anything?"

"About as much as Rebecca Holland. There weren't prints on the apartment's door. The paper was as common as no-see-ums over here, the message could've been made by seven-thousand printer models. To be honest, he's stumped."

"Chief," Charles said, "Thomas Jefferson said, 'Honesty is the first chapter in the book of wisdom.'"

"Cindy LaMond says, what in hell does that have to do with anything?"

I agreed with Cindy but waited for Charles to honestly share some wisdom.

Charles said, "Chief, just thought I'd add a dollop of wisdom. If we all admit we don't have anything worth talking about, there's a chance some wisdom will show through then we can figure out who poisoned the pilot."

Cindy sighed. "Charles, I spend, oh, roughly thirty seven hours a day shoveling pachyderm poop after my guys dump it in my office. Now you throw camel crap on top of it."

Time to guide the conversation back to civil. "Cindy, I'll call if we learn anything."

"I'll be waiting with bated breath. In the meantime, I'll have my guys pick up every young female who could be tall, not thin, not fat, black, or white."

She hung up as Charles was telling her that was a great idea.

I found a parking spot on the street around the corner from Al's. Instead of getting out, I took a deep breath and turned to Charles.

"Charles, you were right, you—"

"Of course, I was," he interrupted. "Umm, right about what?"

"Whether I want to or not, whether it's our business or not, we've got to help the police."

Charles's head jerked my direction. "Whoa, you sound like me."

"Two people perished in the crash; two others were fortunate to have survived. We nearly lost our lives. Someone tried to kill Virgil, most likely because he knows something about the poisoning. The police are stumped. And, what's to say we're not next on his or her list?"

"Chris, I agree. There's one tiny problem. How?"

I wish I knew. Instead of sharing my doubts, I said, "We're going to start by hearing what Bob has to tell me —tell us."

Charles smiled. "Then why are we sitting out here?"

I opened the door to Kenny Rogers singing "Lucille" from the jukebox and Al sitting at his welcome chair. He slowly stood, gave each of us a hug, and said, "Charles, it's good to see you, my friend. It's been too long since you've visited."

Charles seldom visited. His wide smile told me that he was pleased to not only be recognized but being called friend. He thanked Al as I looked around the dark room. Three tables had customers, a fourth had Bob munching a fry.

Al glanced toward the owner and said, "You'd better get back to his throne. He doesn't like me keeping folks from spending money."

Willie Nelson was crooning "Always on My Mind" when Bob reinforced Al's comment and yelled "Old man, get out of the way. Let the paying customers order."

Al mouthed, "See?"

We gave him another hug then headed to the cheerful, friendly owner. Before we slid in the booth, Bob turned toward the kitchen and yelled, "Hey, what's-your-name goofing off back there, get these old farts cheeseburgers, a beer for the one with hair, one of those fruity-tasting, box white wines for the bald one. Chop, chop!"

Bob's atrocious management style was only surpassed by his abundance of rudeness, yet Lawrence chuckled and said, "Yes, master."

"He's the greatest," Bob said through a mouthful of fries. "Don't know what I'd do without him."

I said, "Can't imagine him wanting to work anywhere else."

"Smart ass," Bob said, showing that he treats both customers and employees with the same level of respect.

Charles asked how Al was doing. Bob turned serious and gave an abbreviated update on Al's condition which could be summarized by no worse, no better. He then used the same words to describe how business was since the change in ownership. Lawrence delivered our drinks while Bob rambled on about the excessive cost of beef, beer, and Lawrence's astronomical salary.

He shifted direction and said, "Enough restaurant talk. Repeat this and I'll squash you like a termite." He looked around to see if anyone was spying on him. The CIA, FBI, the ASPCA must've had more important things to do than listen to Bob's nonsense. He continued, "You amateur sleuths are rubbing off on me."

"There you go," Charles said. "Proof you can teach an old dog new tricks."

I said, "Bob, what's that mean?"

"Yesterday I met with Alyssa Kale. Charles, she's my stockbroker. My portfolio has been getting broker. Get it, stockbroker, broker?"

Charles nodded; I groaned; Bob continued, "I wanted to see why she was letting me go broke. Her worthless answer was something about declining international stocks, unrest in the electronics sector, corrections in pork bellies, or pork chops in Great Britain, or something like that, and blah, blah, blah. Bottom line was for me to hang on, things will be okay in the long run. I told her to look at my ample stomach, gaze at my birth certificate, then tell me what the odds are on me being around for the long run."

Charles asked, "What'd she say?"

Lawrence delivered our cheeseburgers, Bob glanced at our food and told what's-his-name to fix him another heaping helping of fries. As Lawrence headed to the kitchen, Bob said, "Hell, I didn't ask you here to talk about my financial health. I remembered how Alyssa was about her ex-hubby the last time I talked with her. She acted like she'd be sadder if a housefly died than she'd be if Tom kicked the bucket. Yesterday, I tried to be sympathetic-like, to say something again about how glad I was he survived the crash."

Charles repeated, "What'd she say?"

Bob stared at him. "I'm getting there. You may not believe this but being sympathetic-like is not one of my strengths. I may not have pulled it off like you, Chris. Alyssa stopped looking at my portfolio on the computer and looked out the window. I waited for her to say something like, 'I poisoned the pilot so he'd wreck the plane to wipe out my jerk of an ex-hubby.'"

Charles said, "Did she?"

"No. She did say she wished he had been."

"She really said that?" Charles asked.

"It was like she didn't mean to say it out loud. She started apologizing, said she shouldn't have said it, that she shouldn't be sharing personal stuff with a client. It threw me off. Not many people feel comfortable telling me stuff. I don't bring out the damned ooey-gooey, touchy-feely stuff in people, so I didn't know how to react. I told her it was okay, whatever the hell that meant. I added she could tell cuddly Uncle Bob anything. It worked. I asked why she felt that way about her ex."

Charles said, "What'd she say?"

"Charles," Bob said, "You have the patience of a drunk waiting for the liquor store to open. The distressed chick said she and her ex were going to court next Tuesday to come to an agreement about splitting the money. I figured if Tom died in the crash, they wouldn't be meeting. Alyssa said that even with the divorce she was still his sole beneficiary."

Charles was persistent. "She say anything else?"

"Yes."

Charles leaned toward Bob. "What?"

"She said, 'Let's sell 500 shares of Marathon Oil.'"

It would be futile to ask if she said anything else about her ex-husband. I said, "Bob, do you think she poisoned Gary?"

"Absolutely."

"Why so certain?" I asked.

"Can't put my finger on it. I'm not much at detecting things. With that said, it was the way she talked about how sorry she was about Gary and Mark's death. It was like she regretted they died while her ex survived."

Charles said, "Like she was sorry she killed the wrong people?"

"Like, I don't know, Charles. It was a feeling."

Al made his way to the table. "What're you talking about, Bob? You don't have feelings."

Bob looked over his shoulder at Al. "I feel you're meddling in a peaceful conversation we're having."

"Peaceful, bull hockey. I came to save my young friends from you ruining their lunch."

"Then why are you standing there? Park your bony butt."

That was Bob's way of telling Al he'd love for him to join us. Al had known Bob since the beginning of time, so he could hear past his friend's bluster. "Don't mind if I do." I pulled a chair from the next table and Al slowly parked his bony butt.

Lawrence brought Al a glass of water and asked if he wanted anything to eat. Al declined then patted me on the forearm. "How's your friend Vernon?"

I was going to ask how Al knew about Virgil, when Bob said, "Damnit old man, I told you it's Virgil."

That answered my question. Al corrected the name

and I shared that Virgil should be released from the hospital this week. Al said good, he hoped he could get to meet our new friend. I wouldn't have gone as far as saying that Virgil was a friend but told Al I'd see if it could be arranged.

Al smiled. "Good. Did Bob tell you about the guy who threw his beer bottle at the jukebox?"

"No," I said as I turned to Bob.

He took the handoff. "You're not going to believe why the troublemaker hurled the bottle at that fine music-playing machine. Ricky Van Shelton was singing "Life Turned Her That Way" one of my favorite country songs by the way. One of Al's Afro buds thought Ricky should be doing a Marvin Gay imitation singing 'Heard It Through the Grapevine.' Unbelievable, right?"

"Abominable."

Bob smiled like he'd won the trifecta at Gulfstream Park.

Charles said, "What happened?"

Bob nodded toward Al. "Old Mahatma Gandhi here told the bottle hurler if he cleaned up the glass, the next drink was on the house."

Al said, "He did. We did. Another race riot caused by blustery old Charmin-white Bob averted."

"Al's generous with my beer."

"Boys," Al said, "The poor man's in the middle of a divorce. Two of his three kids are hooked on drugs. He thinks he may be the next person laid off from the factory. He needs all the breaks he can get, yes he does."

"Speaking of divorce," Bob said, "I saw where Walter Middleton Gibbs was getting one from his long-time sweetie."

I thought rather than divorce, we'd been talking about

the customer who didn't share Bob's opinion of country music.

Al must've thought we'd talked enough about it. "Bob, if you're going to be talking about some rich guy, I'd better get back to the door. Chris, Charles, great seeing you."

He slowly made his way to the door, leaning on chairs along the way.

I said, "Bob, why'd you mention Walter Middleton Gibbs?"

"You're nosy, Charles is nosier. Figured since I told you about the alleged affair Gibbs was having with that double name gal, you'd be interested."

"Charlene Beth," Charles said.

Bob frowned at Charles. "That's what I said."

I said, "Is that all you know about it?"

"Crap, Chris, I ain't wicked-o-pedia. It may have something to do with double-name gal, or good old Walter's wife may dress up like a pansy and hang out in gay bars. Who knows?"

I thanked him for conjuring up that disturbing image as he started in on the super-sized orders of fries Lawrence had delivered.

Chapter Thirty-Five

Three days later, the ringing phone disturbed my morning coffee. Charles was on the other end with, "Ready to go?"

"Where?" I asked, a perfectly logical question, I thought.

"Duh, to pick up Virgil."

"Sure."

"Good. I'll be there in fifteen minutes."

A horn was blowing in the drive five minutes later, so I joined Charles in his Toyota.

"I didn't know today was the day."

Charles smiled as he pulled out of the drive. "He called last night, said the docs did all they could do. The hospital and Virgil's insurance company said he was being kicked out of the resort. I said I'd pick him up. I'm bringing you as a bonus, or if he needs help getting around."

"Did you tell him about the break-in?"

"Nope. Though that'd be a good conversation starter."

Virgil was in the lobby sitting in the insurance-required wheelchair. Crutches were balanced across the arms of the chair. The cast on his leg wasn't nearly as large as the one he wore during our last visit. He had a Gucci shoe on the non-casted leg, the other shoe in his lap.

"Boys, you don't know how glad I am to see you. If that car didn't kill me, I was sure the hospital would if I spent another night here. The rent's cheap, the food, not bad, but a funeral home is more fun than spending that long inside these walls."

We got Virgil in the car and started to pull out of the parking lot when he said, "Want to see where I hung my hat BB?"

Charles said, "BB?"

Virgil chuckled. "Before broke."

Charles said, "We'd love to."

Virgil told Charles to head south on Lockwood Drive instead of staying on the road to Folly. The road turned left and became Broad Street where Virgil gave turn-by-turn directions through streets filled with magnificent homes until we reached South Battery. He had Charles pull across the street from a large, white, two-story mansion with porches across the front on each level. The house sat behind a black, decorative, wrought iron fence leading to a curved walk surrounded by sculptured landscaping. It oozed wealth.

"My new front yard's easier to take care of," Virgil said, with a glimmer of humor. "Look at the view the other direction."

White Point Garden, a six-acre public park, sat immediately between Virgil's former home and where the Cooper and Ashley Rivers met forming the Charleston Harbor. The public park is filled with oak trees, statues, and cannons dating from the Civil War. Virgil, and countless thousands of tourists had a view of Ft. Sumter from the seawall and promenade in the area called the Battery.

We told him how incredible the view was. In a moment of truth, he sighed. "I hated to lose the house, and especially walking out the front door to this view." His sad face turned into a smile. "Oh well, it is what it is. Besides guys, the people on Folly are nicer than my neighbors here."

Charles said, "Except for the one who tried to turn you into roadkill."

"Ah, the exception," Virgil said.

While we were on the topic of his clash with a moving vehicle, we should tell him about the break in.

"Virgil, while you were in the hospital, someone broke in your apartment."

"You're kidding. What kind of lowlife breaks in an apartment of a poverty-stricken, unemployed, bum stuck in a hospital bed? They didn't steal my television, did they? It's the most valuable thing I have. Hell, I paid twelve bucks for it."

Charles patted him on the leg. "The good news is they didn't steal the TV. The bad news is they left a note taped to it."

"An apology for breaking in?"

I shared the contents of the note. Virgil started to say something but stopped with his mouth open.

Charles asked if Virgil had any idea who it may've been.

"That's easy, the person who put me in the hospital."

Charles said, "Can you be more specific?"

"No." Virgil whispered. "Police have any ideas?"

I told him what Rebecca Holland said, adding the police had that information, but nothing else.

"Oh great," Virgil said. "I wouldn't trust Rebecca with my trash, much less her word about what she saw."

That got my attention. "What do you mean?"

Instead of answering, he said, "Let's get out of here. It's depressing looking at what I've lost."

Charles turned at the next street and began weaving his way back to the road to Folly. At the first traffic light, he turned to Virgil. "What about Rebecca Holland?"

"I haven't had much contact with her. I heard she's been in prison."

The light turned green, Charles turned his eyes back on the road, and said, "What for?"

"Stealing cars, maybe embezzlement. That's the story going around, don't know for sure. She didn't happen to mention it during our conversations."

I said, "That why you wouldn't trust her?"

"Not really. I've seen her looking in windows of other apartments. The walls at the apartment are thin, and I've heard her going in and out all hours of the night. Don't know what she's doing. These are only gut reactions."

Charles said, "Do you think she could've been the person who ran you down then broke in your place?"

"Wouldn't put it past her."

I said, "It probably didn't have anything to do with the plane crash if it was her,"

"Does she have a car?" Charles said.

Virgil didn't respond at first, then said, "I've never noticed one. A woman picks her up for work."

"Where does she work?"

"Printing plant in Charleston. That's all I know."

Charles said, "Probably prints counterfeit money."

I didn't think that was likely and figured that was all

Virgil knew about Rebecca. I said, "Virgil, do you know Junior Richardson?"

"Sure, he lives in my building on the other side of Rebecca. Seems like a great guy. Why?"

I asked him if he knew Junior was Cal Ballew's son.

"He mentioned it. Why?"

I explained our friendship with Cal then lightly touched on how Cal didn't know he had a son until Junior appeared on the scene.

"I know he's chef at his Dad's place but didn't know the rest of that."

We pulled on the island where Charles turned left on East Ashley Avenue. A block from Virgil's building, we saw two police cars and an ambulance pulled off the side of the road.

"Crap, not again," Charles said.

Chapter Thirty-Six

The entry to the parking lot was blocked, so we drove past it and pulled over in the front yard of a rental house. We walked; rather Charles and I walked, Virgil hobbled on crutches to the patrol car blocking the entry. In addition to police cars and an ambulance, a coroner's van was in the lot. A Folly Beach Public Safety officer I didn't recognize stopped us with a stern look saying we had to stay behind his car.

I stepped in front of Charles and Virgil, pointed to Virgil, and said, "Officer, this is Mr. Debonnet. That's his apartment." I pointed toward Virgil's door. "What's going on?"

Virgil's door was closed, but the door to Rebecca Holland's apartment was open. An EMT and a public safety officer were coming out.

"I'm sorry gentlemen. I can't let you past this spot. The scene should be cleared in an hour or so."

I repeated, "What's going on?"

"Sir, I'm not at liberty to say."

I saw Trula Bishop coming our way, someone who could share what'd happened. She tapped the other officer on the shoulder. "Officer Smyth, I'll take care of this." She motioned for Charles, Virgil, and me to follow her to the adjacent yard.

The four of us stood in the shade of a live oak and Charles dragged a lawn chair from the house's patio over for Virgil. I introduced Virgil to Officer Bishop.

Trula shook Virgil's hand. "Mr. Debonnet, it's good seeing you're doing so well. The last time I saw you, nobody gave you much hope. Isn't that your apartment back there?"

He thanked her, said Charles and I sprung him from the hospital, then asked how she knew where he lived. She said she was the first officer on the scene after someone left a love letter taped to his television.

Charles wasn't going to let the conversation drift too far from the here and now. "Officer Bishop, what happened?"

She turned to Virgil, glanced at a note in her hand, and said, "Do you know your neighbor, Rebecca Holland?"

Virgil shared what little he knew about her. He left out the part about not trusting her. He asked why.

"I hate to tell you, she's dead."

Charles said, "What happened?"

Officer Bishop gave him a dirty look. "I was getting there, Mr. Charles. She was stabbed multiple times, dead when we arrived. That's all we know."

I asked, "Who found her?"

Bishop looked at the note again. "Cynthia Lawrence, one of her co-workers at S&H Printing. She came to take Ms. Howard to work this morning. Apparently, she picks her up each day. The co-worker knocked. Not getting a response, she tried the knob. The door was unlocked. She opened it a little to yell for Ms. Holland. Her rider was never late, always in the apartment, so when she didn't answer, Cynthia went in and saw Ms. Holland on the floor leading to the kitchen. It was obvious her rider wouldn't be going to work today, or any other day. She called us in a panic."

Officer Smyth moved his patrol car so the coroner's van could exit. We silently watched it go, then I broke the silence with, "Trula, any idea who did it?"

"Detectives from the Sheriff's Office are in there now. From what I heard, nothing stands out. It looks like it happened overnight. We're canvassing the area, but so far, no one answered at the apartment on the other side of Ms. Holland. Of course, Mr. Debonnet was in the hospital."

Virgil said, "When can I get in my place?"

Trula glanced toward the apartment. "It'll be two or three more hours. If you need anything, I'll get it for you."

He said he didn't. I offered that Charles and I would babysit him until he could get in. I asked Officer Bishop if she'd let me know when Virgil could return. She said she would, and the three of us headed to Charles's car.

We piled back in the car before Virgil said, "Got two questions. First one's what in the hell is going on?"

Great question, I thought. Charles said, "What's the second question? It's got to be easier than question number one."

"Know what I haven't had since I got smacked?"

"That's not much easier," Charles said.

"It's a two-part question. The second part is do you know where this bent, folded, near-mutilated hospital escapee can get a cold brew? The answer to the first part of the question is I haven't had an adult beverage since I was holed up in Charleston. Seeing what's happened in my building makes me not want a drink. Guys, it makes me need one."

Rather than answer Virgil, Charles drove to Cal's and parked in a spot that was crutch-aided walking distance from the door. The number of customers doubled when we entered. Reginald, one of Folly's personable locals, was seated at the bar nursing a Bud Light, a middle-aged couple was finishing an order of fries at the table near the stage.

Cal saw us in the doorway and said to sit anywhere. I chose the closest table, so Virgil wouldn't have to hobble far. This was one of the few times I'd been in Cal's without music playing. The eerie silence was broken when Cal delivered us two beers and a glass of white wine.

"Hope this is what you want," he said as he set the drinks on the table. "You look like you need something to wet your whistle."

"You got that one right, Cal," Charles said. "You met Virgil?"

"Haven't had the pleasure. Saw him in here and heard a lot about him." Cal turned to Virgil. "Glad you survived the run-in with the car. They know who did it?"

"No." Virgil said. "Thanks for being concerned. Cal, did you know your kid lives two doors down from me. Nice boy you have there."

"Thanks, pard. He's cleaning the kitchen. I'll tell him you're here."

"Let who know who's here?" Junior said as he headed our way. "Oh, hey, Virgil. Didn't see you."

Cal stepped aside and said, "Don't suppose I'll have to

let him know you're here. I've gotta see if Reginald needs anything."

Junior sat in the other chair at our table and turned to Virgil. "Didn't know you were getting out of the hospital this soon. Good to see you, buddy."

Virgil spent a few minutes sharing his medical condition and Junior talked about how much he enjoyed his job. It was refreshing we weren't having to speak over loud music.

I'd had enough of their reminiscing. "Junior, have you heard about your neighbor, Rebecca Holland?"

"She been arrested?"

Interesting question. I thought about what he'd said the other time we talked about his neighbor, something about if she could be believed. "Why ask that?"

Junior said, "I don't like speaking poorly of anyone, but I wouldn't trust her farther than I can throw her. I figured she finally got caught doing something illegal. What'd she do?"

"Got herself stabbed to death," Charles said.

The room got even quieter. Junior stared at Charles before Virgil broke the silence, "Junior, my buddies here brought me home from the hospital. Our parking lot was full of cops and the coroner. It seems someone killed our neighbor."

"When?" Junior asked.

Virgil said, "Overnight."

Junior tapped his fingers on the table and said, "Who?"

Virgil shrugged. "The police don't know."

"Junior," I said, "when we were talking the other day, you said something about if she could be believed. Now you say you wouldn't trust her. What's that about?"

"Couple of things. It's okay to say it now since she's,

umm, gone. I caught her peeking in my window. Caught her twice. Virgil, I saw her doing it once at your window."

"You caught her," Charles said. "What'd she say?"

"Claimed she heard a strange noise coming from inside, said she was looking to see what it was."

Charles said, "Twice at your apartment, once at Virgil's?"

"She was lying so I didn't waste time pressing her about it. After that, I made sure my door was always locked. The window frame's been painted so many times, no one could get it open. Besides, there isn't anything in there worth stealing."

Nothing as valuable as Virgil's twelve-dollar television, I wondered. "Is that the only reason you wouldn't trust her."

"Mind you, this is only a feeling," Junior said. "She was living there when I moved in. I saw her outside a time or two and asked a few questions."

"Times other than when she was a peeping Tomette?" Charles interrupted.

"Yes."

Charles said, "What kind of questions?"

"Simple stuff. Like where can I do my laundry? Restaurants she'd recommend. It wasn't like I was asking her to divulge secrets. She answered, but the whole time, I had the feeling she was fishing for information."

"What kind of information?" Charles asked.

"Like when I told her I was working for my Dad, she asked how successful the business was, said she'd bet Cal's takes in a lot of cash. Like she wanted me to tell how much. Don't you think that's a strange question to ask someone you just met?"

Charles said, "Sure is."

Not that strange if she thought about stealing it, I thought.

Junior said, "Virgil, how well did you know Rebecca?"

"About the same as you did. I saw her once looking in windows. Thought she was nosy, no more, no less. I heard she had a record. The jail kind, not a recording like your Dad. I didn't trust her."

Marty Robbins singing "El Paso" broke the musical silence and Cal returned to the table, turned the nearest chair around, sat, then folded his arms over the backrest.

"Only so much quiet these old ears can take," he said, I assumed to justify waking the jukebox. "What'd I hear you say about someone being dead?"

Junior told him what he'd learned about his next-door neighbor's death. He asked if his Dad knew her.

"Doesn't ring a bell. When did it happen?"

"Overnight," I said. "Junior, the police will probably be around asking if you know, saw, or heard anything."

"Doubt I'll be much help. Didn't get out of here until two this morning. Think I was half asleep walking home. Someone could've stuck a gun in my face, and I wouldn't have known it. I didn't see anything. I was back here early this morning. Nothing unusual happening around the apartment building when I left."

Ferlin Husky's version of "Wings of a Dove" filled the room, and something Virgil said reminded me of something he'd said the last time we talked about Rebecca Holland.

I said, "Virgil, didn't you say you heard Rebecca had been in jail for embezzlement?"

"That's the rumor."

"And for stealing cars," Charles added.

Virgil asked, "Why?"

I looked at Reginald, still sitting at the bar, then back at the group at our table. "Let me get your reaction. Junior. You said Rebecca gave you a vague description of the person who was in Virgil's apartment."

"It was could've-been-anybody vague," Junior said.

"What if she recognized the person?"

Charles said, "So?"

"Rebecca would know the person she saw was the one who left Virgil's note; most likely, the person who ran him down."

Charles repeated, "What would she have to gain by not telling the police?"

I pointed at Virgil then at Junior, "Both of you have bad feelings about Rebecca." Both nodded. "What if Rebecca found the person she saw and tried to blackmail her or maybe him?"

Junior nodded. "Found her, said something like she saw the person leaving Virgil's apartment and to give Rebecca money or she'll tell the cops."

Cal rubbed his chin. "After that, the person Rebecca was going to blackmail goes to Rebecca's apartment and pretends she's going to pay her. Instead of handing over money, she kills her."

"I wouldn't put it past Rebecca to do something like that," Virgil said.

Junior added, "Me either."

Cal said, "I only see one itsy-bitsy problem with that."

I nodded. "The problem being we still don't know who the person is who ran down Virgil, the person who probably poisoned Gary Isles."

"And the person who knew got herself hauled off to a slab at the coroner's office," Charles added.

Cal leaned forward in the chair. "It seems there may be one other person who knows."

Charles said, "Who?"

"The guy who just got out of the hospital," Cal said, "The one who got a note trying to scare him off."

"Fellas," Virgil said, "if Chris's theory is right, the person who killed Rebecca, tried to kill me, and left me the note, must think I know who it is."

The rest of us nodded.

Virgil shook his head. "Friends, let me tell you right now, I don't know who it is. I assuredly don't."

Chapter Thirty-Seven

We each consumed another drink while talking in circles about who the killer might be, before deciding someone needed to tell Chief LaMond our theory about Rebecca's failed blackmail attempt. I was nominated and elected. I was the sole dissenting vote. Charles said he'd stay with Virgil until his apartment was released for occupancy. I could walk home to call the Chief. I suspected he didn't want to be witness to the barrage of grief Cindy would give me for nosing in police business.

I considered putting off the call. I wasn't certain what the Chief could do with our speculation other than lambast us for thinking it. Despite my misgivings, I called to get the lecture out of the way, or to prevent another lecture from Charles if I'd failed to make the call. Cindy took our playing detective better than I expected, she even asked how Virgil was recuperating. I didn't mention Junior or Cal since it would've been bad enough saying Charles and Virgil had been speculating on the murder. I asked what happened to the Cindy LaMond who'd scold me if I said anything that crossed into her bailiwick. She said she was too tired to give me grief, adding she was frustrated with the lack of progress on the poisoning case, the investigation of Virgil's hit and run, and now the stabbing death of Rebecca Holland. She said there would be one additional death if I shared what she was going to say next. I said I wouldn't repeat whatever it was.

"Chris, the Sheriff's Office and my guys are getting nowhere fast. If you, and yes, I'm going to say it, you and Charles can do anything to put an end to these deaths, go for it. Just promise you won't get killed trying."

"You'll be the first to know if we learn anything. I doubt it'll help, but if you or someone from the Sheriff's Office want to talk to the neighbor on the other side of Rebecca Holland his name is Junior Richardson. He's the chef at Cal's."

Cindy laughed. "Cal has a chef?"

"Not only a chef, the chef is his son."

"Well I'll be a pickled pelican."

"There you go with police lingo again."

"Does Cal really have a son?"

I gave her the abbreviated version of Cal's family history then told her I'd already talked to Junior without getting much information other than what I'd shared with her. She repeated what kind of pelican she was before she said she'd head to Cal's.

That night I couldn't shake thinking Virgil must know something that has the killer worried; worried enough to try to kill him. Who had he talked to about the crash and what could he have learned? He knew Richard and Charlene Beth Haymaker long before the plane went down. They'd had a meal together to celebrate Virgil's sale of his house, plus he'd talked to them since the crash. There's no way Richard had poisoned the pilot since he would've gone down with the plane. What about Charlene Beth? Did she have motive? I remembered Richard's comment at the reception held for Charles and me. It had something to do with her gaining weight. Is that or her alleged affair enough to risk killing four people over?

There's Kelly Isles, grieving widow of the poisoned pilot. What motive would she have? She was unhappy about Gary not letting her work even after she'd been employed at the law firm. I suppose his death would allow her to rejoin the firm. Was that enough motive to kill her husband and risk the lives of three others? Barb had said at the reception Kelly didn't appear sad about her husband's death. Then I remembered Virgil told Kelly he was trying to figure out who poisoned Gary. Was that enough for her to run him down? It didn't seem likely unless he'd said something when he talked with her for her to fear he was getting close—close enough to kill him.

What about Kevin Robbins, Mark Jamison's spouse? He was a pharmacist, would possibly have access to, and know how to use cyanide to spike Gary's drink. He wasn't happy about Mark's failing trucking company which could have syphoned much of Kevin's income to keep it afloat. Was that reason to kill? That by itself may not have been until I remembered the key man insurance policy Mark carried which would make him worth more dead than alive. Did Kevin know Virgil? If he didn't, why would he have tried to run him down? I didn't think he knew him, yet I needed to verify it.

That leaves Alyssa Kale. She'd told Bob she and Tom had a highly contested divorce, were in a battle over money. Money, as any law-enforcement official would say, is a powerful motive for murder. Not only did she tell Bob, she'd shared it with Virgil. What did Virgil tell her about investigating the crash? Was it enough for her to try to kill him?

I then started thinking about the cooler removed from the plane after the crash. Whoever took it had to reach the wreckage by boat. Who among the most-likely suspects had boats? Richard and Charlene had one. She and the twins had been enjoying a day on the water when Charles and I had visited Richard. Add Kelly who told us that Tom Kale's dog Casper enjoyed going out in the boat. I didn't know about Kevin Robbins or Tom Kale's ex, Alyssa. Even if they didn't own one, it would've been simple to rent or borrow one. Finally, Virgil reentered my thoughts when I remembered that he had access to a jon boat he saved while on his trip from wealth to poverty. Could he still be a suspect? If so, why the note in his apartment? Charles and I had already eliminated him, so should I put him back on the list?

Before I went to sleep, another thought popped in my head. What if the murderer was someone we either haven't thought about or someone we don't know? There could be countless people who may've had a grudge against Gary. It was no wonder the police were getting nowhere fast. I knew I was.

Rays of sun peeking through the blinds awakened me the next morning. I had slept later than usual and attributed it to overusing my brain last evening. It could also have something to do with three glasses of wine at Cal's. Water puddled in the back yard, so it must've rained overnight although the sky was clear. I couldn't remember everything about the crash I'd pondered last evening, but I was certain the evening ended with more questions than answers.

Two cups of coffee later, I started thinking about what I did know. Warren Marshall, the airplane junkie, had talked with Gary Isles while the pilot was waiting for the others to arrive. Warren had heard Gary say something about seeing someone he knew there that morning. Warren hadn't seen the person but remembered Gary using the term spouse. Four spouses were at the top of my suspect pool: Kelly Isles, Charlene Beth Haymaker, ex-spouse Alyssa Kale, and Kevin Robbins. Gary wouldn't have been referring to his wife when he told Warren he'd seen someone he knew at the airport, so I marked her off the list, at least for now. Warren may not have associated someone he'd seen that day with Gary, but that didn't mean he hadn't seen the person. It may be another dead end, but I felt the need to talk to Warren one more time.

I called to ask Charles if he was ready for another trip to the airport. This time he didn't ask our flight destination. He asked if we were going to buy a Piper PA-46 Malibu. I told him no, instead of sharing I was impressed he remembered the kind of plane Warren thought we should buy. He also asked when we were leaving. I said I'd be there in thirty minutes, which gave me time to Google the grocery where Kevin was a pharmacist. Fortunately, the store's website had photos of the store manager, the employee of the month, and its three pharmacists. I printed

Kevin Robbin's photo, and found a photo of Charlene Beth on her realtor's website. I couldn't find a photo of Alyssa.

"If we're not going to buy a plane, why are we going to the airport?" Charles said as he slid into the seat.

I shared my thinking and my plan for today.

"That's a sad excuse of a plan."

"I agree, although we don't—"

He waved his hand in my face. "A sad excuse is better than any I came up with."

On that ringing endorsement, we continued our drive to the airport. We parked in the Atlantic Aviation parking lot where there were fewer cars than had been there during our first visit. We were again greeted by the older gentleman who'd been with Warren the first time we visited. He said we looked familiar and I told him that we'd been there to talk to Warren. He reminded us he was Brady then said he hadn't seen Warren all morning, but we should check in the nearby hangar.

A man was pulling a twin-engine, red and white plane out of the hangar using something that looked like a lawn mower attached to the plane's front wheel. There were two single-engine planes parked in the large structure and Warren was standing in the door watching the man. He wore the same red plaid shirt he had on during our first visit.

He saw us approach and smiled. "I recognize you two." He focused on Charles and held out his hand for Charles to shake. "You're, umm."

Charles grabbed Warren's outstretched hand. "Charles, and that's my friend Chris."

"Sure, I remember," Warren said. "Have you come back

to buy the Piper Malibu? I told Mr. Jamison about you. He said he'd give you a deal."

"Not today," Charles said.

I said, "Warren, I've got a question."

Instead of asking what it was, he said, "Do you have a plane, Chris?"

It was the same question he'd asked during our first visit. "No, afraid not. I do have a couple of pictures I'd like to show you." I took the photos out of my pocket, unfolded them, and showed him the one of Charlene Beth. "Warren, did you see this lady out here the day Gary Isles and his friends took off?"

"Does she have a plane?"

"I don't think so."

"Oh," he said. He looked closely at the photo. "She's a nice-looking lady. I see a lot of people around here. I may've seen her."

"The day Gary Isles left on the golfing trip?"

"Don't think so. Who is she?"

"The wife of one of Gary's friends with him on the plane that crashed."

"Is her husband the other man killed?"

"No, he survived."

"That's good," Warren said. "His wife looks nice."

I took Charlene Beth's photo from Warren then handed him the one of Kevin Robbins. "Was this man here that day?"

"Does he have a plane?"

"No," Charles said, losing patience.

"That's too bad. If he ever wants one, I know some for sale."

I glanced at Charles hoping he wouldn't respond. He didn't, and I said, "I'll tell him."

"Did he know someone on the plane?"

I didn't know where the conversation would go if I told Warren that Kevin was Mark Jamison's spouse, so I said, "He's a friend of one of the passengers."

"Is he a doctor?" Warren said.

"He's a pharmacist," I said.

"Oh, I saw the white doctors' coat and thought—"

Charles interrupted, "Warren, was he here that day?"

"I don't recognize him. There were several men, so he could've been."

I was beginning to think our trip to the airport was a waste. I didn't have a photo of Alyssa Kale, and held out little hope that asking about her would get us anywhere.

"Warren, there's one other person I'd like to ask you about. Do you know Alyssa Kale?"

"She doesn't have a plane," Charles said to head off Warren's next question.

"You have her picture?" Warren said.

"No. She's African American, probably in her late forties."

"Let's see." Warren looked around the hangar like he thought she might be hiding in a corner. "Umm, there're two black gentlemen who have planes. One's a new Cessna Turbo Stationair T206H, it's a nice plane. The other's a Commander 114TC."

I said, "Warren, did you see anyone who fit the description of Alyssa Kale the day Gary Isles took off with his friends?"

"No."

Charles looked at me and rolled his eyes.

I silently agreed. "Warren, it's been nice talking with you. Let me give you my phone number in case you think of anything else about the day the plane crashed." I jotted my number on the back of an index card and handed it to him.

He looked at the number. "Want me to give this to Mr. Jamison? He'll give you a good deal on his plane."

Through gritted teeth, I declined.

Chapter Thirty-Eight

"**S**ure you don't want to buy a plane?" Charles asked as we drove past the graveyard. "I know where you can get a good deal on a Piper Malibu."

The phone rang before I could tell Charles where he could stick his Piper. Bob Howard's name appeared on the screen.

"Good morning, Bob."

"What time are you getting here?"

"Where and why?"

"Where do you think? Al said we needed more diversity in this joint. Equal rights for whites and all that."

Since we had to go out of our way to get to the airport, Al's was closer than Folly and it was nearing lunch time. Besides, Bob wasn't calling just to invite us to lunch. "Half hour," I said and hung up on him. It felt better than it should have.

Charles's only comment was, "You buying?"

Traffic was light on Maybank Highway, so we reached Al's sooner than anticipated. Parking was another matter. Al's didn't have a parking lot and depended on-street parking for customers arriving in vehicles. Many were local so they walked. Two blocks later, I managed to squeeze in a spot between an old Pontiac Firebird and a much-newer Kia Sorento.

Al greeted us at the door with hugs, adding a warning that Bob was surlier than normal. I doubted that was possible but thanked him for the warning.

Bob proved me wrong when he yelled over Fats Domino's "Blueberry Hill" blasting from the jukebox, "Get the hell over here and order some food. Got to make enough to pay Lawrence his astronomical salary."

"Sure you don't want to go back and buy a plane?" Charles said as we made our way around three empty tables to Bob's booth.

I ignored Bob's "cheery" greeting and Charles's offer and slid in the booth opposite the burly owner. Lawrence, who normally spent most of his time in front of the grill, joined us as we got seated to ask if we wanted cheeseburgers and our usual drinks.

"Of course, they do," Bob said. "Get frying."

Lawrence resisted knocking Bob's drink in his lap before heading to the kitchen.

"Damned fine cook," Bob said. "His waitin' on tables skills could use some work. Need to train him better."

Bob training Lawrence *waitin' on tables* skills would be like a Chihuahua training fighter pilots.

I glanced back at Al who'd returned to the chair by the door then turned to Bob. "How's Al doing?"

"Wish I could tell you he was great, but he's far from it."

Charles said, "He still showing up every day?"

"Yes, but he's not staying as long."

"Sorry to hear it," I said.

"Me, too," Bob said as he looked at Al. "Me, too."

Lawrence returned with our drinks; Bob told him he needed to get back to the kitchen to make sure our cheeseburgers didn't burn. Lawrence had been a short-order cook long before high school students had been born, probably before most of their teachers. Bob had never fried a burger, cheese or otherwise, in his life. That didn't stop him from giving Lawrence directions.

"Yes, boss," Lawrence said and left.

Bob said, "Caught the killer?"

I wasn't ready for the transition from frying burgers to catching killers. "No."

"You're slipping in your old age. Fortunately, your good buddy Bob has a clue for you." He leaned back in the booth then grinned.

Instead of applauding what he considered to be a clue, I said, "Going to share it?"

"I learned from a friend of a friend who got it from his cousin that the Real Estate business of one formerly successful realtor is sucking wind."

I was stuck on Bob having a friend. Charles wasn't hung up on that. He said, "Who's the formerly successful realtor?"

"Double first-name Haymaker. My source says she hasn't sold anything worth more than an anthill in the last six months."

"Is that the clue?" I said.

"Part of it."

Charles said, "Do you think she poisoned Gary Isles so he'd crash and kill her husband because she hadn't sold anything recently?"

"Charles," Bob said, "if you'll keep your trap shut, I'll tell you the other part of the clue."

Charles kept his trap shut, not because Bob told him to, but because Lawrence had returned with our food. Charles had stuffed his mouth with cheeseburger, then motioned Bob to continue.

"My friend also told me his friend who happens to be a lawyer said he knew from a reliable source that Richard has a prenup saying if Charlene Beth divorces him she gets zero, *nada*, zilch. Now I'm not a detective like Charles, and sometimes you, Chris, but that sounds like what you detectives call a big-ass motive."

"How would your friend's friend, or friend of your friend's friend, know about the prenup?"

"Crap, Chris. I'm not a lawyer, not a friend of my friend's friend, not a psychic. I have no idea. The point is there's one. Unless your brain is fried from old age, you should remember I'm the one who told you Walter Middleton Gibbs filed for divorce. And, I'm the one who told you the rumor that he's having a fling with the double-named hussy. Do I have to do all your work?"

Bob was right. Those reasons were more motive than Richard's comment at the reception about his wife gaining weight, more accurately, her negative reaction to his comment. I told him about our conversation with Warren at the airport.

"There you go," Bob said as he grabbed a fry from

Charles's plate. "A slam dunk. All the credit goes to me. Charles, sign me up to your detective agency."

Charles said, "Bob, I don't—"

Bob grabbed another fry off Charles's plate, waved it in Charles's face, and turned toward the front door. He yelled, "Al, call the sign company. Order us a big-ass sign for out front. I can see it now. *Al's Bar and Detective Agency.*"

Fortunately for us, unfortunately for sales, there were no other customers, so Al treated Bob's declaration like he did most of his others. He ignored him.

I also ignored it. "Bob, Warren didn't say he saw Charlene Beth at the airport that morning. He said he may have. Walter Middleton Gibbs may've filed for divorce, may be having an affair with Charlene Beth, and her business may be off. None of that proves she poisoned the pilot while trying to kill her husband."

"Chris, what more do I have to do?" Bob said. "I've got it. Why don't I call her and have her show me a trillion dollar-house? I'll say, 'Charlene Beth, I'll take it. Write it up. While you've got a pen in your hand, why don't you write a confession telling my good friend Chris Landrum you poisoned the pilot?'"

Charles stifled a smile and said, "Bob, get it notarized."

Bob did have good points—about Charlene Beth, not about the new sign or the confession. I reluctantly told him so. He was less helpful when we discussed how to prove Charlene Beth was guilty. Al joined us, and we turned the discussion to his family and how they were doing. We finished eating and I was paying Lawrence for lunch, when the phone rang. I didn't recognize the number and started to let it roll over to voicemail, when Charles grabbed it and answered for me. He had as much patience as a hungry baby chipmunk.

He handed me the phone. "It's for you."

Duh, I thought. "Hello."

"Chris, this is Brady at Atlantic Aviation. Warren was just in here. He said you'd showed him pictures of people who might've been here when Gary Isles took off the day of the crash."

I told him yes, that Warren wasn't sure about seeing any of them.

"One of them sounded familiar from Warren's description. I could look at the photos to see if I'm right. I'll be here another hour if you could come now."

I told him where we were and were ready to leave. We'd be at the airport within the hour. I told Charles, Bob, Al, and now Lawrence who'd been on the phone and what he wanted. I asked Bob if he wanted to go with us.

"Nope, I'm the brains behind the detective agency. You underlings do the legwork."

We left on that delusional note.

The trip to the airport took longer than I'd hoped. A wreck on Maybank Highway forced traffic to detour through a housing development. By the time we arrived, I was a nervous wreck. It didn't help that Charles kept tapping his fingers on the console while mumbling something about me driving faster. We were pushing the outer limits of the hour when we parked. Brady was lounging on the chair where we'd first met him. He stood and glanced at his watch.

"Thanks for waiting for us," I said.

"Have the photos?" he said, clearly in a hurry.

My hand was shaking as I unfolded the pictures. The

image of Kevin Robbins was on top and Brady looked at it for no more than two seconds before shaking his head.

"It wasn't a guy. Warren said you had a picture of a gal."

I slipped the photo of Charlene Beth over Kevin's.

Brady tapped the photo and smiled. "That's her."

"You sure?" I asked.

"Yep. I don't forget a pretty gal."

Charles stepped closer to Brady. "You're certain she was here that morning?"

"Yep. I didn't pay much attention to it until a little later."

"What made you pay attention then?"

"About the only folks who come around here are pilots, passengers, an occasional salesperson. Once I thought about it, I realized she wasn't here to fly anywhere. Struck me as odd."

I said, "Where was she?"

"Out by the hangar. I wouldn't have seen her if I hadn't gone to the car to get some papers I forgot to bring in."

Charles said, "Don't suppose you saw her around a cooler Gary had with him?"

"Nope. She was on the opposite side of the building from Gary and his plane."

I said, "Was she here after the others arrived and the plane took off?"

"Don't know. I only saw her when I was outside. After I came in, I didn't see her, or Gary, or the others again." He lowered his head and his voice when he added, "Gary was a good guy. I'll miss seeing him around here." He looked at his watch. "Guys, I've got to go."

I thanked him, and Charles and I started to the door,

when I remembered one more question. "Brady, did the police talk to you about any of this?"

"Nope. I wasn't here the day after the crash. My better half convinced me I needed to go with her to visit her sister up in Georgetown. My sister-in-law had back surgery, so my wife wanted to see how she was doing. The poor women had three surgeries in two years, and—"

Charles interrupted, "So the police didn't talk to you."

Brady looked at his watch again, glared at Charles, and shook his head, "No, they talked to Warren. You may've noticed he's a little slow on the uptick. Get him started talking about airplanes or aviation and he'll talk your ears off. Anything else, well, you know."

We certainly did. "Did he tell you what they talked about or what he told them?"

One more glance at the watch, then Brady smiled. "Yep. None of the cops wanted to buy a plane."

Brady was close behind us as we left the building. We watched him pull out of the lot and called Chief LaMond to let her know what we'd learned.

She answered with, "Chief LaMond. How may I help you?"

It wasn't an insult or her asking how I was going to ruin her day. I knew she couldn't talk so I asked how long she'd be tied up.

"This budget meeting should be over in an hour or so. May I get back with you then?"

I said yes. She said she'd meet me at the Surf Bar. I told her I'd be there.

Charles watched me set the phone on the console. "Chris, we know who the killer is, so what do we do now?"

"I take you home. Then I'll go home and pace the floor until we meet Cindy at the Surf Bar."

"That's all? There's a killer out there and we know who it is."

"That's why we tell the police and leave it in their capable hands."

Charles sighed. "I guess."

Chapter Thirty-Nine

After leaving Charles at his apartment, I started thinking about what we'd learned. I was certain Charlene Beth had poisoned Gary. I was tempted to drive to City Hall, barge in the budget meeting while yelling I knew the name of the killer. Sure, the Chief would be tempted to shoot me, but wouldn't it be worth it? A few seconds of rational thought led me to conclude waiting a little longer to tell her would be okay. A bit of paranoia seeped into my head as I realized Virgil's life was still in danger. The killer, now known as Charlene Beth Haymaker, had made one attempt on his life. What was to stop her from trying again?

Instead of going home or barging in on a budget meeting, I drove to Virgil's apartment in hopes of finding him safe. I pulled in the parking area and was relieved to see him sitting on a concrete bench at the far end of the property. He was leaning back against a table and was on the phone. His crutches were leaned beside him keeping him company.

He waved me over while still talking on the phone. It was in the upper seventies and partly cloudy, so I was content to join him and enjoy the glorious March day.

Virgil suddenly moved the phone away from his ear, stared at the device, and said, "That's funny."

I didn't know if he was talking to me or the person on the phone. He slid the device in his pocket making me think he'd addressed his comment to me. "What's funny?"

"That was Richard."

"Richard?"

"Richard Haymaker. I was thinking more about the crash. I asked him to tell me again everything he remembered. Charles would've been proud of me. I'm catching on to this detective stuff."

"What'd he say?"

"Nothing I didn't know. I suppose part of being a detective is running into dead ends."

"What'd he say that was funny?"

"He was talking when the phone cut off. Dead air."

"Was he in the car? There're several dead spots where phone service cuts out."

"Could be it, except he isn't in the car. He's on his boat."

"By himself?"

"Charlene Beth is with him."

It hit me hard. Virgil wasn't the only person in danger. After all, Charlene Beth caused the crash to kill her husband.

"Where were they?"

"Don't know; didn't ask. He yelled early in the conversation at Charlene Beth to be careful of the oyster bed, something about them being sharp, could scratch the boat. Does that help?"

"Sounds like they're in the marsh. What exactly was he saying when the phone went dead?"

"He wanted to meet me tomorrow."

"He say why?"

"No. He sounded like it was important, though. I was asking him when and where then the call cut off. Why's that important?"

I realized I'd been holding my breath. I exhaled. "Because Charlene Beth poisoned Gary."

Virgil jumped up, then returned to the bench. "You're kidding. How do you know?"

I told him about Brady's identification.

"Chris, what if Charlene plans to kill Richard? Today. Kill him in the marsh. What if—"

"Virgil, we don't know anything. Let me call Chief LaMond to tell her what just happened."

The call went directly to voicemail. I left a brief message for her to return my call as soon as she could. I said I knew who the killer was, that she might be getting ready to strike again.

"Let's try to find them," Virgil said as he jumped up a second time. This time he grabbed the crutches.

"Virgil, we don't have a boat. Besides, even if we did, there are countless places out there where they could be."

Virgil smiled, not the reaction I had expected. "I can get a boat. Let's try."

If Richard wasn't already dead, he could be long before Cindy called back. Against my better judgment, I said, "Where can you get a boat? Your jon boat isn't fast enough."

"Met a guy in the bar before I had the run-in, slam-in with the car. He lives near the end of East Ashley Avenue on the marsh side. Has a fifteen-foot Boston Whaler he keeps behind his house. Has a little dock. Says he doesn't use it as often as he used to since he travels with work. Told me I could borrow it whenever."

Ten minutes later, we pulled in Virgil's new friend's drive. I asked if the man was home and Virgil said his truck wasn't there, so he was probably out of town. Virgil added he knew where the key was hidden. He went to find it as I stood on the dock and stared at the attractive, blue and white striped hull with a white interior. My fear of water kept me from stepping off the land-bound dock onto the boat. I took a deep breath and told myself the boat was more stable than the kayak I'd been in on my last trip to the marsh.

Virgil waved a key in my face and said, "Let's go."

We managed to get the engine started and the vessel untied when I silently said a prayer. I tried Cindy's phone again only to receive the same recording. I then called Detective Callahan and had better luck. I told him what'd happened. He told me to go home, he'd take care of it. I said it was a good idea. I didn't tell him home wasn't my destination.

We headed west to where it didn't take long to realize there were numerous creeks, and narrow waterways weaving through the marsh. It was high tide which made it even more difficult. Some of the narrow streams weren't navigable at low tide, but at high tide they opened to more possibilities. More possibilities to miss the boat.

We had to make several go-left or go-right decisions which made me realize the futility of trying to find the

Haymakers. They could be anywhere, if they were even out here. We rounded a bend when I spotted a decent-sized vessel stopped. I'd never seen the Haymaker's boat so didn't know if it was them. Virgil slowed then asked me what we should do. I asked if he knew what the Haymaker's watercraft looked like.

"No. What now?"

The question was answered when I heard a child squeal and saw a dolphin surfacing beside the stationary watercraft. A woman's laugh filled the air. It wasn't Charlene Beth. I told Virgil to approach and stop when we were beside the other boat.

The child who'd been delighted by the dolphin smiled at us. She waved as her mother put her arm around her daughter. The mother said hi.

We returned her greeting adding, "Have you seen another boat out here?"

"A couple of skiffs, oh yeah, an Alumacraft 1860 Bay."

I asked if she noticed who was on the Alumacraft.

"Didn't pay much attention. It was a man and woman. Why?"

I told her I was looking for a friend and asked where she'd seen the other boat. She pointed in the direction where we were headed then said for us to take a left where the creek split. I thanked her adding for them to have a great rest of the day. I hoped that would be true for us.

Chapter Forty

I didn't know what an Alumacraft looked like, but figured it'd probably be the only boat in the direction she'd sent us. Virgil was careful to stay in the middle of the channel and asked me what our plan was when we found the Haymakers.

Sounding like Charles, I said, "We'll figure it out when we get there."

Virgil steered with his left hand as he pointed a crutch at something he saw around the curve. "We can start figuring. I think that's it."

I looked where he was pointing. The boat was white with a red stripe on the side. It was a few feet longer than the craft Virgil had commandeered. I had no idea what to expect. Virgil said he was going to pull even with it on the starboard side.

We edged closer to the side where I had an unobstructed view of most of the deck. The only person I saw was Charlene Beth standing behind the wheel. She had on black shorts, a light-yellow linen blouse, and tennis shoes.

"Wow!" Virgil said. "Is that you, Charlene Beth?"

I thought he'd pulled off the surprised look. Charlene Beth must not have been as convinced. She looked at him with a stoic face then glanced at me. "What're you doing here?"

"My friend Chris wanted to show me where the plane crashed. The boat belongs to a friend." Virgil looked over the side of Charlene Beth's boat. "Where're Richard and the twins? Thought they'd be with you on such a nice day."

Charlene Beth smiled for the first time. "The twins are with our neighbor. She was taking her toddler to the mall, asked if she could take the twins."

Virgil pulled a few inches closer to the other boat so I could see the entire deck. He then said, "What about Richard?"

"He came but one of his clients called needing a printout of his portfolio. Took him back to the house so he could go to the office to get it. I'd better be moving along."

I didn't see Richard but a large red spot on the deck looked convincingly like blood. A splatter of the red was also on the gunwale by the front port cleat.

Virgil reached over to pull our boat closer when Charlene Beth turned her head, catching me looking at the stain. She muttered a profanity. Before Virgil reacted, she reached down and pulled a five-foot-long boat hook from the deck. She grabbed his collar with the curved brass hook at the end of the pole.

Virgil was off balance when Charlene Beth yanked the pole dragging my friend with it. His shoulder hit the gunwale as he reached for the aluminum railing. He missed and toppled into the saltwater. I leaned to help Virgil when she reached under the steering wheel and pulled out a pistol.

My *figure it out when we get there* plan was woefully inadequate.

"I should've done this when you started nosing around about the crash," she said before firing two shots my direction. Her marksmanship skills weren't as good as her boat hook maneuver. A bullet punctured the gunwale, the other ripped through the back of the seat. I didn't give her a chance to succeed on the third shot. My fear of water was surpassed by my fear of a bullet. I dove overboard then treaded water while the boat provided a barrier between Charlene Beth and me.

Instead of another gunshot, the roar from her Evinrude filled the air. I glanced around the side of our boat to see Charlene Beth speeding away. I then remembered Virgil on the other side of our craft.

I held onto the boat and slowly moved around it. "Virgil, are you okay?"

Garbling sounds were followed by, "Can't swim." Then more garbled sounds.

I hurried around behind the boat and saw the top of Virgil's bobbing head. In much of the marsh, the streams were shallow enough to touch bottom. This wasn't one of those spots. He was eight feet from the boat. His flailing arms slapping the water propelled him farther away. I yelled for him to stop struggling, but doubted he heard me. I pulled myself up on the side of the boat enough to grab two life vests from under the rear seat.

There wasn't time to put one on, so I pushed it under

my chest and dog paddled to Virgil. He'd stopped struggling and was floating face down. We were six feet from the jagged shore, pluff mud, and oyster shells clinging to the edge. The boat had drifted much farther than that from us, so the best chance to save him was to push him to the uninviting mud and marsh grasses.

My feet finally touched bottom so I could push Virgil up enough to keep his head above water. I caught my breath then shoved him toward a more solid piece of earth. I sank up to my shins in the mud. It felt like I wasn't going anywhere. Was he alive?

I struggled to push his unmoving body to firmer ground. It took me three tries to get him out of the water. I barely had energy to pull myself up to dry land. If there was any chance of him making it, I'd have to perform CPR. Time was critical, but if I didn't have the energy to lift my arms, I'd be useless. I put my head down and took two deep breaths to garner the strength to help my friend.

Virgil was on his side. I flipped him onto his back, then … then what? I'd taken a CPR course forty years ago. I racked my brain to remember what to do. I put my ear near his mouth and listened for breathing. My heart was beating so fast I couldn't tell if I was hearing him or me. His chest wasn't rising and falling so I guessed he wasn't breathing. I put two fingers on his neck to find a pulse. Nothing. I took another deep breath, placed the heel of my hand on his chest, covered it with my other hand, then began rapid compressions. I knew I should press a certain number of times a minute but couldn't remember how many. Was I helping or were my efforts futile?

My question was answered when I felt his arm move

against my leg. He coughed. I turned him on his side as he coughed up water. He tried to speak. I told him to remain still, that he'd be okay. Was I right? The only other sounds I heard were my breathing and birds squawking in the distance.

Virgil turned his head toward me then mumbled, "Am I alive?"

I assured him he was before exhaustion overcame me. I collapsed beside him. I looked at the clear blue sky and gave thanks for both of us surviving. I reached for my phone only to find it wasn't in my pocket. It's probably at the bottom of the stream. Virgil asked what happened to Charlene Beth. I told him how she'd left us in the water. I asked if he still had his phone or if it was in the boat.

"Was in my pocket." He patted each pocket. "Not now."

"That's okay, mine's gone too. It doesn't matter, they'd be waterlogged, useless."

He asked if I could see our boat. I sat and looked around. Our way out of the marsh was about thirty yards behind us, nosed into the mud on the opposite side of the waterway. I felt strength returning to my legs, so I told him I'd try to get the boat. This time, I put on the life vest before swimming back to our ride. It took two efforts before I mustered the strength to pull myself up out of the water enough to climb on board. I looked around to make sure neither of our phones had landed in the boat before we hit the water. All the search yielded were Virgil's crutch and sunglasses. He'll be pleased.

Virgil moved better than I would under similar circumstances. He was waiting for me on the edge of the solid ground as I edged the boat close enough for him to step aboard. He thanked me for saving his life, thanked me for finding his sunglasses. I couldn't tell which he was happier about.

He was moving better, but in no condition to pilot our ride. I wasn't certain how to retrace our voyage to the dock, but thought I recognized the dense marsh at the spot where the plane crashed. If I were right, I thought I could find my way to the Folly River Boat Ramp, so I headed that direction. Besides, I figured it was safer than going the direction that Charlene Beth had exited.

I showed him the spot where the plane crashed.

He nodded then suddenly pointed to the left. He yelled, "What's that?"

I slowed the boat and turned to see where he was pointing. It appeared to be part of a red raft caught in the marsh grasses. I turned the boat and moved closer to the object. I was shocked to see the red was a shirt, a shirt worn by Richard Haymaker.

Virgil was reaching down to pull the body to the boat before I brought our craft to a complete stop. It took both of us to pull the six-foot-two body up enough to get it onboard. Virgil lost his footing and slipped under Richard as they both flopped down on the deck.

Virgil slid out from under the lifeless body and said, "Is he dead?"

Richard's soaked hair was matted, his shirt had what appeared to be a bullet hole below his shoulder. I pushed the sleeve up exposing a clean entry wound and a not-so-clean exit wound on the other side of his arm. Water had washed the blood out of his shirt and off his arm, so I couldn't tell how much he'd lost. I felt his neck for a pulse. It could've been my imagination, but I thought I detected a slight movement. The boat was rocking, so I couldn't be certain if it was a pulse or the movement of the boat. Richard's eyes popped open. It startled me so much that I fell back, coming inches from smacking my head on the gunwale.

"Hey, Richard, how're you doing?" Virgil said as if he'd run into Richard in the grocery.

I laughed when Richard mumbled, "Huh?"

The wound began bleeding. Clearly, he wasn't doing well. I pulled my shirt off then told Virgil to press it against Richard's arm. I told Virgil to stay with him while I piloted us to the dock to find help.

I began thinking we were lost until I saw houses on Folly that backed up to the river. Five minutes later I crossed under the bridge to the island and approached the Folly River Boat Ramp where a pickup truck was pulling a boat out of the water. I yelled for the two men with the truck to help as we hit the side of the ramp. One grabbed our bow, the other looked at Virgil then Richard and asked what happened. Instead of answering, I asked him to call 911 to request both medical assistance and police.

I shut off the motor and moved beside Virgil. Richard was able to hold my shirt against his arm. He appeared more alert than he'd been earlier.

I said, "Richard, what happened?"

Instead of answering, he said, "Where's Charlene Beth?"

We shared what little we knew then again asked what happened.

"She said she wanted us to take a pleasant ride through the marsh. The weather was nice, the kids were with a neighbor. I thought it was a good idea. I was talking to Virgil when we lost cell service. Then we were near where the plane crashed. I said something about how strange she'd been acting since that day."

"What do you mean?" I asked.

"She's been distant. Saying little. I'd heard a rumor about her and some guy in Charleston. Since we were out with no distractions, I figured I'd share the rumor with her. You know, saying how silly it was, knowing it couldn't be true."

He pulled the shirt away from his wound, grimaced, then looked at it. The bleeding had slowed. He returned the shirt to his arm.

"What'd she say?"

"Nothing, not a damned word. She pulled a gun out from under the wheel, pointed at me, pulled the trigger. Chris, I didn't even know she had a gun. Thank God she wasn't a good shot." He pointed at his arm. "Got me here. It knocked me out of the boat. Thought I was a goner. Honest to God I did."

Sirens from emergency vehicles headed out way. Officer Bishop was first to arrive.

"What happened, Mr. Chris?"

I told her Richard's wife shot him, that she was the person who poisoned Gary Isles. I said they might catch her at the house then added the twins were with a neighbor. Bishop got the address from Richard, then radioed for someone to go to the house. She asked Richard what Charlene Beth was driving. He told her a white Lexus SUV but didn't know the plate number.

One of Folly's fire trucks arrived next and two EMTs rushed over. One asked if I was okay. I told him yes, so he went to check on Richard, while the other one tended to Virgil. A crowd had begun to gather. A man I'd seen in

Bert's a few times offered me a T-shirt he had in his truck. I accepted and felt like Charles when I noticed the University of South Carolina logo on the front.

I smiled, not only because of the shirt, but more because I was alive.

Chapter Forty-One

C harles said, "I can't believe you didn't take me on your peaceful boat ride through the marsh."

It was at least the fiftieth time he'd said it, or similar words, in the six days since I docked the bullet riddled boat at the boat ramp. We were on our way to a party at Tom Kale's house. This time, to celebrate me saving Virgil and Virgil and me saving Richard. I didn't think a party was necessary but didn't have the heart to say no to Tom, especially after he told me he'd already invited several others.

The party was also to celebrate the capture of Charlene Beth Haymaker by a Columbia, South Carolina, police officer two and a half hours after she picked up her kids from the neighbor's house. She'd been pulled over for speeding. Thank you police vehicles with on-board computers.

Tom's drive was full when we arrived, three cars were parked along East Ashley Avenue. We were greeted at the door by Kelly Isles carrying Casper. I gave Kelly a peck on the cheek, Charles kissed Casper. Kelly said the party was in full swing, for us to follow her up to the deck, the same spot of the earlier reception for Charles and me. I was surprised to see Cal, standing behind his antique mic and strumming the opening to "Farewell Party." He wore his Stetson, an orange Folly Beach T-shirt, and black jogging shorts.

Tom was in deep conversation with Bob Howard, so he didn't see us arrive. Virgil did see us. He was down to one crutch, but I don't think it hit the deck as he rushed to greet us. He had a beer bottle in his other hand. His Gucci shoes had lost much of their luster after their trip through the marsh. His sunglasses were bent.

"Here's the hero," he said as he gave me a hug. I was pleased when he also hugged Charles. That probably kept my friend from fuming the rest of the afternoon.

Bob moved away from Tom and stood in front of Cal and mouthed the words to "Chiseled in Stone," the song Cal was singing. Cal finished, saw me standing with Charles, tipped his Stetson my direction, and said, "Guys and gals, our guest of honor has arrived."

I turned several shades of red as everyone broke into applause. Virgil put his arm around me. Bob pushed his way through three people standing close together and tapped me on the arm. "Where's beautiful Barb? I'd much rather see her than your ugly mug."

What's not to love about Bob, I thought. "She's at work, Bob. Isn't that where you should be?"

"Hell no. I couldn't pass up free booze and those little sandwich-thingees you have to eat a dozen to equal a sandwich. Besides, since I'm the one who figured everything out and helped you nearly get yourself killed saving two guys, I had to be here to make sure you didn't take all the credit."

"Thanks, Bob. I needed that."

He tapped me again on the arm, pivoted, then headed to the bar.

I spotted Junior leaning against the railing watching his Dad begin another song. I walked over to say hi. He smiled and nodded toward Cal. "I love Dad's enthusiasm. I only wish I'd known him years ago. He's a great guy."

"Have you told him that?"

Junior smiled. "Couple of days ago. I apologized for being such a pain in the ass. We decided to leave Cal's the way it is, except for finishing the paint job. It's his life, his love. It's keeping him young."

"That's great. I know he feels good about you being here."

Cal announced that he was taking "a pause for the cause," set his guitar on its case, and ambled over to Junior and me.

"Welcome to the shindig," Cal said.

I told him I was surprised he was here and not at the bar.

"All the drinkers will wait for me to open in a couple hours."

Chief LaMond was next to arrive. She was off duty and wore a green blouse and tan shorts. She came over, looked around, then said, "Any dead bodies?"

I told her I didn't know of any.

"That's a surprise. Can you handle being around all living folks?"

"I'll manage."

She looked around again, then said, "Where's Richard?"

That was one question I knew the answer to. "Home. He wanted to stay with the kids. They're too young to understand where their mom is. He said he'd feel bad about leaving them."

Cindy smiled, "Here's a phrase I don't often get to use. Smart man."

"Funny," I said.

"Did you hear Charlene Beth's attorney is trying to work a deal with the district attorney? Leniency if she admits to poisoning the pilot, killing Rebecca, and trying to knock off her hubby, twice."

"What are the chances of that happening?"

"About as good as me winning Miss America. I'd better say hi to the host." She left me standing at the rail where Virgil spotted me.

"Virgil, how much trouble are you in with the guy who owned the boat? He probably didn't appreciate the bullet holes."

"Wrong, my friend. Oh, so wrong. He thinks they're wonderful. Said it gives him a great conversation starter, gives his boat character. He said I could use it any time. Want to go out on the marsh with me?"

I smiled instead of shouting, "Never!"

About the Author

Bill Noel is the best-selling author of nineteen novels in the popular Folly Beach Mystery series. Besides being an award-winning novelist, Noel is a fine arts photographer and lives in Louisville, Kentucky, with his wife, Susan, and his off-kilter imagination. Learn more about the series, and the author by visiting www.billnoel.com.